Praise for *Reconstructing Natalie*

"Laced with refreshing wit and stunning insights, this memorable tale will lift your spirits!"

—Robin Jones Gunn, author of *Gardenias for Breakfast* and the Sisterchicks® novels

"No way can you read *Reconstructing Natalie* without laughing, weeping, cheering, wincing, and above all, rooting for this feisty young woman in her battle to overcome a disease that has claimed far too many of our friends. Be prepared for unflinching descriptions of what it's *really* like to deal with breast cancer on a daily basis, including all the highs and lows—the goofy, the icky, the embarrassing, and the tragic moments—shared with honesty, humor, and heart by a talented author who has truly been there."

—Liz Curtis Higgs, author of *Mixed Signals*

"*Reconstructing Natalie* is a funny, heartwarming tale . . . Bravo!"

—Kristin Billerbeck, author of *With this Ring, I'm Confused* and *She's All That*

"I'm crazy about Natalie! She's funny. She's smart! She's real! She has a crush on Johnny Depp for heaven's sake! And, by the way, she just happens to have breast cancer. Laura Jensen Walker doesn't dodge real-life issues. Bad stuff happens, but it doesn't consume her characters. On the contrary! It makes them more interesting! There's an energetic flow that moves Natalie (and the reader) joyfully beyond the crisis to experience sweet romance and deep fulfillment."

—Sue Buchanan, author, speaker, cheerleader, and a breast cancer survivor

Reconstructing Natalie

Reconstructing
NATALIE

Laura Jensen Walker

WestBow™
PRESS

A Division of Thomas Nelson Publishers
Since 1798

visit us at www.westbowpress.com

Published in Nashville, Tennessee, by WestBow Press, a division of Thomas Nelson, Inc.

The following Scriptures are quoted in this book:
Chapter 18: 2 Corinthians 5:1 NIV
Chapter 19: Song of Solomon 1:2, 4 NIV
Chapter 22: 2 Corinthians 4:17 KJV
Chapter 25: Psalm 91:15–16 KJV; Psalm 23:1–6 KJV
Chapter 30: Psalm 139:14 NIV
Scriptures marked NIV are from the HOLY BIBLE, NEW INTERNATIONAL VERSION, Copyright © 1973, 1978, 1984 by International Bible Society. Used by permission of Zondervan Publishing House. All rights reserved.
Those marked KJV are from the King James Version of the Bible.

Publisher's Note: This novel is a work of fiction. Names, characters, places, and incidents are either products of the author's imagination or used fictitiously. All characters are fictional, and any similarity to people living or dead is purely coincidental.

ISBN 978-0-7394-7206-4

Printed in the United States of America

For my mother, Bettie J. Eichenberg,
a longtime breast cancer survivor who's
always been my biggest cheerleader,
with all my love and gratitude.

And in memory of Linda Gundy and Jane Valenzuela,
who fought the good fight for so long
and are now at home with their Lord,
not having to fight anymore.

To God be the glory.

But those who suffer He delivers in their suffering;
He speaks to them in their affliction.

—JOB 36:15

It is never too late—in fiction or in life—to revise.

—NANCY THAYER

chapter *one*

I'm obsessed with breasts.

Not in the lesbian sense. I'm a card-carrying heterosexual woman with a serious crush on Johnny Depp. And I never really noticed them before. Breasts, I mean. They were just a fact of life. Like day and night. Sun and rain. God. And Krispy Kremes.

But now that I'm about to lose mine, I can't stop staring at them everywhere I go. The mall. Work. Church. The gym. Even my parents' house. (Sorry, Mom.)

Large ones, small ones, black ones, white ones, perky, even sagging—to me, they're all a thing of beauty.

My name is Natalie. I'm twenty-seven years old. And I have breast cancer.

Oh yeah. And I'm single. There goes my dating life down the toilet.

I never dreamed *I'd* get breast cancer. That was for older women. Right? I mean, you can't even get a routine mammogram until you're forty. There's gotta be a reason for that.

Right?

• • •

I discovered the lump by accident.

Wish I could say it was during my regular self-exams, which I learned how to do during a women's health class in college. But my monthly self-exams were more irregular than regular. And I never could tell one lump from another anyway. They all felt the same to me. Squishy.

Like more than half the women on the planet—including my sixty-seven-year-old mother, I had fibrocystic breasts. Lumpy, in other words. But to my knowledge, there's no history of breast cancer in our family, so I really wasn't worried when I felt the lump while trying on a gel bra at Victoria's Secret.

My best friend, Merritt, and I were goofing around one Saturday at the mall, wondering how we'd look if we were both a little bigger in the boob department.

Although I needed more help than she did.

We each tried on one of those padded gel and water bras like they use in Hollywood all the time. And Merritt, who'd grabbed a black double-D, was vamping for the dressing-room mirror, sucking in her cheeks, making her lips all pouty, and trying to look appropriately sexy as she admired her now-bountiful cleavage beneath her straining white poet's blouse.

I shook my head. "Too Anna Nicole Smith."

She swung her tomato-red (this week) mane and examined her double-basketball profile. "But they helped her marry a millionaire. Who knows? Maybe they'll do the same for me."

"Right. And then you'd have to sleep with a guy who's as old as your grandfather. Correction, great-grandfather."

We scrunched up horrified faces. "Eew!"

Faster than a Hollywood marriage, Merritt whipped that bad boy off from beneath her blouse and dropped it on the reject pile. Then she glanced at me and did a double take. "Hey, whaddya know? You've got boobs!"

"I know! Can you believe it?" I turned sideways and scrutinized my B-cup self. "The double-fried-egg girl finally has curves."

"You've always had curves. They're just small." She stared at my basic black T-shirt as I pirouetted in front of the mirror. "But, honey, those double fried eggs are now a couple of blueberry muffins. You *have* to buy that miracle-worker bra."

"Nope." I took a last regretful look at my curvy front. "With me, what you see is what you get."

"I know. I know. Little Ms. Candid and Up-front. But what would it hurt to be a little mysterious every now and then?" She twirled in her gauzy Indian broomstick skirt over leggings, lowered her head, and made her eyes all exotic and inscrutable. "Men like that in a woman."

"Well, they're not going to get it from me. I wouldn't know how to even begin to be mysterious." I turned my back and unhooked the lacy pink bra while Merritt busied herself collecting all the lingerie we'd tried on. As I lowered the straps off my shoulders, my hand grazed my left breast and I felt something.

A lump. Not squishy.

Time to cut down on my caffeine intake. I'd read somewhere that too much caffeine can increase fibrocystic lumps.

"Hey, heads up!" I tossed the bra over my shoulder to join the others on the reject pile.

• • •

Pushing open the door of her midtown Victorian apartment half an hour later, Merritt sang out, "Honey, I'm home!"

"Me, too, honey," I echoed, even though I didn't live there.

Jillian raised her shaped-and-waxed eyebrows over her cappuccino. "So what'd you buy?"

"A T-shirt." I raised my lone shopping bag high. "It's this great coral color. And only $9.99 at Target."

She rolled her eyes. "Nat, one of these days you've got to branch out from your discount stores." She glanced at my jeans. "And your jeans and T-shirt uniform."

"You're such a snob, Jilly." I gave her an affectionate grin. "Besides, I do so branch out. At work I wear khakis or dress pants and the occasional skirt. And I have a tailored jacket for meetings."

"Whoa. Really pushing the fashion envelope there."

Merritt was trying to skulk behind me in an evasive maneuver. But Jillian spotted her.

"Not so fast, roomie. Show me what you got for your date tonight."

My best friend exchanged a resigned look with me, shrugged her shoulders, and lifted her hands, empty palms up. "Nada."

"You two! What am I going to do with you?" Jillian slid her slim, designer-clad self off the retro kitchen bar stool and advanced toward us. "How do you expect to get a guy if you don't even make a little bit of an effort?"

"Uh, have you forgotten? I've already got a guy." I popped an Altoid into my mouth, enjoying that heady peppermint rush. "And Jack doesn't seem to have any complaints about my casual style."

"That's right," Merritt said. "And you guys have been together—what? Two months now?"

I thought back to our first date and did some mental calculations. "One month and seventeen days. But who's counting?"

"Whoa, I'm impressed, math girl. You're usually not good with numbers." Merritt turned a dazzling smile on Jillian. "And speaking of numbers, I'm not even thirty yet. You know what they say—forty is the new thirty, which goes to follow that thirty must be the new twenty, which means I'm really only eighteen. Besides . . ." She waved her hand airily. "If a guy's hung up by how I dress, he's not for me."

"At least tell me you'll change out of those paint-spattered leggings." Jillian raised a French-manicured hand to her brow, her sparkling new solitaire winking in the light, and shook her head in dismay. "I can't believe you went out in public like that."

Jillian's the fashionista in our trio of friends. A personal shopper at Nordstrom, she lives, breathes, and eats what's in and what's out, what works and what doesn't in the world of fashion.

Merritt and I, not so much.

I'm more a Target and Old Navy girl myself. In fact, the first time Jillian said "Jimmy Choo," I said "Gesundheit." But I'm willing to spend a little more money on a fabulous accessory to pull a whole outfit together, like a brooch or a designer belt. I might be casual, and I might be thrifty (Jillian has another word for it), but I do have flair if I say so myself.

And Merritt? Well, Merritt's an artist, so she has this funky, bohemian, retro, thrift-store vibe goin' on. She gravitates toward long, flowy skirts over tights or leggings and boots (combat or cowboy), often paired with a men's jacket over a billowing blouse or tank top. She's a modern-day Annie Hall. (Or Mary Kate Olsen with a little more padding. But don't ever tell her I said so.)

"I can't help it that *someone* in this room"—Merritt wriggled her eyebrows at me—"woke me up at the crack of dawn. Since I got dressed in my sleep and without benefit of caffeine, I just threw on the closest thing."

"Ten o'clock is not the crack of dawn, Batgirl. Maybe it's time to leave your cave and enter the sunshine." I beckoned to her. "Don't be afraid. Come to the light. Come to the light."

"I'll light you." Merritt grabbed an Art Deco lamp from the end table and brandished it at me.

"Watch out!" Jillian yelped.

Too late. The lamp cord caught on a can of Diet Pepsi and tipped it over onto the cream-colored carpet.

Jillian yanked some paper towels from the kitchen and raced to mop up the spill. "How many times have I asked you not to leave your half-full cans of soda lying around?"

"Sorry." Merritt grabbed the can of spot remover she kept in the end-table cabinet, and the two of them tag-teamed to clean up the mess.

"Good work, guys." I strode to the table. "But if I might make a humble suggestion? If you move the lamp to the back of the table like so"—I pushed the lamp to the back corner and angled it—"that won't happen again." I stood back and surveyed the table with a critical eye, then adjusted the coasters and angled the magazines as well. "There."

Merritt smirked. "Well, thank you, Ms. Home Makeover."

Jillian shook her head. "Actually, it looks a lot better. You have a great eye, Nat."

"And you can cook," Merritt added. "If Jack doesn't marry you, maybe I will."

I stuck out my tongue at her and looked at my watch. "Whoops, gotta go." I winked at Merritt. "Have fun on your date tonight. Call me later."

• • •

Merritt, Jillian, and I have been friends since the eighth grade. We bonded in girl-power solidarity when Doug Anderson, the captain of the junior varsity football team, slipped me a note in art class that said, "What color undershirt are you wearing today?" As my flat-chested, undeveloped self cringed and turned every shade of red, Doug and several of his jock pals sniggered. Merritt, who sat next to me and whose hair was then a two-toned blue, saw the note. She didn't say anything. But a few minutes later, she accidentally tipped a container of thinned-out orange acrylic paint into my tormentor's lap.

"Hey!" Doug jumped up as the class exploded in laughter.

"Oops. Sorry." Merritt widened her eyes and looked all innocent. "Guess I wasn't watching what I was doing."

The bell rang then, and Jillian, the head of the JV cheerleading squad, who at thirteen already filled out her perky cheerleading uniform in ways I never could, shot Doug a withering glance and linked arms with me and Merritt. "C'mon, girls, let's go to lunch. I'm starving."

We were fast friends from that moment on. Which is kind of strange considering how we were all so different.

Jillian came straight out of Central Casting as the pretty and privileged yuppie blonde cheerleader—except she never had that mean-girl thing going on. She is now engaged to Bill, a successful real-estate wheeler-dealer she met when she helped him upgrade his wardrobe.

Merritt, who was abandoned at birth and raised in a series of foster homes, is kind of a cross between Pink and Gwen Stefani with a voluptuous dash of Kelly Osbourne thrown in. On her own since sixteen, she is a fabulous artist—her oils are as bold and colorful as she is—and I just knew she'd make it really big someday. But until then, she was working as a graphic artist for a PR firm here in downtown Sacramento.

And me? I'm somewhere in-between.

After getting my B.A. in business, I worked my way up to executive assistant to one of the partners of a major capital city accounting firm. I was the go-to girl for everything in that office. And I was a sure bet for the office-manager position that would open up pretty soon, when the current manager retired.

Impressive, huh?

Okay, so the partner was my dad and the current office manager was my mom. So what? I still had to start at the bottom like everyone else.

After twenty years of marriage, my career-minded mom got pregnant at the age of forty. What she thought was early menopause was actually me. So to say my folks doted on me would be putting it mildly. But I couldn't have asked for better parents. Dad's a doll, and Mom—okay, Mom can be a tad, well, *opinionated*. In the same way that a Mack truck is opinionated. If I didn't know that she's gone to the same neighborhood church all her life, I'd swear she was Jewish. *Oy*.

Mom named me after her favorite movie star, Natalie Wood, because she'd loved her in *West Side Story*, plus I had dark eyes and dark hair like Natalie. When I was little, Dad always called me Snow White. Once we saw *Pocahontas* though, with her hair flowing behind her as she ran like the wind, he exchanged one Disney princess for another. And even after I grew up and it became clear I wasn't going to look like any of those movie stars, real or fictional, my parents still managed to make me feel pretty.

After that embarrassing art-class incident, for instance, Mom took me to Macy's and bought me five A-cup bras—three white, one nude, and one navy. (Black would have been a bit too racy for her thirteen-year-old daughter.) "Don't you worry about being small, honey," she whispered to me in the dressing room at Macy's. "When you're older it will be a blessing."

Merritt said my parents and I were a little too close and I needed to break free and spread my wings a little. But I have *so* spread my wings. After we graduated from high school, we went to Paris, just the two of us, for three weeks and had a blast. Merritt was in artist heaven as we strolled through Montmartre and spent hours at the Louvre and the Musée d'Orsay. My best moment was seeing the Eiffel Tower up close and personal while munching on a croissant.

Then, halfway through our trip, the coolest thing happened. My parents, who'd never been to Europe in their lives, let alone Paris, surprised us with a visit.

I still don't know why Merritt got so upset.

Personally, I was a little tired of youth hostels and protein bars by then, so it was paradise to stay in a nice hotel in a room adjoining my parents and enjoy pâté, coq au vin, and chocolate mousse when we dined.

Not to mention the Belgian chocolates on our pillows. Talk about bliss.

Merritt always told me it was time to leave the nest, but I had a pretty sweet deal going. I had my own place, a cute mother-in-law cottage that Dad built in the backyard for my nana when she came to stay with us in her final years. When I was twenty-three, Nana passed away and I moved into the three-room cottage—where I only paid three hundred dollars a month, I might add, a rental steal in California. I was thinking of moving in with Merritt and Jillian, but my folks showed me the financial wisdom of staying put.

My parents didn't want me to pay rent, but I insisted. My independence was important to me. And I loved my cottage. You should see what I did with it. It's amazing what you can do with some good basic pieces (my grandmother's antiques), some fabric, and lots of imagination.

We lived on a quiet, tree-lined street in an older suburb of Sacramento, the state capital of California, where the most common variety of tree is the Modesto ash, with a few maples and birches thrown in. Unfortunately, the Modesto ash only has a fifty-year life span and our little suburb was forty-nine years old. So the trees were really starting to show their age, most of them filled with mistletoe.

Mistletoe is only romantic at Christmas. Trust me on this—it's a parasite. So once or twice a year, a scruffy-looking guy in a rattle-trap truck knocked on all the neighborhood doors and offered to get rid of the mistletoe for a mere forty bucks. For years my dad did it himself, but once he turned sixty-two, his back couldn't take clambering up in the tree anymore. So now we paid the forty bucks. Except we'd let it go recently—tax season was always crazy at the firm—and the mistletoe was really getting thick.

I coasted to a stop at the end of our driveway, reveling in the beauty of the gorgeous spring day. I looked up at the ash that shaded my porch and made a mental note to get the tree guy's phone number from Mom. Then, grabbing my purse and shopping bag, I locked my car and headed to the front door of my cottage.

Before I got there, I was assaulted with a powerful blast between my breasts.

chapter *two*

G otcha!"
     Peals of delighted laughter bubbled forth from the tow-
headed little neighbor boy clutching the garden hose's high-
intensity spray nozzle.

Dropping my bag and purse, I sprinted toward him, my shirt
drenched and a river of water running down my jeans. "You are
so gonna get it!"

He shrieked and let go of the hose, running for cover in his
backyard.

"You may run, but you cannot hide. I'm gonna get you." I
grabbed the hose and squirted his skinny retreating back with a
gentle blast that made him shriek again.

"Hey, what's going on?" A sandy head popped up from behind
a soapy Mustang convertible in the driveway next door.

"Daddy, save me." The boy ran and hid behind his father's
broad back.

Suddenly conscious of my soaking T-shirt, I crossed my arms

over my chest but still made sure to keep a firm grip on the hose. "Turnabout is fair play."

My shirtless neighbor Andy grinned at the sight of my dripping clothes, then arranged his features into a stern look before turning to his four-year-old. "Josh, did you spray Aunt Natalie with the hose?"

"Yeah. I got her really good." His sapphire eyes shone. "A total sneak attack. Really cool. Just like you taught me."

My eyebrows lifted.

Andy looked sheepish—for about a millisecond. "But what else did I teach you? Is Aunt Natalie wearing shorts or a bathing suit?"

Josh scuffed his feet on the driveway and hung his head. "No."

"Then I think you owe someone an apology, don't you?"

He nodded and trudged over to me, eyes downcast. "Sorry you're not wearing a bathing suit, Aunt Natalie."

I covered my mouth to hide the watermelon grin splitting across my face.

"Josh . . . ," Andy warned.

He expelled a loud sigh. "And I apologize for drenching you too."

"Apology accepted." I knelt down and hugged him. And while I was hugging him, I discreetly raised the spray nozzle dangling behind his back and blasted his dad full in the chest.

"Hey!"

I shot Andy a triumphant smile. "You guys aren't the only ones who know how to do a sneak attack."

* * *

Andy Jacobs is my dearest male friend in the world. Three years older than me, he and I had been pals since we played in the sandbox together. Our mothers had always hoped for an alliance, especially since Andy took me to my senior prom—after my long-time boyfriend Billy broke up with me the week before. But we were just best buds. Still are.

Andy's the brother I never had.

Over the years, I've cried on his shoulder about my share of disappointments and breakups. But he's only cried on mine once. That was three and a half years ago, when his wife walked out after deciding the white-picket-fence-and-mother-in-the-suburbs bit wasn't for her.

Andy, who had bought his childhood home from his parents when they downsized to a condo, attended the same neighborhood church as I did, and really believed in the whole "for better, for worse" thing. He had never sought a divorce.

Even when his Sheila didn't write or call for more than a year.

He faithfully wore his wedding ring, didn't date, and was an excellent father to his son. Then, thirteen months after she abandoned her family, I opened my cottage door one day to find Andy on my stoop, a vacant stare on his face.

"Sheila's pregnant," he said. "She's living in Vegas with some guy who works at a dog track, and they want to get married before the baby's born."

I held him in my arms as he wept.

* * *

"So, Nat, what are you and Jack doing tonight?" Andy asked, tugging gently at my long braid.

"Nothing. He's doing the male-bonding thing with his brother." I made a face. "They're going to that World Wrestling Federation exhibition. Ugh. But what about you?" I gave him an innocent look.

"I noticed you chatting with Sara Sedberry this morning. Things looked pretty cozy between you two. Anything happening there?"

"Nope. She just needed some help with a clogged sink."

Sara was a single mom who lived around the corner and went to our church. I'd been conniving to get the two of them together for a while. She wasn't the first person I'd tried to set him up with either. But Andy rarely dated. And when he did, he never brought the woman home to meet Josh. "I'm not going to have my son get all attached to someone and then be devastated if it doesn't work out. I won't do that to him. It's not fair. When I bring someone home—if I ever do—it's because she's *the one*," he'd told me once when I quizzed him about his love life (or lack thereof).

Now he scooped up his son and tickled him. "Me and Joshie have big plans for tonight, don't we, buddy?"

Josh nodded between giggles. "We're having hamburgers and mac 'n' cheese and watching *The Incredibles*!"

"For only the seventeenth time." Andy rolled his eyes.

"Wanna come, Aunt Nat? You can bring brownies if you want."

"Oh, I can, huh?" I raised my eyebrows. "I think if I come, I'd better bring a green vegetable too. What'll it be? Peas, green beans, or broccoli?"

Josh scrunched up his wise-old-soul face. "I don't like broccoli. Even though it's good for you, it doesn't taste good."

"I'm with you, buddy." Andy gave me a plaintive smile. "Peas, please?"

• • •

If Andy's the brother I never had, Josh is also the nephew I would not otherwise have had. And although Andy has a sister in Texas,

I'm the only aunt Josh has here in town. He's called me Aunt Natalie since he learned to speak, and he learned early. That kid's precocious with a capital P. His vocabulary continually amazed me. And amused me, because I never knew if he'd sound like a four-year-old or a twenty-year-old.

I peeled off my wet T-shirt and jeans and stepped in the shower, shaking my head. *"I apologize for drenching you."* Most kids his age would just say, "I sorry."

As I was toweling off, I felt the lump again—sort of like a hard little pea.

I pulled on my basic white terry-cloth robe and headed to the kitchen, where I put on the kettle. "Sorry, Jean-Luc," I said, addressing the strong-but-smiling image of my favorite starship *Enterprise* captain taped to the inside of the cupboard door. "Instead of my customary 'Earl Grey, hot,' I need to switch to some caffeine-free Good Earth."

Opening the other cupboard door, I lusted over my collection while I waited for the water to boil. Sigh. Front and center was my Johnny, so sensitive and adorable in *Finding Neverland*. And all around him were the runners-up I drooled over: Ty Pennington, the hunky carpenter from *Extreme Makeover Home Edition*—I loved his muscles and his humor and that husky voice. But also Viggo Mortensen, strong and noble in full Aragorn regalia. And last, but not least, Clay Aiken.

Yes. Clay Aiken. I got goose bumps a few years back when he sang "Unchained Melody" and "Bridge over Troubled Water" on *American Idol*. And like millions of other voters around the country, I think he was robbed. But that hasn't stopped him from shooting to the top of the pop charts. (So there, Simon.)

Brad Pitt flexing his fabulous pecs in his *Troy* costume used to hold a place of honor next to Clay. But after dumping Jen for Angelina (how could he do that to *Rachel*?!)—down he came. Now there's an empty space just waiting to be filled.

But I was not in any hurry. Serious consideration needed to be given to the best candidate for the coveted cupboard-door slot. Orlando Bloom was a major contender, but so were Clive Owen and Hugh Jackman. What can I say? Those British and Aussie accents made me go all weak in the knees. Of course, for sheer all-American appeal and charisma—and that yummy devilish gleam in his eye—you couldn't beat Matthew McConaughey. There's a reason *People* magazine voted for him as having the best abs. Mmm.

I kept my lust collection under wraps, of course, especially when Jack was around. Didn't want him to think I was stuck in junior high. And wouldn't want to make him jealous either, especially since he's gorgeous enough to belong right up there with the others. Dark, spiky hair, blue eyes, runner's bod—what a combination!

I glanced at the picture of us on the fridge, taken last month on our third date, playing miniature golf with some friends of his. Jack's right behind me, having just whispered something funny in my ear, and I'm laughing, my head thrown back. His buddy snapped the picture just as my ponytail smacked Jack in the face, giving him a beard on his theretofore clean-shaven chin. My fingers reached up to trace his lips above the ponytail beard.

That was the day we first kissed.

Mmm again.

• • •

Just as the kettle began to whistle, my front door cracked open.

Every Saturday afternoon without fail, Mom came over for my

dirty clothes and a cup of tea. Since there weren't a washer and dryer at my place, she always took my laundry to their house and did it for me. I'd protested at first, but it made her happy, so who was I to deny my mother happiness? Besides, laundry's about the only domestic-goddess skill my professionally oriented mother is good at, so I liked to encourage her.

I pulled out another mug and quickly shut my fantasy doors. I kept my collection out of Mom's sight too.

An empty laundry basket appeared in the kitchen doorway, followed by my color-coordinated, not-a-hair-out-of-place mother.

"Did you have fun shopping with Merritt today?" Mom asked hopefully. "Get anything new?"

"Yep. A T-shirt."

"Oh, honey, when are you ever going to start wearing something besides jeans and T-shirts?" She set down the laundry basket and smoothed her gray slacks, removing a minuscule piece of lint. "You live in them."

"That's 'cause they're comfortable." I poured the boiling water over the tea bag. "You and Jillian must be in cahoots."

"Is that cinnamon I smell?"

"Yep. I was in the mood for some Good Earth today."

No way was I going to mention the caffeine—or the lump. *Terms of Endearment* was one of Mom's all-time favorite movies. Knowing her, she'd immediately start wringing her Shirley MacLaine hands and cast me in the dying Debra Winger role.

I poised the spout over her mug. "Want some?"

"Thanks." She plopped down on one of my white metal bistro chairs. "Do you and Jack have plans for tonight? Since the weather's so nice for April, your dad's planning to throw some steaks on the grill. I got some salad in a bag and some potatoes to nuke."

"Sorry." My lips turned down in a pout—Dad's steak was fabulous. "Jack's out of town with his brother watching pumped-up men on steroids with one-word names wrestle each other. And I'm going over to Andy's to watch *The Incredibles*—Josh's current movie du jour. We're having hamburgers. But if you have any leftovers, maybe you could save me some . . ."

I threw her a pleading look, and she laughed.

"Anything for you, my darling little carnivore. If you're good, Mother may even go to the freezer and bake you a pie."

chapter *three*

I hated going to the ob-gyn.

Is there anything more humiliating than putting your feet in those stirrups? I always felt like a wishbone about to be snapped. And why is it they always have the table angled to face the door? Is it too much to ask for a little modesty and discretion? C'mon, work with me, people! I lived in mortal fear of flashing the whole doctor's office.

And do they have stirrups for men? I don't *think* so. All they have to do is bend over and cough. Big deal. So much more dignified.

But dignified or not, this had to be done. So I sat there on the edge of the table and tried to make the best of things.

The doctor's assistant took my blood pressure, then handed me one of those flat, blue vacuum-packed gowns that's a hybrid of paper towel and waxed paper.

"The doctor will be right with you," she said.

And the race was on.

Since I didn't know if I was going to have one minute or fifteen before the doctor arrived, I yanked off my shirt in one fluid
motion and undid my bra with one hand while trying to open up
the gown with the other. As usual, it wouldn't cooperate—I just
knew I was going to rip it. So there I stood in full frontal glory,
fumbling with the sky-blue folds, keeping one nervous eye trained
on the doorknob for the first hint of movement.

Ah, success at last. I pulled on the flimsy gown and gingerly
tied it shut with the plastic belt (which also looked like it would
rip in a heartbeat). Then with all embarrassing body parts safely
covered, I reached under the gown to pull down my pants and
underwear. I hung all my clothes on the back of the door, tucking
the underwear neatly out of sight under the jeans and T-shirt.
Then I was sitting at the edge of the table, looking down at my
chipped blue toenails (courtesy of Merritt), waiting for the doctor.

It must have been a slow day, because I only had to wait seven
minutes. I had lain back and was in the midst of playing con-
nect-the-water-stains on the ancient ceiling when a couple of
brisk raps at the door made me sit up quickly. A head of Little
Orphan Annie curls shot through with gray poked in first, soon
followed by the angular, freckled, fifty-something form of Dr.
Laura Calhoun. (She's nothing at all like the more famous Dr. Laura,
I might add.)

"Hi, Natalie. How are you?" She gave me a warm smile.
"Haven't seen you in a while."

"I know." I had the grace to look guilty. "It's been a couple of
years since my last pap."

She checked my chart. "Three, actually."

"Really? That long, huh? Sorry. I kept forgetting to reschedule
my missed appointment."

"That's what they all say." She grinned. "The only ones more unloved than gynecologists in the medical profession are dentists."

Dr. Calhoun made small talk to put me at ease while she pulled out the stirrups, eased me back onto the table, and began the exam. She chatted about the romantic comedy she'd seen over the weekend, then segued into favorite reality shows. She liked the one where the rich executive always said, "You're fired!" I was hooked on the heartwarming home-makeover show. I was in the midst of describing in minute detail the fairy-tale bedroom of the daughter in the latest installment when her fingers, which had been playing piano on my left breast, stilled.

"Feel that lump, huh, Doc? Don't worry. I've already cut back on the caffeine."

"That's good. Too much caffeine can cause tenderness and swelling in some women." She frowned. "Where are you in your cycle? Breasts always get lumpier before your period."

I tried to do the math in my head. "I think I should start in about two and a half weeks."

Dr. Calhoun continued examining my breasts, moving over to the right one and then returning again to the left. Then she headed south for the part I always dreaded.

"Just relax." She advanced upon me with the shiny metal shoehorn thingy.

"Right. Tell that to my clenched thighs." I looked up at the water stains again, squinting slightly until they ran into a vision of someone floating in the ocean. Then I shut my eyes and imagined myself languidly floating in the Pacific.

"Okay, all done. You can open your eyes now." She peeled off her latex gloves, dropped them in the disposable-waste can, and washed her hands while I gratefully pushed myself up to a sitting position.

"Tell you what," Dr. Calhoun said. "Just to be on the safe side, I'd like you to get a mammogram."

"A mammogram? Don't they hurt?"

"Nah, they're just a little uncomfortable."

•   •   •

A *little* was stretching it.

Did you ever notice that doctors have their own unique vocabulary? "Just a little stick now." Yeah, right.

Now I knew how it felt to be a hamburger patty on a George Foreman grill—and on my lunch hour, no less.

After the technologist raised the grill cover and my breast popped back to its normal, unsquished shape, I waited in the dressing-room cubicle at the breast-imaging center, clad in yet another waxy blue gown, and thumbed through the latest issue of *People*.

A knock on the cubicle door interrupted my drooling over a picture of Orlando Bloom.

"Natalie?" The kind, middle-aged tech in kitten-print scrubs who'd just finished squashing my breasts opened the door. "Your mammogram was difficult to read. It often is in younger women because your breasts are so much denser, so the radiologist wants us to do an ultrasound too. We're just waiting for the okay from your referring physician."

"Aren't ultrasounds what they do when a woman's pregnant?" I flashed back to the *Friends* episode when Rachel couldn't see her baby but pretended to Ross that she could. "I'm *so* not pregnant."

"Ultrasounds are used for many reasons—including giving us a better picture when a mammogram can't."

"Oh, okay." Another first to share with Merritt and Jillian.

The ultrasound was a little strange. A female tech squirted some warm gel-goop on my breast and rolled a thingy that looked like a Star Trek phaser over the lump—which showed up as black wavy lines on the TV-looking screen.

I was tempted to change the channel but decided against it.

• • •

Dr. Calhoun called two days later to tell me that the lump looked a little "unusual." So just to be safe (*again with the "just to be safe" bit?*) she was referring me to a breast surgeon so I could get an expert opinion. And a needle biopsy.

Now I was getting seriously freaked out.

"It's just a precautionary measure," she reassured me. "Don't worry. Most lumps are benign."

"It's not the lump I'm worried about. It's the needle."

Ever since a nasty tetanus shot as a kid, coupled with a painful blood draw from a novice lab tech when I was fifteen— she kept digging and digging in the needle, trying to capture a "rolling" vein—needles have not been my friends.

But I figured I could do what I always did in her office—shut my eyes and think of the ocean.

• • •

After I hung up, I went online and Googled "breast needle biopsy." I learned that, as my ob-gyn had said, most breast lumps are benign. But when I saw a picture of the needle, I began to shake.

The shaking started all over again the following week, when

the thirty-something breast surgeon, Dr. Karen Herris—another woman, yes! I wasn't comfortable with strange men feeling my breasts—started explaining the procedure. I squeezed my eyes shut and just nodded and said uh-huh as she talked. I was so freaked out by the needle prospect that the words "lump feels a little suspicious" didn't even register at the time.

Before I knew it, it was all over.

"Okay, you can open your eyes now. We're finished."

Cautiously, I opened one eye. "Are the needles put away?"

"Yep. All gone."

"Now what?"

Dr. Herris stuck a nickel-sized bandage over the tender spot. "We'll send this to the lab, and I should have the results by late tomorrow afternoon." She picked up my chart and a pen. "Where will you be around five o'clock so I can call you?"

• • •

I know it sounds clueless. Maybe I was in denial—or just stupid. But to tell the truth, I was just relieved the biopsy was over. Okay, I'd done the right thing—taken care of the problem. Even better, I'd managed to do it without freaking out my mother, although it took some little white lies about running errands away from the office.

I honestly didn't think much about the results. I was too busy thinking about Jack and our weekend plans.

At 5:07 the next day, I'd just turned off the freeway and was approaching a stop sign when Pachelbel's Canon rang—unknown number. I flipped open my phone as I coasted to a stop. "Hello?"

"Natalie?" Dr. Herris said gently. "I'm afraid I have news you aren't going to want to hear . . . It's cancer."

chapter *four*

Cancer?

I couldn't breathe. *Cancer kills people.* My fingers strangled the phone as hot tears coursed down my cheeks.

A car honked behind me, and I turned the corner in a daze.

I don't want to die. Please, God. Not now. I haven't even had sex yet! Not really. How can I have breast cancer? Me? Two-fried-eggs Natalie? There must be a mistake. I'm too young . . .

Dr. Herris was still talking, and I tried to focus in on what she was saying, but I just couldn't wrap my head around it.

Will I lose my breast?

The only thing that really registered was when she said there was no rush for me to decide what to do—the lump was small and had probably been growing for a while.

Why didn't that reassure me?

Hanging up, I continued driving and tried to think of anyone I knew who'd had breast cancer. Anyone at all. Oh yeah. Mrs. McCaffey from church who always wore velvet or floral turbans. *She died. Remember?* Not a good example. I wanted success stories.

I wracked my brain and finally thought of Edie Falco from *The Sopranos.* And, um . . . Olivia Newton-John. And . . . Melissa Etheridge. That was better. It was so brave and cool when she performed at the Grammys bald.

Bald? I fingered my thick French braid.

Forget my breast. Will I lose my hair?

The title song from Merritt's favorite retro soundtrack started spinning in my head: *"long, beautiful hair . . ."* Not to be vain or anything, but people were always complimenting me on my hair. The thickness. The shine. The natural wave. It was definitely one of my best features—and one of the first things that caught Jack's eye.

I was jogging through the park one Saturday. No, I'm not a runner. I don't even work out regularly. But now and then it feels good to break a sweat, especially after being cooped up in an office all week. So I was jogging through the park one Saturday morning in a baggy white T-shirt and running shorts, my dark ponytail bouncing against my sticky T-shirt, when all of a sudden I heard a wolf whistle behind me.

I stopped short, turning around to glare in righteous feminist indignation at the sexist pig who had dared to emit such an inappropriate, politically incorrect Neanderthal mating call.

And collided smack into said sexist pig, tumbling us both to the grass.

After Jack, the sexist but drop-dead gorgeous pig, made sure I was okay and apologized for his wolfish catcall ("Not something I normally do, but I couldn't help myself. Your hair looked so beautiful and gleaming in the sun . . ."), he managed to charm me into a date.

We'd been seeing each other ever since. And Jack still loved my hair. He was always playing with it, and he liked to run his fingers through it when he kissed me.

Jack! How am I going to tell him? How do you tell your new boyfriend you have cancer? And not only cancer, but breast cancer?

I jerked the car over to the side of the street, and horns blared.

Smart, Sherlock. You don't need to worry about dying from cancer. You'll just buy it in a car accident instead.

I fumbled in the glove box for a tissue, then blew my nose and checked my face in the mirror.

Nice.

It looked like an entire tube of mascara had been finger-painted on my face. I spit on a tissue and tried to wipe off some of the damage.

No good. I rooted beneath my seat until I found an old water bottle with a little water left. I wet the tissue and tried again. Much better. I tilted the mirror down so I could see my boobs. I stared at their reflection long and hard, but they didn't look any different than they had that morning when I got dressed for work.

I looked again. Intently.

They *were* different, though. One of them had this deadly thing growing inside it, like the monster in *Alien*. Only I didn't want it to explode out of my chest the way it exploded from that guy's stomach. I wanted to kill the monster first, before it could kill me. But I needed to know how. Knowledge was power.

With fresh resolve, I started my car and pointed it in the direction of the library. I checked out several books—by doctors, nurses, and plain, everyday women who had already walked this cancer road ahead of me—before heading home.

Home. How would I tell Mom and Dad? They fretted and fussed over me when I had a little sniffle. How would they ever handle this?

I grabbed my cell to call for backup. But Merritt wasn't answering. Neither was Jillian, and I knew she was still at work anyway. Jack was in Chicago on business; he wouldn't be home until the next day. And this wasn't really something I wanted to tell my boyfriend over the phone. Much better to do in person.

In person . . .

I glided into the driveway, turned off the engine, and started to open my car door. But the stack of books on the passenger seat screamed out *breast cancer*, so I casually draped my sweater over them, making sure that no words showed through.

Taking a deep breath, I scurried next door before Mom or Dad could catch sight of me. I knocked on Andy's back door, determined to ease into it casually. But when he saw my face and asked me what was wrong, I blurted it out: "I have cancer."

Andy blanched and pulled me inside. He shut the door and wrapped me in a great big hug. And I started crying again for the third time that hour—great, gulping sobs that caused snot to run down my nose and onto his U2 T-shirt. He stroked my hair and made soothing noises of comfort.

I knew he was also praying. He's a praying man.

When my sobs finally subsided into hiccups, he patted my back, handed me a paper towel so I could blow my nose, and led me to the kitchen table. "Now tell me everything."

Afterward, he gripped my hands and looked at me with eyes filled with tender, big-brotherly love. "Hey, look, whatever you decide to do, I'm behind you all the way. Whatever you need, I'm there, Nattie. We're going to get through this."

"You mean that?"

He nodded.

"Okay." I blew my nose again—this time a nice, feminine honk—brushed the last traces of tears away, and gave him a wry smile. "I'm going to take you up on that. You need to come with me now to tell my folks. You know how my mother can be."

"No problem. I got your back."

• • •

"Mom, Dad, I have something to tell you."

They looked from me to Andy, who was glued thigh-to-thigh to me on the couch, his hand tightly holding mine. Mom's eyes widened, and her mouth began to curve in a delighted smile.

"It's not what you think." I dropped Andy's hand and jumped up, in a hurry to get it over with. "Look, I don't want you to worry, because everything's going to be fine." Pushing the stack of newspapers to one side, I sat on the hassock in front of Mom's wingback. "But"—I took a deep breath—"today I found out I have breast cancer."

"What?!" All the color had drained out of my mother's face.

"You're kidding," Dad said.

"It can't be—there must be a mistake." Mom's fuchsia finger-nails dug into the armrest of her chair.

"That's right." My father's eyebrows beetled together. "Doctors are always making mistakes." He jerked his recliner to its full upright position. "Who do they think they are, scaring people that way?"

I touched his knee gently. "It's not a mistake."

His leg trembled beneath my hand, and he leaned over and grabbed me tightly, his voice choking. "No. Not my little girl."

"It's okay, Dad. It's okay." I patted his shaking back and met my mother's streaming eyes. "Really. The doctor thinks they caught it early because the lump is so small. It's going to be fine."

Mom swiped at her eyes, then joined us in a brisk group hug. "Well, of course you'll be fine," she said in that determined tone I knew so well. "We'll make sure of that."

"All of us." Andy strode over and joined the pileup.

"That's right." Dad released me to pull out his handkerchief and blow his nose.

"So what'd the doctor say you should do?" Mom asked. She had already reverted to business mode.

"The first thing is for me to learn everything I can so that I can make an informed decision about my treatment." I grabbed my water bottle and took another swig. "I checked out several books from the library to skim this weekend, and I want to research some Web sites—"

"I can help with that." Mom rustled through a pile of papers and magazines on the cluttered end table and finally extracted a pad of paper. "I'll Google it and print out everything we need to know."

Dad looked at a loss. Then he snapped his fingers. "And I'll call Stan Johnson, my golfing buddy. He used to be the head of oncology at Capital before he retired. Stan's a good man. He won't steer us wrong."

I made my way back to the couch.

"What's wrong, honey?" Dad followed me, concern creasing his brow. "Are you in pain?"

"No. Just a little tender from the needle biopsy yesterday. But I—"

"What?" Mom gave me an incredulous look. Her voice rose. "You had a biopsy yesterday and didn't tell us?"

"I didn't want to worry you." *Besides, it was supposed to be* "*nothing.*"

"Who went with you?" Mom shot a suspicious glance at Andy.

He held up his hands. "Not me. I just found out too."

"No one went with me. I went by myself, Mom. I'm a big girl, remember?"

"You didn't even take Merritt?"

"Did someone say my name?" My best friend appeared in the living-room doorway in a tie-dyed tunic and orange leggings. "I knocked at the back door, but nobody answered, so I just let myself in." She looked around the room at all our strained faces. "What's going on?"

I clapped my hand over my mouth. "I totally forgot. We're supposed to go out to dinner and a movie tonight."

And then for the third time that day, I had to tell someone I loved that I had cancer.

chapter *five*

"Hey, check it out, Nat. This woman has really great boobs." Merritt turned one of the library books my way. "Look at her before and after. What an improvement, huh?"

"That's putting it mildly." I gazed at the torso of the middle-aged woman before her double mastectomy and then after her surgery and reconstruction were complete.

Can you say perky?

Reading the caption below the picture, the fifty-three-year-old woman was quoted as saying that both she and her husband "loved" her "new, nonsagging set" and that it had revitalized their love life.

I blinked. *TMI.* Too much information.

Merritt and I had ditched the dinner-and-a-movie idea. Instead, we were eating pizza and thumbing through the stack of books I'd brought home. The artist in her was entranced by the black-and-white picture book depicting breast cancer patients of all ages, colors, and shapes.

I turned the page and laughed out loud. One sixty-something woman had opted against reconstruction when she had her single mastectomy. Instead, she had chosen to have a yellow smiley-face tattooed over her scar. The scar was the smile. "Good for you, Grandma! Very cool."

Merritt grinned. "I could do something like that for you. Maybe your favorite dessert—a hot-fudge sundae with a cherry on top. I could sketch it in removable marker and then have the tattoo guy just fill it in."

"No thanks." I made a face at her. "A little too suggestive. Besides, that would involve a needle. And to outline and color in that whole area? Repeated in-and-out needle torture." I shuddered, remembering how I'd passed out when I accompanied Merritt to get her Free Bird tattoo.

She twisted her leg to admire the small blue bird in the shape of a flowing V on her left ankle. "Good thing the guy didn't flinch when you fell down, or I'd have had Free Willy instead." Her face lit up. "Hey, what about the Eiffel Tower? You loved that, and it would just be an outline. No coloring in."

"Not in this lifetime." I picked off a stray onion from my mushroom-and-sausage half and stuck it back on Merritt's vegetarian side. "Thanks for calling and telling Jillian for me. I couldn't go through that again. I didn't even answer the phone when Jack called earlier."

Merritt raised her eyebrows a little but nodded. "No problem."

"I kind of thought Jillian might drop by, though . . ." My voice trailed off.

"Give her some time, Nat." Merritt gave me a gentle look. "Remember, her mom died of colon cancer when she was eleven, so she's a little freaked out. And scared."

"Well, I'm scared too."

"So am I." She squeezed my hand. "But the difference is we know you're not going to die."

"We do?" This was the first time since my diagnosis that any-one I loved had spoken the *D*-word aloud. Leave it to Merritt to address the elephant in the room.

Merritt shook her now-jade-tipped pigtails vigorously. "Yep. Not an option." She grabbed another one of the thick how-to-cope-with-cancer books from the stack and read aloud: "Breast cancer is not the death sentence it once was. With all the treat-ments available today, if caught early, it can be treated success-fully." She looked up at me. "And yours was caught early. That's what the doctor said. Right?"

"Not exactly. She said she *thinks* it was caught early because the lump is so small."

"Well, we're going to think positive." She tossed a book my way. "Okay, you read what they have to say about the different treatment options in that one while I check out this one. Then we'll compare notes."

"I have a better idea." My eyelids fluttered at half-mast. "Why don't you take that with you and give me a book report by Monday? And I'll go to bed and start reading again in the morning."

• • •

True to my word, after inhaling Dad's primo blueberry pancakes at breakfast with my folks Saturday morning, I grabbed a few of the cancer books and headed outside to read in my weathered Adirondack chair. But after a couple of hours, I got bogged down. They were all so medical and technical and overwhelming.

Except for one little hot-pink one.

The author—not a doctor, nurse, or medical professional—was an average woman just like me, except that she had been newly married when she was diagnosed. She shared funny and inspiring anecdotes of how she serenaded farewell to her breast and "took control" over the cancer by choosing to get her head shaved before all her hair started falling out in clumps.

I fingered my braid again. I wasn't sure I could do that.

But the most hilarious part was when she wrote about being so proud of her new prosthesis that she wore it around the house all the time rather than going braless as she always had in the past. A couple of days after she got the fake boob insert, a plumber came over to fix the toilet. She was busy scrubbing the bathtub when all of a sudden the prosthesis fell out and landed on the edge of the tub with a loud *smack*—right in front of the male plumber.

I laughed so hard I snorted out my tea.

"That must be a really good book."

"Jack! What are you doing here?" I snapped the little pink book shut and turned it facedown in my lap.

"Well, that's a nice welcome," he teased. "I just got back into town and came right over to see my best girl." He leaned down and twirled his finger in the curl at the end of my braid. "Miss me?"

I flung my arms around his neck, dropping the book in the process. "You have no idea."

* * *

At church the next morning, sitting between Mom and Dad in our regular pew, I flipped through the bulletin while the choir began their opening session of praise music. I skimmed through the announcements for the seniors' potluck, the young couples' camping trip, and the request for Vacation Bible School volunteers.

Not this year. I'm taking a break.

When I got to the prayer requests, I blanched. There, right between Evelyn Carmichael's stroke and Henry Wilson's gout flareup, screamed the words, "Natalie Moore, Breast Cancer." *With a capital* B.

"Mom," I hissed in her ear.

"What?" she whispered back.

"You called my name in to the church prayer chain?"

"Of course." She shot me a puzzled glance. "That way everyone can be praying for you."

"No wonder every man was averting his eyes from my chest when he said good morning." I clenched the bulletin. "I didn't want the whole world to know."

"It's not the whole world." She squared her beige, rayon-blend shoulders. "We've been members here for over forty years. These people are our *family*."

"Not all three hundred and fifty of them!"

Dad shushed us as Marilyn Black began her bordering-on-the-operatic-but-not-in-a-good-way solo.

I slunk down in the pew, crossed my arms over my fried-egg chest, and closed my eyes in an effort to appear caught up in the music. But Marilyn's wobbly vibrato on top of the billboard about my boobs was simply too much for my battered psyche.

When the time came for the greet-each-other-with-a-brotherly-hug point of the service, old Mrs. McCormick grabbed me from behind in a bone-crushing embrace and prayed into my ear, "Jesus, oh sweet Jesus, please spare this young girl's life." Her tears wet my neck. "We know that You are the Great Physician who can heal all our afflictions, so we pray that You heal Natalie." Her skinny arms gripped me tighter, and her heavy lavender cologne nearly strangled me. "Unless, of course, You want her home with You. Not our will, but Thine."

"Uh, thanks," I murmured just as Faith Thomas from the pew in front reached for my hand with both of hers. Twice divorced and on the husband hunt again, forty-something Faith took a more practical tack: "Don't worry, honey," she murmured, patting my back. "As small as you are, most men won't even notice the difference."

Angie Williams, Faith's plus-sized, forty-year-old shadow and trolling partner, hugged me and said, "Oh my gosh, Natalie! When I heard, the first thing I thought of was my sister-in-law's cousin in Wisconsin. She had breast cancer, too, and died the day before her thirtieth birthday."

More than enough brotherly love going around today for this girl, thank you very much.

Time for Dave, our associate pastor, to read the announcements. I slunk even lower in our side pew, expecting the worst. But although his eyes flicked in my direction, he didn't mention my name.

Whew. Saved by the compassionate pastor.

Determined to beat a hasty retreat before our whole church family descended upon me, I excused myself to go to the ladies' room while Pastor Bob, our senior pastor, was still wrapping up his sermon.

I hid in one of the stalls for a while, checking out the Christian graffiti: "God rocks!" "My boss is a Jewish carpenter," and "What would Jesus do?"

Not deface public property, I thought. *Although there was that one time in the temple . . .*

Finally, knowing I couldn't put it off any longer, I left the narrow metal sanctuary, washed my hands, and used the paper towel I'd dried them with to open the restroom door. I tossed the paper towel in the trash with a backward glance on my way out. In the process, I managed to body slam Dan Martin, who was just exiting the men's room.

"Whoa, careful." He grasped my arms to keep me from falling. "You okay?" His good-looking, eligible-lawyer face flushed, and he made sure to look only above my neck.

"I'm fine. Thanks." *Only dying of embarrassment.*

He dropped my arms and fidgeted. "Uh, a few of us are going to Macaroni Grill for lunch. Want to join us?"

It was my turn to fidget. I crossed my arms in a protective chest maneuver. "Well, uh—"

"*There* you are, Nat," a familiar voice behind me said. "I've been looking for you everywhere. Ready to go to La Bou?"

I whirled around, mouth agape.

Merritt linked her arm with mine and gave Dan an apologetic smile. "You don't mind if I kidnap my best friend, do you?"

He shook his head as he took in her frizzy green hair, her tie-dyed tank and skirt, and the silver navel ring flashing in the middle of her exposed midriff. He waved good-bye weakly as Merritt led me away.

"What are *you* doing in church?" I whispered.

She gave me a devilish smile. "Saving you from Mr. Spit-and-Polish Conservative." She shuddered. "Did those loafers really have tassels?"

"Never mind the tassels, heathen-girl. Let's hurry and get out of here before the roof caves in." Once outside, I looked around the parking lot. "Where's your bicycle?"

"I hitched."

"What? How many times have I told you—"

"Relax, Mom. Bill and Jillian dropped me off on the way to their megachurch."

"God's going to get you for scaring me like that."

She looked heavenward and sighed. "Just add it to the list."

• • •

At La Bou, our favorite neighborhood lunch spot, I ordered my usual—a half sandwich of turkey and jack cheese on a croissant and a half Caesar salad—while Merritt went her standard veggie route: a cheese, avocado, tomato, and lettuce sandwich with tons of sprouts and the Oriental salad.

I sent a quick text message to my folks so they wouldn't think I'd run away, then dug into my salad. "Mmm, no one in town can touch La Bou's Caesar. Yum. Thanks for suggesting this."

"Anytime." She took a sip of her bottled water and asked casually, "So did Jack get back yesterday?"

"Uh-huh."

"Well, how'd he take the news?"

I pointed to my full mouth, then held up my index finger in a "just a minute" gesture. I needed that extra chewing minute to formulate my response. I swallowed and took a drink of water. "He was pretty shocked, as you can imagine."

"Well, sure. We all were." She gazed at me intently. "And?"

And he acted as if I'd just told him I had AIDS, and he could catch it.

But I wasn't about to tell Merritt that. She'd tell me to leave his sorry butt and never look back. And I wasn't about to do that. I liked his butt too much, especially in jeans. No, I needed to give Jack the benefit of the doubt. And a little time. After all, I'd just dropped a huge bombshell in his lap. He needed time to process it. Then everything would be fine.

I hoped.

"And?" Merritt prompted again.

"Well, he was a little freaked out. And, of course, concerned for me."

Her tense posture relaxed. "So how was the show?"

"The show?"

"The musical? Didn't you guys have tickets to a play last night?"

"Oh yeah. But we were both too tired to go. He was still jet-lagged from that long flight, and I was pretty worn out from this whole emotional roller coaster, so he gave the tickets to a buddy of his."

"Let me guess." She waggled her eyebrows Groucho Marx style. "You stayed in and snuggled together watching *Trading Spaces* instead?"

"You know me so well."

Yes, I had watched my favorite decorating show last night, but I'd done it alone—with a full box of tissues at my side that was empty by the end of the night. Jack had pleaded exhaustion and said he still needed to unpack and do "a ton" of laundry before going back to work on Monday, so could we have a "rain check" on our date?

That was something else I didn't plan to tell Merritt. She'd immediately jump to the wrong conclusion. I decided to redirect the conversation. "So did Jillian TiVo that supermodel competition again and make you watch it?"

"Nah. Bill had a softball game, so she went to cheer him on, and I had the whole apartment to myself." Merritt let loose a blissful sigh. "No one to bug me about drinking soda in the living room or putting my feet up on the coffee table."

Nice, I thought. Jillian could cheer her fiancé on, but she couldn't even stop by or pick up the phone to see how I was doing?

When Merritt went to the restroom, I checked my messages to see if Jack had called or texted. Nothing. I quickly sent him a breezy text telling him I was having lunch with Merritt and checking that we were still on for tonight—we were going out for Mexican with some of his friends from work.

All the way home after I dropped Merritt off, I kept checking my cell, but still no response. The blinking light on my answering machine when I opened my front door made me a happy and seriously relieved girl. *His cell probably just needed recharging.*

I hit the play button and grabbed a water from the fridge, wondering which pair of jeans I'd wear tonight with my new coral T-shirt.

"Hi, Nat." Jack's voice sounded strained. "I'm afraid we're going to have to cancel for tonight. I'm absolutely buried in work, trying to get ready for my big presentation tomorrow. I'll probably be up half the night. Sorry. I'll talk to you soon."

The call had come five minutes after I texted him from the restaurant—when he knew I wouldn't be home yet.

"Coward." I threw my water bottle at the answering machine, sending it crashing to the floor.

• • •

Sunday night passed in a blur of tears. I didn't want either my folks or Andy to know that Jack had stood me up, so I closed all my blinds, turned off the lights, and watched *Extreme Makeover Home Edition* in bed with my headphones on. Watching Ty and crew rebuild the home of a widower with three kids whose pretty young wife had died of cancer, I blubbed my way through almost a whole box of tissues—and it was an episode I'd seen before.

I didn't even know I had fallen asleep until I woke up numb two hours later. When I got up to go the bathroom, my foot had fallen asleep. I stumbled and fell when I got out of bed, grabbing at my quilt as I went down. Unhurt, I lay on the thick-pile carpet for a while, my great-grandmother's crazy quilt cocooning me, remembering back to when I was little and took my blanky everywhere I went. Finally, my bladder reminded me of why I was up. I shook my foot back and forth, tingling it awake, and made my way to the bathroom, the quilt trailing in my wake.

After brushing my teeth and scrubbing the dried tears from my face, I shambled back to bed, bunched my quilt tightly around me, and continued with the nightly ritual I'd been doing since I was eleven—brushing my hair a hundred strokes before going to bed.

chapter *six*

Monday I was happy to return to work and normalcy, thankful that the puffiness in my eyes had gone down considerably in the night. I still had to use a lot of concealer, though.

I always arrived fifteen minutes before everyone else to unlock the doors, organize my desk in descending orders of to-do piles, from the most urgent to the least, and provide backup in case the phones got busy early.

Amber, our new nineteen-year-old receptionist, was habitually late. Since she was also supposed to start the coffee, I usually wound up doing that, too, so that the partners would have a fresh cup when they arrived.

Today I was also eager to check my e-mail while no one was around. Jack liked to send me funny messages at work. Since he'd had to cancel the night before, and we hadn't gotten to see each other much over the weekend, I was hoping he'd have flooded my in-box with funnies.

I readied my keys but discovered to my surprise that the door was already unlocked. I pushed it open with my hip, my hands full of purse, newspaper, herbal tea, and muffins I'd picked up at Starbucks on my way in.

"Omigosh, Natalie!" Amber, who had a tendency to dress inappropriately for the office in skirts that were too short and tops that showed her belly button, jumped up. "Let me help you with that."

Last week I'd had to have a diplomatic talk with Amber about not showing her tummy or too much leg in the office. And I was pleased to see she'd taken the talk to heart. Today she wore pants and a tucked-in top that completely covered her stomach. Problem was the low-rise black pants were so tight they looked sprayed on, and her V-neck yellow knit top revealed way too much cleavage.

I started to say something, then sighed. *She might as well enjoy her boobs while she can.*

Amber relieved me of the paper and muffins and sent me a look of sympathy from beneath her heavily mascaraed lashes. "I'm so sorry."

"For what?"

"About the, you know"—her voice lowered even though no one else was in the office—"*breast* cancer." Her eyes flicked to my chest. "How are you feeling? Are you scared? I'd be scared to death. I didn't know you could get breast cancer so young. I thought it was just for older women. What are you going to do?" She followed me to my desk.

"Boy, word sure gets around fast." I set my tea and purse down carefully. "I just found out Friday on my way home from work."

Amber looked uncomfortable. "Uh, your mom, I mean Ruth, called and told us over the weekend so it wouldn't be such a shock when we came in today."

"Us?" I stared at her. "Who's us?"

Amber twisted a hunk of hair around her finger. "Me and Gregg."

Gregg Hamilton was my dad's partner in the accounting firm. He was also a family friend I'd known all my life.

"Uh, Natalie?" Amber looked miserable. "Your mom, I mean Ruth, asked me to call the rest of the office and tell them for her."

I could have killed her.

The front door opened, and behind Amber's size-four frame I saw a pair of pressed khakis and a black polo shirt with a silver head rising from the collar. "Nattie!" Gregg rushed over and enveloped me in a bear hug, surrounding me with his familiar smell of coffee and cigars. "Whatever you need, you tell us, sweetie. Whatever we can do, you just let us know. We're with you all the way." He whispered in my ear, "You're going to beat this, kiddo. You're young and strong."

I blinked back tears. "Thanks, Gregg. Can you excuse me for a second?"

And for the second day in a row I found myself hiding in a bath-room stall. This time, though, I wished I could stay there forever.

No such luck.

My mother's worried voice intruded. "Honey, are you okay?"

Sure, for a woman who's got a big red C hanging on her chest.

I felt a new affinity for Hester Prynne.

I exited the stall. "Mom, we need to talk."

• • •

Jack was missing in action.

He hadn't returned any of my calls or text messages, and

when I went by his apartment, he was never home. Or at least he didn't answer the door.

I was tempted to waylay him at work, but my pride stopped me—the little I had left.

"I don't understand," I sobbed to Merritt after a week with no word from him. "How can he just disappear like that? I thought he cared for me, that I meant something to him." I cried harder.

"Jack's a jerk." Merritt scowled. "Forget him. You're better off without him."

"She's right."

"Andy?" I said thickly, looking at him with blurred eyes. "What are you doing here?"

"Your door was open and I knocked, but you didn't hear me." His face darkened. "But I heard you, and I agree with Merritt. You're better off without that jerk." Andy hugged me and raised a tissue to my runny nose. "Now blow."

I did.

He handed me another tissue. "And again."

Andy picked up the poker from my fireplace and slapped it against his palm. "Now tell me where this jerk lives, and I'll go pay him a little visit." He glowered. "Nobody messes with my little sister unless they want to sleep with the fishes."

I giggled through my sniffles. "Are you supposed to be Tony Soprano or Sonny Corleone? You need to work on your accent a little."

"And the whole menacing thing needs some work too." Merritt glanced at Andy's Daffy Duck T-shirt and worn Top-Siders and chuckled. "You're just not threatening enough, Mr. Boy Next Door."

• • •

Jack wasn't the only one who couldn't deal with my cancer.

Lynn, a friend and secretary in the office next door with whom I went to lunch a couple of times a month, was always busy when I invited her to split a sandwich.

"You'd think I had some horrible communicable disease or something," I groused to Merritt as we sat in her favorite independent bookstore-coffeehouse drinking decaf chai. Luckily we were tucked away in the religion section, which didn't see a lot of foot traffic.

"Uh, hate to break this to you, but you do. It's called cancer."

"Disease, yes. But not communicable. It's not catching like measles or chicken pox."

"No, but the outcome can be more intense."

"Oh well, it's their loss anyway." I picked up a copy of *In Style* magazine someone had left on the table and began flipping idly through it.

"I don't suppose, uh, that Jillian has said anything about me."

Merritt shook her head and looked annoyed. "Actually, I've barely seen her. She's either at work or out with Bill or in her room with the door closed. I think she's avoiding me too."

"Well, that's just wrong!" I spat out in frustration. "Maybe I should call and talk to her."

"Let's give it a little more time," my friend soothed. "I know Jillian. She'll come around."

"Well, I hope so." I took another sip of chai to calm me down and turned a page, staring down at a glossy shot of Salma Hayek's celebrated chest.

"Do I really need boobs?" I cast a rueful look down at my own chest. "What have mine ever been but a source of embarrassment? It's not as if they're even a necessary part of the body. They don't really serve any function other than nursing babies, and since I don't see a baby on my horizon anytime in the near future, that's not an issue."

"True," Merritt said "Besides, when and if that day comes, there's this wonderful invention called a bottle. And then you don't have to worry about flashing your boobs in public while you're breast-feeding Junior."

"I hear that!" I high-fived her, then lowered my voice. "Of course, there's the sexual aspect. But since I'm not having sex, that's not an issue either."

I frowned. "Although, once I get married, it will be. How will my husband feel about being married to a breastless woman?"

Husband. "And how am I ever going to get a husband without boobs?" I wailed. "I couldn't even keep a boyfriend, much less a husband."

"Jack the jerk doesn't count. There are plenty of other men out there."

"Right. And most of them like breasts. Everyone knows men have an inordinate fascination with boobs." I flipped through page after page of Hollywood fashion beauties—all displaying perfect cleavage. "Without boobs, how am I supposed to fascinate? Sure, there's my brilliant mind, scintillating conversation, rapier wit, and kindness to small children and animals, but guys are visual. Right?"

Merritt started to say something, but I didn't give her a chance. I was really on a neurotic roll now. "Granted, it's not like I've ever had a lot in the chest area, but at least there was *some-thing* there."

"Think positive. Not everyone's a boob man."

"Maybe not, but they still usually expect them to come with the package." I slumped down in my chair. "I'll never get married.

And I'll probably never date again either. I can see it now. I'll spend the rest of my life alone in my little mother-in-law cottage with my surfboard chest, *Golden Girls* DVDs, and seventeen cats."

"Going a little overboard, aren't we?"

"Everyone knows you can't be an elderly spinster without a bunch of cats. It says so in the old-maid manual."

"I know. Page three. Got it memorized. But you can only have ten cats."

"Why?"

"'Cause I'm bringing seven." Merritt steepled her fingers and looked at me over them. "Which means you're going to need a bigger house."

"Speaking of bigger . . . I could always get fake boobs. They've worked well enough for Pamela Anderson. And no one's ever going to call *her* a spinster." I tapped the magazine. "Supposedly she had her implants reduced, but she still looks like she might pitch forward and fall off her skinny stilettos at any second."

"If she did, those babies might pop. And then what a mess there'd be."

I snorted. "Now that's a disaster flick for you—silicone flooding the streets."

"Yeah, I can see it now. *Attack of the Killer Implants.*"

• • •

Hours later, back home, I looked out my front window at the mistletoe still in the ash tree. If we didn't get it cut out soon, the tree would eventually die.

Then I looked down at my breasts and decided.

My weapon of choice in the cancer battle was going to be a

modified radical mastectomy followed by chemotherapy. Trans-
lation: I'd have them cut the whole thing off, including some
lymph nodes, then kill off any stray cancer cells with the chemo.

But there was something else to decide.

The needle biopsy, in addition to showing the cancer, also
showed a biological marker the doc called LCIS, standing for
"lobular carcinoma in situ." (I'd written it down so I wouldn't forget. All these medical terms were making my head spin.)

LCIS meant I was at high risk of developing breast cancer, but
that risk was equally divided between both breasts. So even if I
had the one breast removed, there was still a chance it could show
up in the other, possibly in a more aggressive form.

Like I really wanted to wait around and live in constant fear
of that happening. That wasn't living. That was Russian roulette.

"So if I *were* to develop cancer in my other breast," I'd asked
Dr. Herris, "how soon could that happen?"

"No way of knowing," she'd answered. "Could be two years,
could be twenty. Or it could be never. We don't have a crystal ball.
And we do want you to be around for a long time."

Before heading to bed, I surfed the Net and checked out several cancer boards where I read stories of other women—several
of them young like me—who'd had *both* breasts taken off at the
same time as a preventive measure. That way they wouldn't have
to live in constant fear that the cancer would show up in the other
breast someday.

I turned off my laptop and sat in the dark for a long time,
thinking and praying.

Bottom line? I knew breasts were a big deal to guys, and I rather
liked my own personal set. Small as they were, they were still mine.
But my life was worth a lot more to me than boobs or even guys.

There was so much I wanted to see and do yet. I ticked them off in my mind.

Visit the Grand Canyon. I couldn't believe I'd never done that.

Scuba dive in the Caribbean. I'd always wanted to swim with the fishes—but *not* courtesy of the mob.

Ride a gondola in Venice, which had to be at least as romantic as Paris.

Watch Josh grow up. That was a big one.

Maybe go back to school or own my own business someday. I didn't really want to work in an accounting office forever.

Learn to tap-dance. Yes, tap-dance. If Richard Gere could learn for *Chicago,* why couldn't I?

And of course, get married and have my own home and someday place a grandchild in my parents' arms.

I was pretty sure that being boobless might make that last dream a little harder to achieve. But being dead would absolutely nip it in the bud.

So I sighed and decided.

If removing my breasts could buy me time for any of those things I longed to do, then I was all for getting rid of those puppies.

The sooner, the better.

chapter *seven*

Omigosh, is that Joan Rivers?" Merritt whispered.

"Shh." I looked around the packed waiting room at the taut, wrinkle-free faces of the fifty- and sixty-something women in their five-hundred-dollar outfits and Italian shoes and felt seriously out of place in my Target shorts and Payless sandals. Until I spotted a fortyish woman in a floppy hat whose makeup-free face was in no way taut and whose feet were shoved into three-dollar flip-flops. She inclined her head to me in a nod of recognition, and as she did, I noticed another woman beyond her in an ill-fitting wig.

Statistics say one in eight . . .

I did a quick head count of the room: twenty-two. Pretty close.

"Natalie Moore?" A trim brunette in pink scrubs motioned for me to follow her.

Wow. This is more like it. No blue-paper-towel gowns here. I slipped on the beautiful kimono, enjoying the silky softness against my skin.

There was a soft knock on the door. Pink-scrub woman, whose name tag read "Heather," entered with a camera and asked me to open my gown.

I looked over at Merritt, who grinned, then back at Heather. "You've gotta be kidding."

"The doctor needs this for your file."

"Don't worry. I'll make sure they don't upload to the Internet." Merritt shot me a sly grin from her seat in the corner. "That would be my job."

I stuck my tongue out at her as Heather left.

Another light rap on the door signaled the entry of a petite woman of indeterminate age with light-brown hair pulled into a loose knot on the top of her head. "Hello, Natalie, I'm Dr. Taggart. Ellen Taggart." She shook my hand. "I understand you're considering a prophylactic mastectomy as well as the modified radical in your left breast?"

"Prophylactic?" Merritt's eyebrows flew upward.

"Preventive. Sorry. I forget that most people associate that term only with preventing pregnancy. Here we're talking about preventing cancer in your other breast." She looked at my chart. "I'd like to examine you now." She glanced at Merritt.

"Don't mind me." Merritt pulled out a small notebook from her canvas carryall. "I'm just here as Natalie's secretary, taking notes and reminding her of questions she might forget to ask."

Dr. Taggart delivered an approving nod and turned to me. "I'm sure you must be feeling a little overwhelmed with all the information we doctors have been bombarding you with."

"A little?"

She rotated her fingers in a circular motion on my left breast. "So Dr. Herris referred you?"

I nodded.

"She's an excellent surgeon. We work together a lot." She finished her exam and had me sit up. "Why don't you get dressed now? Then Heather will show you to my office, where we'll discuss your reconstruction options."

Dr. Herris had said that if I opted for reconstructive surgery, then I had to decide *before* my mastectomy (or mastectomies), because many plastic surgeons liked to start the reconstruction in the operating room at the same time as the mastectomy. That was the case with Dr. Taggart, who would insert "tissue expanders" in my chest after Dr. Herris removed my breasts. She explained that the tissue expander started out like a limp balloon. "This balloon is slowly filled with injections of saline over a period of time, which helps stretch the tissue to make room for the final implant. That will be inserted later, and the expander will be removed."

"Hey," said Merritt, "she's gonna pump you up." She spoke the last words in a silly German accent like those guys we'd seen on *Saturday Night Live* reruns.

"And once the implant is inserted, I'll tattoo a nipple onto your breast mound." Dr. Taggart gave me a mischievous grin. "I went to a tattoo parlor to learn the technique."

"Nat, you'll finally get your tattoo!" Merritt chortled.

I paled. "Um, Doc, I kind of have this thing about needles . . ."

"Not to worry. You don't have to look. And I guarantee you won't feel a thing."

"Huh?"

"I've had other patients who are phobic about needles," she said. "But after a mastectomy, it takes awhile to regain feeling in your chest area again, since nerves also get cut out in the process. So you don't feel a thing when I 'pump you up'"—she grinned over at Merritt—"or even when I do the tattoo. Some of my patients even get to the point where they watch in fascination as the needle goes in."

Not me. Not in this lifetime.

Dr. Taggart continued, "Now, about your implant—do you want the same size as your current breasts? Or something a little larger?"

"Hey, here's your chance to be Dolly Parton." Merritt wiggled her eyebrows at me. "Or Lindsay Lohan before she went and got all thin and anorexic-looking."

"Uh, no thanks." I didn't want to do anything quite so drastic, but I also figured I might as well get *some*thing out of this whole cancer thing. "I was thinking maybe a B-cup? Kind of medium. More like Jennifer Aniston."

• • •

Merritt and I babbled all the way back to her apartment about the new and improved set of breasts I'd have in just a few more months. "You're going to look great, and just think of all the cool clothes you'll be able to wear."

We giggled together, but the giggling faded as I came face-to-face with a nervous Jillian for the first time since my diagnosis.

Jillian took a couple of tentative steps my way, her voice quavering. "Nat, I'm sorry I haven't come over to see you. I just—"

"You just what?" Merritt whirled on her roommate, her eyes flashing. "You just couldn't be there for one of your oldest and dearest friends? You just couldn't put your own fears and family history aside and offer a little support?" She began to shake. "No, when the going gets tough, you just abandon your friend. Real Christian of you."

I stared dumbfounded at Merritt as tears coursed down Jillian's cheeks. "Take it easy, Mer. It's okay. I understand."

"You do? And that's why you've been bummed that she hasn't come over or even called *once* since your diagnosis?"

Jillian cried harder. "I'm so sorry. I know I should have come to see you right away, but it brought back so many memories of my mom. I just couldn't handle it. And then I felt all guilty, and that made it worse."

"It's okay," I soothed. "Really."

"No, it's *not* okay." Merritt whirled on me now. "You're just saying that because you're the good girl who doesn't like to make waves. But, Nat, you've gotta start standing up for yourself—even if it's uncomfortable, and even with your friends and family—or you're never going to make it through this." She blinked angry tears from her eyes. "Now tell Jillian how you really *feel* about her desertion."

Jillian winced and stared at the floor, her silent tears plopping on the carpet.

How I really feel? My eyes welled up. "Merritt's right," I said slowly. "I have been hurt that you didn't come see me. Or call."

"Or even send a card," Merritt prompted.

I lifted my chin. "Or even send a card. Just a few words to let me know you were thinking of me or praying for me or something."

Jillian's head snapped up. "But I *was*. I *am*," she choked out. "I haven't stopped praying since Merritt first told me."

"And Natalie would know that *how*?" Merritt asked.

Jillian's wet eyes locked with my equally wet ones. "Because she knows that I love her."

Merritt snorted. "Sure have a funny way of showing it."

A sob escaped Jillian, and she flung herself into my arms. "I'm sorry, Nattie," she hiccupped. "I'm sorry. I'm an awful friend. I've been absolutely terrified ever since I heard, and I just didn't know what to do." She clung tightly to me, her body trembling. "I didn't know what to do for my mom, either."

I hugged her and patted her back, my tears falling onto her shoulders. "It's okay. It's okay."

Merritt appeared next to us, holding up a roll of toilet paper. "Pull off a little and blow."

Jillian sniffled and released me, sighing. "That's my refined roommate." But she pulled some squares off the proffered roll and blew. All three of us did.

I pushed back my hair from my hot face and said, "Okay, enough with the tears now. And the anger and negative emotions." I smiled at Merritt to soften my words. "From here on out, I'm going strictly for the positive approach. Now, Jilly, let me tell you all about my new boobs."

"I'm dying to hear. And what's this I hear about cool clothes?"

"Well, *Rachel* . . ." Merritt and I had dubbed Jillian that ever since she got her upscale personal-shopper job.

The three of us were huge *Friends* fans. We'd started watching the show together in high school when it first began and every Thursday night thereafter. When it went off the air, we'd mourned. But now, thanks to the magic of DVDs, between the three of us we owned every season.

"I still think Rachel and Joey should have gotten together instead of her and Ross," Merritt added, picking up the *Friends* conversation from where we'd last left off.

"No way." I popped an Altoid.

"Rachel and Ross were meant to be," Jillian said. "They had a child together, for goodness' sake."

"Besides, she and Joey were more like brother and sister. That would have just been wrong." I shuddered. "It would have been like me and Andy getting together."

"But it was the *only* time in ten seasons that Joey was ever in love," Merritt argued. "Ross was in love a few times, with a few different women. Besides Rachel, there was Emily from England; Charlie, the gorgeous paleontologist—whom he stole from Joey, by the way—"

"He did not!" I shook my purse at her. "She and Joey mutually realized that they didn't have anything in common and split up. And besides, Ross never loved Charlie; he just thought she was hot and liked the fact that she was a fellow scientist."

"I'll grant you that one, but Ross was a serial husband." Merritt began ticking off on her fingers: "Let's see, there was the drunken Vegas wedding to Rachel when they weren't even dating anymore. And Emily, whom he called Rachel at their wedding— and don't forget his first wife, Susan."

"Who left him after deciding she was a lesbian," Jillian said.

"Okay, fine." Merritt sighed. "But I still wanted Joey to wind up with Rachel."

● ● ●

I was staring at breasts again. Now that I had made the decision to have mine cut off, I seemed to see them everywhere.

After leaving Merritt and Jillian's, I decided to swing by the McKinley Park Rose Garden so I could stop and smell the roses— literally—before heading home. Mom and Dad first took me to this beloved Sacramento landmark when I was a little girl. I can still remember how staggering the sights and smells of all the hundreds of roses were back then.

I felt the same way on that May afternoon.

I wandered through the grassy curved paths, enjoying the experience of being off work on a weekday and marveling at all the different colors and varieties of roses. Over the years, under Dad's green-thumb tutelage (he's the gardener in our family), I had learned their names: Mr. Lincoln, Rio Samba, Brigadoon, Joseph's Coat, and more. But my favorite was the Double Delight, a creamy white with the vivid pink-bordering-on-red tips. When I was a kid, I always thought it was funny to call them Double-Ds.

Now, in my breast-obsessed state, I could only snicker that a rose and a bra could have the same name . . . before I got distracted by a woman jogging by in bicycle shorts and a sports bra. Then off in my peripheral vision I noticed a young couple, arms woven around each other. But it wasn't his anemic stick legs under baggy teen gangsta shorts that caught my eye, but rather her skintight, midriff-baring tank top stretched over perfect breasts.

Soon I'll look like that. Except I won't dress quite so obviously.

I sat on one of the sun-faded wooden benches, discreetly watching every pair of breasts that went by, while that old hot-dog jingle played over and over again in my head. *"Fat ones, skinny ones, double-Cs and Ds; wide ones, narrow ones, even some down to their knees . . ."* I was tempted to run up to every woman and yell, "Don't take your boobs for granted. You don't know how long you'll have them. Do breast self-exams! Get your mammograms!"

I didn't do that, of course. I just prayed for every pair that passed by.

I also wondered how many of them were real.

Ah, there's a pair that doesn't bounce. Dead giveaway.

• • •

That night at dinner with my folks—Dad's chicken-and-veggies stir fry—I broke the news to them. "I've decided on a bilateral mastectomy, followed by reconstructive surgery and chemo."

"Good plan, honey." Dad covered my hand with his. "Best not to mess around with cancer. You want to cut that disease out."

Mom zeroed right in on the *B*-word. "Bilateral?" She furrowed her brow. "But that means—"

I took a deep breath. "That means I'm going to have a double mastectomy."

"But you only have cancer in the one breast." She gripped her fork. "Don't you?"

"Yes. Right now." I took another deep breath. "But I also have these biological markers that put me at risk for developing cancer in the other one someday too. My other breast is a time bomb, and I don't want to live my life waiting for it to go off."

She looked at me over her bifocals. "Nice analogy."

"Makes sense to me." I speared a piece of chicken. "Anyway, I'd rather defuse the bomb now."

"But isn't that rather extreme?" Her mouth tightened. "You don't *know* that you'll get cancer in your other breast. I can't believe a doctor talked you into this!" She threw her napkin down on the table. "Let's get a second opinion."

"The doctor didn't talk me into this," I said evenly. "It was my decision. A hard decision, I might add, but one that I made after a lot of researching and thinking and praying." I sighed and continued softly. "It's my body, and I have to make the decision that I can live with. I choose not to live in constant fear."

Mom twisted her napkin and swallowed hard. "I just think a second opinion might not be a bad idea."

I looked from her to my father. "I really need your support on this."

Dad sent Mom a warning look and gave my arm a reassuring squeeze. "You've got it, honey. All that matters is that you beat this, no matter what it takes. We're behind you all the way. Right, Ruth?"

She nodded and gripped her fork tighter.

"Look at it this way, Mom. I'll get a new and improved, perfectly matched set out of it, which might necessitate a few other changes as well. I might even expand my wardrobe."

She looked at me sideways and snorted.

• • •

Early the next morning, on his way to play golf, Dad dropped by my place for a cinnamon roll and a visit. The two of us possess a serious sweet tooth that Mom doesn't share. So when Dad wanted to satisfy his craving, he sneaked over to my house, knowing I always kept a stash of something sugary on hand.

I nuked the cinnamon rolls, added some butter, and set Dad's in front of him. I poured more coffee into his favorite mug, which he'd brought with him.

He took a bite, closed his eyes, and released a rapturous sigh. "Your mother doesn't know what she's missing."

"Yes, she does. Inches on her hips." I stole a glance at my dad's potbelly and patted my own slight pooch. "And stomach."

"Aw, honey, you look great just as you are. You're nice and trim, with just the right amount of curve." He took another bite, then wiped his mouth with a napkin. "Men don't like super-skinny women unless they live in Hollywood. And the women there are all plastic anyhow, all tucked and plucked and inflated beyond—"

He choked on his roll, realizing what he'd just said.

"It's okay, Dad. My personal inflation will be of the less-is-more variety."

He gulped his coffee, his face reddening. "Nattie, I just want you to know how proud I am of how you're handling all this. I know your mother and I have been a little overprotective of you over the years." He set down his cup with a shaky hand, his voice quavering. "And it really tears me up that we couldn't protect you from this." A tear leaked down his cheek, and he dashed it away. "But we're going to fight this with you every step of the way. We Moores are from hardy stock, you know. Why, your ancestors fought in the—"

"Revolutionary War," I finished with a fond smile. "I know. And I *am* going to beat this. I promise."

• • •

After Dad left, I showered and pulled on shorts, a T-shirt, and a pair of flip-flops to go work in the garden. Dad's knees don't allow him as much movement as they used to, and Mom's thumb isn't the least bit green, so it's my job to do all the weeding and pruning. As I started out the door, I noticed Dad had left behind his beat-up stoneware coffee mug, the one inscribed with "Golfers take their time."

Whoops, better return it before he gets home. He'd be lost without that cup.

I rinsed it out and headed toward my folks'.

My parents and I have an *Everybody Loves Raymond* drop-in policy (without all the yelling). We're always in and out of each other's houses and rarely knock, so I slipped into their kitchen quietly, not wanting to wake my mom, who is *so* not a morning person. I set the mug down on the kitchen counter—the cleaning lady had come yesterday, so it was fairly clear—and turned to go. But then I heard a muffled noise coming from the direction of their bedroom.

"Mom?"

No answer.

I made my way through the family room and down the hall. As I drew near their partly open door, I realized my mother was crying.

And not just crying, but sobbing.

I'd never seen my mom cry like this. I hesitated outside her door, wondering whether to intrude or not.

"Why my daughter, God? Why not me? It's not fair," Mom railed between sobs. "She's so young! Take me. Take my breasts instead. I don't need them anymore. But my daughter does. She hasn't even had a baby yet." She sobbed louder. "This is *my* baby! I know you promise not to give us more than we can handle, Lord, but I just can't handle this!"

I turned and tiptoed back down the hall, careful to shut the kitchen door quietly behind me.

If my strong, efficient mother couldn't handle this, what made me think that I could?

chapter *eight*

G ot your eyes closed?" Jillian asked.

"No peeking," Merritt warned.

"I'm not peeking. But I am seeing those red stars behind my eyelids, so you think maybe you could hurry this along a little?"

"All right. On the count of three, open." Jillian raised her voice. "One . . . two-oo . . . threeeeeeeeee!"

I blinked at the cake. And howled. It was baked in the shape of two boobs, with two very strategically placed candles.

Merritt strummed her air guitar, struck a rock-star pose, and began to sing. And not "Happy Birthday," either. No, this was the song they always played at the end of sporting events, the one with all the *na-na*s and the *hey-hey*s, each culminating in *good-bye*. Except she changed the first verse to "Nat, you don't need them; you're getting a new pair . . ." and wrapped up with "Kiss them good-bye." Jillian and I joined in on the *na-na-na*s, and our girl group rocked out my living room.

Destiny's Child had nothing on us.

Finally, Merritt bowed and did her trademark Elvis "thank you very much" impression. "So make a wish already and blow out the candles," she said.

We all knew what my wish was—that tomorrow's surgery would go well and Dr. Herris would be able to remove not only my breasts, but every trace of the cancer. For that, though, I needed more than just a wish.

Jillian knew. "Before Natalie makes her wish, I'd like to say a quick prayer."

For once, Merritt didn't protest.

Jillian prayed that God would guide the surgeon's hands, that I would not be anxious or fearful, and that none of those who loved me would be, either, but that we would rest in the Lord and trust Him.

"Amen!" I blew out the candles.

She handed me a knife to cut the cake—and I solemnly sliced into the red-velvet-cake (my favorite!) mammaries. Then Merritt directed my attention to a vivid handmade poster she had propped in front of my Art Deco armoire. I couldn't believe I hadn't noticed it before. It was fabulous. A gleaming luxury ocean liner was pulling away from port, complete with colorful streamers and waving friends and relatives. And at the top, painted in startling pink, orange, and lime strokes, were the words, "Boob Voyage!"

"You are so twisted." I hugged her. "That's why we're best friends." I picked up the poster and examined it closely. "This is fabulous! I love it!"

I'd told my friends and family that I didn't want to be all serious and worried the night before my surgery. Instead, I wanted to laugh and have a good time and give my breasts a proper send-off. And Merritt and Jillian had more than taken me at my word.

I looked around at all the food and decorations, appreciating all the work they'd done to make this a special evening. Except . . . wait a minute, something wasn't quite right.

I tilted my head. *Ah.*

I straightened the magazines on my tufted yellow ottoman, which does double duty as a coffee table. I moved my matching club chair to its proper angle. Then I adjusted the beaded shade of the vintage floor lamp that had been my grandmother's.

"Told you." Merritt winked at Jillian.

"What?" I looked from one to the other, who were both grinning at me.

"Little Miss House Beautiful. Everything has to be picture-perfect." Merritt smirked. Then she gave me a sly look and pushed my fanned magazines off the ottoman and onto the floor.

"Hey, what are you doing?"

Jillian moved the easy chair closer, then plopped down on the couch, patting the cushion next to her. "Have a seat, Nat."

Which I did—after I picked up the magazines.

Merritt sank into the easy chair and pulled a packet of colorful cards from her canvas carryall and set it on the ottoman. "We know how much you love to play Taboo, but tonight we thought we'd play Ta*boob*."

Jillian giggled. "Merritt made new cards—all having something to do with breasts instead."

And play we did, laughing ourselves silly as we noshed on yummy foods from one of the wedding caterers Jillian was considering.

I forked up another mouthful of a delicious vegetarian side dish. "Yum. This is really good tabouli."

Merritt shot me a devilish look. "That's not tabouli. It's ta*boob*li."

I snorted and choked on a piece of tomato, quickly washing it down with a cup of fizzy wedding punch.

Jillian gestured to her skewer of lamb and vegetables. "So I guess this would be shish ke*boob*?"

Now it was Merritt's turn to snort. Which quickly morphed into a guffaw, which culminated in hysterical, uncontrollable hooting we all joined in on.

"I know," I gasped through my giggles. "At your wedding, Jilly, you should have all breast-related foods in my honor." I gave a dismissive wave. "Forget that 'it's all about you; it's your day' rubbish. Instead, put your poor, pathetic, boobless friend first, and you'll receive a megacrown in heaven." Chin in hand, I pondered the possibilities. "Let's see, you could have, um . . . *boob*ecued chicken breasts—"

Merritt scratched her head. "Mammary and cheese!"

"Three-boob salad," Jillian and I said in unison, high-fiving each other.

"And for dessert, homemade breast pudding with whipped cream." Merritt licked her lips.

"Or cherries boobilee."

"I prefer crème booblée." Jillian stuck her nose in the air.

"Boobenberry pie."

"No, no." I clutched my side. "Even better." I paused for dramatic effect. "Strawberry-rhuboob pie!"

"Stop!" Merritt doubled over. "I'm going to wet my pants!"

"Oh, that reminds me—we don't want to forget the boobly for the wedding toast." Jillian raised her glass of punch.

And once again we were off.

When the laughter subsided, Merritt took a final bite of cake, then pushed her plate away. "Ugh. If I eat any more, I'm going to pop."

"Me too." I undid the button on the waistband of my khaki capris as Clay Aiken ended the final song on his CD—much to Merritt's relief. The room grew quiet.

Jillian glanced at her watch. "It's getting late. We'd better open presents now."

"Presents?" I frowned. "It's not my birthday."

"No, but it is your *boob*day." She passed me an elegant gift bag with light-green and white tissue paper fanning out the top and tied with a pale green moiré ribbon. Inside was a pair of mint-green pajamas and a squat, heavy jar of something.

"The p.j.'s are by Karen Neuberger," Jillian pronounced. "Oprah's favorite. She says they're the most comfortable she's ever worn." She sent me a tentative look. "I thought they'd be good while you're recuperating, especially since you can wear them all day . . ."

"They're perfect." I brushed the plush softness of the jammies against my cheek, then peered at the jar. "But what's this stuff?"

"That's Laura Mercier Crème Brûlée Soufflé Body Crème." Jillian exhaled a rapturous sigh. "It's got vitamins and shea butter for moisturizing, but isn't heavy or greasy." She gave a secret little smile. "Bill loves the way it makes my skin feel."

Merritt and I exchanged a look.

Jillian blushed. "I'm talking about my arms."

"Uh-huh."

"Okay, my turn." Merritt thrust a flat parcel at me.

"Uh-oh. Should I be scared by the plain brown wrapper?"

Except that it wasn't plain. Far from it. As I examined the wrapping, I noticed it was decorated with sidewalk café scenes drawn in colorful crayon, with the Eiffel Tower beckoning in the background.

"I don't even need to open this." I clutched the package to my soon-to-be-gone chest. "The wrapping paper alone is a great gift. In fact, I think I want to frame it." I tilted my head at Merritt. "Then when you're a world-renowned artist, it'll be worth a fortune, and I can sell it on eBay."

"Well, if you don't want what's inside"—she reached for the package—"I'll gladly take it back."

"Hands off, bucko. This is *my* present."

"Then hurry up and open it already."

"Patience, patience." I wagged my finger at her. "It's a virtue. Remember?" I undid the tape slowly, careful not to rip the paper, then folded Merritt's art-wrap and set it off to one side before lifting the lid of the flat box.

A riot of blue silk met my eyes. Slowly I removed a colorful, hand-painted tunic. The vibrant, whirling waves of blue ranged in hue from vivid turquoise to deep cobalt, shot through with swirls of white. "Oh, wow." I stared at Merritt, my voice barely a whisper. "This reminds me of our trip to Mendocino last summer and the waves crashing on the beach."

"So you really like it?" She raised worried eyes to mine. "I was afraid the colors might be a little too bright for you. But I thought—actually, Jilly and I thought—that since you're starting over with a new set of boobs, you might want some new clothes to go along with them."

Jillian rushed in. "You're about to begin a new chapter in your life, so why not make more of a splash?"

My eyes filled. "It's absolutely beautiful." I gently stroked the luscious fabric. "And I don't just like it. I love it!" I held it up against my front. "I've never seen anything like it."

Merritt beamed. "I remember how your plastic surgeon said it will be a few months before construction's finished on your new boobs, so I thought the tunic could serve as a little camouflage in the meantime."

Slipping it on over my white T-shirt, I went to admire my new present in the bathroom mirror. I turned right, then left, checking out the view from all sides. "It looks great. Fits perfect."

Behind me in the mirror background, I could see Merritt waving something white and flowing. "I also found this cool oversized cotton shirt at my favorite thrift store that I thought would be good, too, since it might be a little while before you can wear T-shirts again."

I looked in the mirror again, but this time at my snug T-shirt beneath the tunic, and burst into tears.

Merritt dropped the blousy shirt and rushed to my side. "I'm so sorry." She put her hands on my shoulders and met my wet eyes in the mirror with her own horrified ones. "I could cut out my tongue."

"Here you go." Jillian tapped her on the shoulder.

We both saw it at the same time. Jillian was extending the cake knife to Merritt.

Another emotional outburst followed—only this one of laughter. "Good idea, though; then I'm not the only one going under the knife." I grabbed the proffered knife—still covered with crumbs of red velvet and smears of frosting—and advanced upon Merritt. "So would this would be considered a tonguectomy?"

"Maybe more of a foot-in-mouthectomy." Merritt still looked stricken.

"It's okay. Really. Better for me to face reality now." I crossed over to the table to cut us three more pieces of cake. "Besides"—I stole a glance back at Jillian, rolling my eyes as I did—"you'll finally get me to wear something other than T-shirts. Maybe this is a sign that I'm supposed to upgrade my wardrobe."

"Yes!" Jillian's eyes gleamed. "I'll help you."

"I thought you might. But I draw the line at Manolo Banana and all those other high-end brands."

"Blahnik," Jillian corrected reverently.

"Whatever. Po-tay-to, po-tah-to. Spending that much money on a pair of shoes is just wrong."

Merritt nodded in happy thrift-store agreement.

Jillian started to respond, but we'd had this discussion before. I held up my hand. "Hey, I'm happy to spread my fashion wings a bit, but I have no aspirations to be the next Sarah Jessica Parker." I grinned. "Although I wouldn't mind the throng of admirers she left in her wake."

"Not to worry." Jillian put her hands on her hips. "When I'm finished with you, the men are going to be knocking down your door."

I looked down at my soon-to-be-gone chest. "Not when they realize my knockers are gone." I cringed. "I can't believe I just said *knockers*. Eew! Sorry. I'm not quite myself these days."

"I'll say. Sounds like you're channeling some good ol' boys now." Merritt cupped her hand to her ear. "Wait, I think I hear the faint sound of 'Dueling Banjos.'"

"Could we go back to the men knocking down my door? Although it's more like they'll be running away from my door."

"Stop that!" Jillian sighed in exasperation. "Any man would be lucky to get you."

Merritt, her mouth full of cake, said, "Hear, hear." A glob of frosting dropped and landed on her chest.

Her chest. Which housed her breasts. Her real, voluptuous,

cancer-free breasts. My eyes flickered from hers to Jillian's slightly less voluptuous but equally real breasts.

Don't go there. Remember: Look ahead. To your future. This surgery tomorrow will enable you to have a future. Focus on what you'll gain, not what you'll lose.

"Hey, know what I just realized? I'll never have to worry about the sag factor." I smirked. "When you two have that middle-aged droop goin' on, I'll still be proud and perky."

• • •

I'd just tried on my pretty new pajamas—can you say soft as a baby's behind?—when there was a soft knock on my door.

It was Andy, bearing a book and a grin. "I waited 'til the girly coast was clear. I wanted to give you something before tomorrow—"

At that moment it really hit me.

Tomorrow, tomorrow. At this time tomorrow . . . my breasts will be gone. Forever.

All at once I had an unexpected desire to flash him, just to have a loving record of a part of my body soon to disappear. The picture in the plastic surgeon's office wasn't the same thing.

What I wanted—suddenly, inexplicably—was for a man I loved and trusted to see me, *all* of me, before a part of me was gone.

Who better than my surrogate brother and dearest friend in the entire world?

Andy followed me into the room and sat next to me on the couch, extending the hardbound book. "It's a journal. I thought you might like to keep a record of your cancer journey."

A record. Unbidden, the tears began to flow. Again.

Andy held me and let me weep. Then he prayed.

At last I sat up, pulled away from him, and without saying a word, pushed my hair out of my eyes and began to unbutton my pajama top.

He understood. I saw it in his eyes.

He reached toward me, and for a second I thought he was going to help me with the buttons.

Instead, he took my hand and placed it gently in my lap.

"Nat, there's no need." Andy placed his hand gently over my heart and said, "This is who you are."

He looked deep into my eyes and softly stroked my cheek. "And this."

He cupped his hand over the top of my head. "And this. Not your breasts."

And then I lost it all over again.

• • •

Another knock at the door sent me scurrying for the tissue box.

I wiped my eyes and blew my nose and gave Andy a grateful kiss on the cheek. "Grand Central Station," I said, flinging the door open wide.

My parents stood there holding a gift bag.

"What? Is this Christmas or something?" I ushered them in. "Come in; join the party."

"Actually, I need to get back to Josh." Andy nodded at my parents and ruffled my hair. "Don't forget what I said. I'll be praying. See you tomorrow."

He ducked out the door just as Mom zeroed in on my red nose and puffy eyes. "You've been crying. Is everything all right?"

"Yeah, Mom, I'm all right. I'm just . . ." My eyes lit on the gift bag, and I went for distraction. "Is that for me?"

Inside was a rich emerald green chenille robe and matching slippers.

"I thought that color would be perfect for you. It looks so good against your dark ha—" Mom stopped and busied herself picking up paper plates. "Looks like you girls had quite a party." She paled when she noticed the "Boob Voyage" sign.

"Yep. Merritt and Jillian went all out. Wish you could have joined us."

Dad squeezed my hand. "Actually, honey, your mother and I were wondering if you'd like to join us." He cleared his throat. "We thought you might like to sleep in your old room tonight."

I started to refuse, but then I thought of how nice it would be not to be alone tonight of all nights. To feel safe and protected like when I was little and Dad kept the scary monsters at bay. "Sounds good, actually."

At my folks', I headed to the linen closet to get a washcloth, but Mom stopped me. "Just use the one in the hall bathroom, honey."

I stared at her. "But that's the guest washcloth . . ."

"Well, you're our guest tonight, aren't you?" She gave me a bright smile.

Now I knew my mother was worried. Never before in my entire life had she let me use one of the guest washcloths. It was one of her quirks—the rest of the house could go to pot, but she liked to keep the hall bathroom practically untouched between her weekly visits from Maxi Maids. So she'd drilled into my head growing up that the washcloths and towels in that bathroom were for display only and never, ever to be touched, except by guests.

"Okay then." I returned her bright smile and closed the bathroom door in a daze. After brushing my teeth and washing my face, I slowly unbuttoned my pajama top in front of the bathroom mirror, cupped my breasts, and wept quietly.

chapter *nine*

It was three days after my surgery, and I felt gross.

My hair was greasy, and I smelled like something the cat dragged in. I had two small football-shaped plastic containers hanging down on each side of me, filling up with disgusting bodily fluids from the drains beneath my arms.

Oh yeah, *and* my bandaged chest hurt like hell.

As a good Christian girl who'd grown up in the church and even taught Sunday school, I rarely used profanity. But no other word was strong enough to describe the pain. "Like the dickens" was something Aunt Bee and Opie would say. Not exactly in today's twenty-something vernacular.

Besides, right now, the last thing in the world I felt like was a girl, much less a good one.

• • •

Can I just say what a shock it was to see the area formerly known as my breasts?

When Drs. Herris and Taggart showed up in my hospital room the morning after my surgery to check to make sure everything was "viable"—no signs of infection or anything around the site—I told them I wasn't quite ready to see my chest yet.

I turned away as Dr. Herris lifted the bandage. "Everything looks good."

"That's a matter of opinion." I stared out the hospital room window. But then, after a few seconds, I couldn't stand the suspense. Slowly, I turned my head and glanced down.

I'd always been flat-chested, but not to this extent. The strangest thing was not to see any nipples. Just a thin red line across each breast—correction, former breast—where they used to be.

"I look like a boy!" And I burst into tears for the zillionth time since my diagnosis. All the tears I'd shed since first hearing the dreaded C-word were enough to start our own salt lake in California.

Dr. Taggart touched my shoulder. "Hey, you're going to give me a complex. This is some of my best work." She sent me a gentle smile. "The first time is difficult, I know. But as soon as you recuperate from surgery, we'll be starting the tissue expansion. In a few months you'll have some drop-dead gorgeous breasts. Trust me."

"Where's Aunt Natalie?" I could hear Josh's high-pitched voice outside the half-open door, followed by a light knock.

"Just a moment," Dr. Herris called out from behind the modesty curtain she'd pulled around my bed. Dr. Taggart slipped out after saying she'd see me soon, and I could hear her making small talk with Josh and Andy before she left. Dr. Herris reapplied the bandage, pulled the front of my gown back up, and tied it around my neck, then gave me a questioning look.

My eyes darted to the box of tissue, which my arms, propped

up and cushioned as they were by pillows on each side, couldn't quite reach. She plucked one from the box and blotted away the tracks of my tears, then gave me a thumbs-up before opening the curtain.

"Well, hi there. Are those for me?" She squatted down to Josh's level.

Josh clutched the bunch of daisies in his hand and shook his head. "Nuh-uh. This bouquet is for Aunt Natalie. You have to get your own."

"Josh!" Andy frowned.

Her eyes twinkled. "That's okay. I understand. After all, I'm not the one who had surgery. Right?"

Josh nodded.

Dr. Herris bid me good-bye and said she'd be in touch while Josh scampered over to my bed and thrust the daisies at me. "These are for you."

I started to reach for them, but as I did, an excruciating pain shot through my arm. I bit my lip to keep from crying out but couldn't prevent a hot tear from coursing down my cheek.

Andy relieved his son of the flowers and set them on the hospital nightstand. "Josh, remember I told you Aunt Natalie has an owie?"

"Yes, but I don't see any Band-Aid." He looked me over curiously, and his eyes widened as he caught sight of the IV. "Just the straw sticking out of her arm. Ooh, does that hurt?"

• • •

I was finally home and sore as all get-out, with greasy hair, yucky, smelly things hanging down from each armpit, and a mummylike bandage across the upper half of my body. And I was dying for a shower. The sponge baths in the hospital didn't quite do the trick, but my plastic surgeon said a shower was out for a couple of more days.

Aside from all that, everything was just peachy.

Oh yes, and I was back in my old bedroom at my parents' house as if I'd never left. Talk about a shrine. Mom had left everything exactly the way it was when I moved out, with the exception of the things I'd taken with me. My parents had insisted that I come home with them after I was released from the hospital so they could take care of me more easily, and I'd been too weak to argue.

It made sense really. I couldn't lift anything. Moving my arms was tricky. I wouldn't be up to cooking.

But I was getting a little stir-crazy and longing to be home in my own place again.

I shifted in the white iron daybed, trying to get comfortable. Pillows supported me on each side, and I was only able to sleep lying flat on my back—another thing to adjust to, since I usually slept on my side. But when I tried to the first night, I thought I would pass out from the pain.

• • •

"I feel like one of the women on *Survivor*," I said to Merritt, who'd come over to spell Mom in the caretaking department. "Except I'd never eat bugs or slugs." I looked down at my chest. "Or maybe wear a bikini top."

Merritt wrinkled her nose, her tiny emerald stud on the outside of her left nostril sparkling as she did. "I'm thinking you smell like one of those *Survivor* castaways too." She fanned the air in front of me. "We need to give you a bath."

"Natalie's father and I can give her a bath later." Mom brought us some water. "I was just trying to wait another day or two since the doctor doesn't want her bandages to get wet."

"I don't want Dad to see me naked," I protested. It was bad enough that a thousand and one doctors, nurses, lab technicians, and the like—both male and female—had already poked and prodded me every which way since this whole cancer thing began. All modesty and decorum got thrown right out the window in the hospital. But I still wanted to maintain a modicum of privacy. And I drew the line with my dad.

Best friends were another story.

"Besides"—I jutted out my lower lip at my mother—"the doctor said I couldn't *shower* for two more days. As long as I keep my bandages dry, a bath would be okay."

My mother looked doubtful. "Well, all right. Give me just a sec." She hurried out of the room and returned moments later with a roll of plastic wrap.

"You've gotta be kidding." I rolled my eyes.

Mom handed the roll to Merritt. "Now don't make it too tight over her bandage. And it gets really warm in that plastic wrap, so don't make the water too hot, either." She looked at her watch. "I have to run, or I'm going to be late for that meeting with the insurance rep. I should be back in just a couple of hours. If you need me, you've got my cell, right?"

Merritt nodded, her mouth twitching.

We held it together until we heard the back door slam, then convulsed with laughter. Merritt held her side. "And your mother would know how hot it gets in plastic wrap exactly *how*?"

"I don't even want to know." I shuddered, remembering the plump middle-aged woman in *Fried Green Tomatoes* who'd greeted her husband at the door clad head-to-toe in Saran Wrap and gold pumps.

Merritt looked at the plastic wrap in her hand, then at me, and we started giggling all over again.

"Ooh, stop, stop. It hurts." I pressed my arms against the sides of my bandage.

After we made the laborious, agonizing trek to the tub, Merritt washed my back and shampooed my hair.

"I feel like that woman in *Out of Africa*." I closed my eyes.

"Meryl Streep. Except I'm not Robert Redford."

I snorted. "That's for sure." The warm, soothing water enveloped and refreshed my tender, aching body; the plastic wrap kept the water at bay. "Florence Nightingale, then."

"Nope. Just someone with a locker-room-smell intolerance." Merritt started singing, "I'm gonna wash that grease right outta your hair."

• • •

"I want these disgusting drains *out*," I told Dr. Taggart. "That is, if you can even find the entry points in the middle of that dense forest that's sprung up under my arms." I shuddered. "How soon can I shave again?"

"Let's give it another few days. And it would be best if you used an electric razor." She pulled a fat syringe off the metal tray and approached me. "Just pretend you're in Europe, where underarm hair is considered sexy. Or at least it was when I was there twenty-some years ago."

"No thanks." I turned my head so I wouldn't see the needle and tensed, waiting for the prick on my skin.

"Let's see how much fluid buildup you have. Relax now."

"I hate needles."

"Now there's a news flash." Dr. Taggart busied herself beneath my arm while I looked up and away at the ceiling, trying not to think of the inevitable jab to come.

"There's still a lot of fluid in there. We'll need to wait a couple of more days to remove the drains." She slid her metal stool away from me and held up the nearly full syringe.

"What do you mean?" I swiveled my head around. "You already stuck me? I didn't feel a thing."

"I told you about that, remember? The nerves were cut during the surgery, so you won't have feeling there for a while."

"Really? Cool."

She approached with another syringe—this one full of saline. "Ready for your fill-up?"

"Go for it, Doc. Pump me up."

• • •

Everyone was staring at me. I just knew it.

As I carefully slid into the pew next to my parents—just over a week after surgery, I was moving slowly—I could feel every pair of eyes in the sanctuary fixed on me.

I closed mine and tried to focus on the service.

Afterward, Pastor Bob embraced me gingerly, and everyone made a concerted effort not to look beneath my chin when they talked to me. "Glad to see you back, Natalie . . . So happy the surgery went well . . . Blah, blah, blah . . . You look great! We prayed for you . . . Blah, blah, blah . . . If you need anything, just call." I smiled and nodded and made the expected responses. But out of the corner of my eye, I noticed a couple of teenage girls staring.

Now I knew how the Phantom felt without his mask.

I wanted to scream at them, *Hey, I used to have boobs just like you.* But of course I didn't, because I'm a good girl and that would have been out of character.

Dan, the good-looking lawyer man, came up and gave me an awkward around-the-shoulders side hug that made me wince. He dropped his arm as if scalded. "I'm so sorry. I didn't mean to hurt you."

"That's okay." I slowly released air out through my teeth.

He stepped back and ran his hand through his hair. "So how are you feeling? You doing okay?"

You mean for a woman without boobs?

"Fine. Thanks so much for—"

Just then Faith Thomas barreled over with Angie, her shadow, in tow. "Natalie, honey, so good to see you up and around so soon. How are you feeling?" Her man-seeking-missile eyes flicked to Dan, even though he's at least a decade younger than she is. "Anything I can do?"

"Thanks, but I'm fine. A little tired, maybe." But Faith's gaze had already shifted beyond me. She moistened her already-shiny lip-glossed lips.

"Nat, you about ready to go?" Andy came up behind me and touched me gently on the shoulder.

I smiled at him as we walked away. "Thanks for getting my back."

"It's a nice back." His eyes widened as he realized what he'd said.

"Yep," I teased. "It's just my front that needs some work."

"I didn't mean—"

"Just giving you a hard time."

Mom joined us then. "Your dad's bringing the car around to the front so you won't have to walk so—"

"Hey, Ruth, how 'bout if I bring Natalie home?" Andy turned to me. "That okay with you?"

I nodded. "Can we go for a little drive first? I really need some fresh air."

Mom started to protest.

"We won't go far, and I promise the second she gets tired I'll bring her home," Andy reassured her. "Okay?"

"What about Josh?"

"My folks needed some grandchild time, so they're taking him to the zoo this afternoon."

"I don't know." Mom bit her lip. "Natalie really shouldn't overdo it—"

"Hello. Still in the room here." I sighed. "I'm a big girl now, Mom. Remember? Just because I'm staying back home for a couple of weeks doesn't mean I'm a teenager again."

"I know that." She tensed her shoulders. "I just don't want you to do too much too soon."

I leaned over and kissed her on the cheek. "I won't. Promise. All I'll be doing is sitting in the car. Nothing strenuous. Tell Dad I'll be back soon. Love you."

And we were off.

• • •

The minute we turned the corner, I asked Andy to pull over and put the top down on his convertible. "Are you sure?" He cast me a doubtful look. "It's a little windy today."

"That's why God made sweaters." I flicked my eyes down to the cardigan Mom had gently tied around my shoulders, the ends camouflaging my new breastless state.

"I'm not sure that's such a good idea—"

"If you don't put the top down, Andy Jacobs, I'm going to put *my* top down right here, right now."

"Okay, okay. Chill out."

"Now let's fly." I leaned my head back.

"Within the speed limit, of course."

"Of course." I slid him a sly glance. "At least in town."

Once we left the city and were flying down the freeway, I warned Andy to brace himself. Then I screamed into the wind, my hair whipping across my face.

"Feel better?" He looked at me out of the corner of his eye.

"Much."

"So spill. What's got you all worked up?"

"My mother makes me crazy. She still treats me like I'm thirteen."

"Your mom always makes you crazy. That's nothing new. What's really going on?"

I slumped down in my seat. "I hate being this walking advertisement of breast cancer. And I hate everyone knowing and feeling sorry for me and acting like they have to handle me with kid gloves or something. Why can't people just treat me the way they always have?"

"They don't know how to respond." Andy drummed his fingers on the steering wheel. "People never know what to say, so they wind up saying stupid things without thinking. They're not trying to be mean; they're just clueless." He gave me a gentle look. "Cancer's scary in the first place, Nattie. And you add the *B-word* to that—buh-buh-b-reast—especially in church, and people get all uncomfortable. Especially guys."

"I'll say. Did you notice how they all got red-faced and couldn't look at my chest? I mean, come on." I scowled. "You men. Just can't keep your mind off sex."

"Hey, God made us that way for a reason." He started to pat my arm, then remembered and patted my knee instead. "But that's not the only thing on our minds, you know. Some of us like laughter, conversation, intense discussion, working together. Honest, Nat, if your chest or lack thereof scares a guy away, then he's not the guy for you."

"So where *is* the guy for me?"

"He's out there. Somewhere." Andy glanced at me, grinned, and started singing the duet from *An American Tail*.

"Oh thanks. The best you can come up with is a song a mouse sang?"

"What can I say?" He lifted his shoulders. "My viewing habits are limited to animated films. Comes from living with a four-year-old."

"At least you could have picked something from *Beauty and the Beast*."

He launched into a full-throated version of "Be Our Guest."

I joined in. Or tried to. But the results weren't pretty.

"You never could sing."

"Maybe not, but I can beat you at Scrabble any day of the week, Jacobs."

"Oh yeah?"

"Yeah."

"You're on, Moore. Anytime, anyplace."

chapter *ten*

A little to the left. No, too much." I shook my head. "Now it's crooked. Go just a smidge to the right . . . Perfect!" I frowned. "But now that chair beneath it doesn't work. It looks too busy."

I scanned the living room from my reclining vantage point. "Bring it over here by the couch. No, not up against the wall. Pull it into the room a few inches and angle it toward the couch. There you go. That's great."

Merritt sank into said chair—a Mission-style recliner—and plucked her blouse away from her sweaty skin, flapping it back and forth to cool off. "I need a break, Ms. Decorator Nazi."

"Me too." A glistening Jillian flopped down on the floor, her back against the leather-and-wood couch.

"This was your idea," I reminded them.

"Yeah, but we didn't know you intended to do an extreme makeover on our whole living room." Merritt grumbled and gulped her Diet Pepsi. "We just wanted your advice on where to hang my new pieces."

"And do you like them where they are now?"

"I love them." Jillian looked up at Merritt's bold oils on the walls.

"They've never looked better," the grumpy artist known as Merritt acknowledged. "But I didn't plan on spending my Saturday morning rearranging all the furniture in the apartment."

"Wish I could help." It was two weeks after my surgery, and although the hideous smelly drains had at last been removed, I was still sore and unable to lift heavy objects. I couldn't even raise my hands too high over my head yet, even though I was faithfully doing the walking-my-fingers-up-the-wall exercises the doctor had ordered.

"You've been a *big* help." Jillian lifted her hair off the back of her neck. "Without your direction, we'd probably have a thousand nail holes in the wall."

"Yeah." Merritt chugged her Pepsi, then let loose a little burp. "And now we only have seven."

My girlfriends, knowing I was bored out of my skull at my folks', had invited me over on a mission of mercy under the pretext of needing my opinion.

"This is the most fun I've had in a while." I shifted on the couch. "Watching *Wheel of Fortune* with my parents every night is getting pretty old."

"We need to get you out more," Merritt said.

"I hear that." I shifted my position on the couch and grimaced. "But I'm not quite ready to put on my dancing shoes yet. I've got some other things on my mind."

. . .

It was in my lymph nodes.

The cancer.

It had already jumped from my breast to my lymph nodes.

Out of the nineteen nodes the surgeon removed, two were positive for cancer. This meant that instead of having stage-one cancer, the earliest and "safest" level of the disease, I'd moved up the cancer ladder to stage two.

When she called with the results of my lab work, Dr. Herris said my cancer was "an aggressive, rapidly growing type," so she wanted me to meet with an oncologist and get started on chemo "soon."

Aggressive? Rapidly growing? A wave of fear threatened to overwhelm me. All this trouble—the pain, the weakness, the loss of my breasts—would it all be for nothing?

I knew I shouldn't be afraid of dying since I'm saved and all. I knew that when I died I'd go straight to heaven and the arms of Jesus. But right then, to be honest, that wasn't very comforting.

I longed to be in the arms of a husband, or at least a boyfriend. In lieu of that, I took the next best thing.

Andy stroked my hair as I wept against his solid, comforting chest. "I don't want to die," I wailed, clinging to his shirt.

Something wet dripped onto my hair. I pulled back and saw Andy's face streaked with tears. "Hey, you're not supposed to cry."

"Says who?"

"Tom Hanks and all the testosterone manuals."

He wiped his face with the back of his hand. "Tom Hanks?"

"Yeah. In *A League of Their Own*. He said, 'There's no crying in baseball!'"

"This isn't exactly baseball."

"Oh. You're right." I hesitated, thinking, then grinned up at him through my tears. "But it's boob-ball."

"Nice."

My tackiness achieved the desired effect. The corners of Andy's mouth turned up. "Anyone ever tell you that you have a real way with words?"

"All the time. In fact, those Monty Python guys have asked me to collaborate with them on their Broadway sequel to *Spamalot*."

"Make sure I get front-row seats."

"Always."

• • •

At work, everyone was kind and solicitous. Too solicitous.

"Natalie, would you like a cup of tea or some juice, maybe?" Amber hovered over my desk my first day back.

"Here, Nat, let me get those files for you," Randall, one of the accountants, offered when I started to lift some thick folders into the top drawer of the filing cabinet.

I'd been going crazy just staying home, so I'd finally returned to work part-time. But now I was going crazy at work.

My mother, who prior to my diagnosis had been handing more and more of her office-manager duties over to me in preparation for her retirement at the end of next year's tax season, now started taking them back.

I headed to the supply room to take inventory, since we'd been running low on some things just before my surgery, and was surprised to discover everything fully stocked. The same thing in the break area. The coffee, creamer, sugar, tea, artificial sweeteners, and hot chocolate bins were all full to the brim.

Returning to my desk, I started to type up the monthly reports. Usually my fingers flew over the keyboard at a hundred words per minute, but they weren't moving as fast today. I flexed them the way the doctor had encouraged me to.

Then again, my fingers didn't really need to move fast. I stared at my computer screen. This month's figures had already been entered.

I looked around for my mother, but she was nowhere to be found. "Amber?"

"What do you need?" The receptionist was beside my desk in a heartbeat. "A glass of water? Some Tylenol? Do you want to lie down in the break room for a little while?"

Shaking my head, I tapped the screen in front of me. "What's up with this?"

She flushed. "Oh. Your mo—I mean—Ruth—already updated the monthly report. We weren't sure exactly when you were coming back, and she didn't want you to be overwhelmed with work when you returned."

It's not work I'm overwhelmed with.

The back door opened, and Mom reappeared bearing a couple of white deli takeout bags. "Here're the sub sandwiches. Come and get it, everyone."

I longed for bed. My own bed. In my own house.

After lunch, when Amber and Mom were cleaning up, I phoned Merritt, whom I knew took a later lunch hour. And when she arrived, I made my excuses to everyone and left. One good thing about surgery—it gives you a get-out-of-jail-free pass for a while. Especially when your bosses are your mom and your dad.

Merritt helped me gather up all my bits and pieces from my parents' house and got me all settled back into my own place again, with my chenille throw next to me on the couch in case I got cold, water and cell phone on the end table, and remote within clicking distance.

"Okay? Got everything you need?" She took a final glance around the room.

"I'm fine. Thanks." I shooed her away. "Now go. Get back to work."

When Merritt left, I waited a few minutes to make sure she didn't return, then slowly got up off the couch, padded into the kitchen, and opened the cupboard door to my gallery. "Hi, boys. I really missed you." I scanned them over with a greedy eye. "Jean-Luc, I think it's time for a little Earl Grey. Hot."

• • •

"Natalie Louise, *what* do you think you're doing?" Dad towered over me, hands on his hips, blocking the TV.

I flicked my eyes up to his. "Well, I was watching *Oprah*, but I can't quite see it right now."

"You know what I mean." He folded his arms over his chest. "You shouldn't be home alone. The surgeon said recovery takes four to six weeks."

Wait. This was supposed to be Mom's role, not Dad's. What was going on here? Was I in a parallel universe or something?

I shook my head to clear it. I wasn't going to let the element of surprise throw me. If I could have, I'd have crossed my arms over my chest to show my father I meant business. But I knew that would hurt, so I settled for a determined look instead. "And I plan to recover the rest of the way right here in my own home."

"That's ridiculous! You can't—"

"Knock, knock. Can I come in?" Andy's voice floated through the screen door.

Dad raised his voice. "Natalie and I are in the middle of something right now. Can you come back a little later?"

"Andy?" I yelled. "Get in here. I need reinforcements."

He entered the living room, my mom close on his heels.

Oh great. Now I've had it. *Even Andy can't withstand the power of the two of them at once.*

Dad brightened when he saw Mom. "Good. Now you can help me talk some sense into your daughter."

"What sense is that, dear?"

He frowned. "Why, to tell her to move back home until she's completely recovered from her surgery, of course."

I sent my mother a beseeching look. "It's not like I'm going to be across town or anything." *Although if I was smart, I would be.* "I'm right in the backyard."

"But what if you need something?" Dad asked, his forehead creased with worry.

"Then I'll call you." I held up my cell. "See? I've even got you and Mom on speed dial. Merritt too. And Andy and Jillian."

"But I don't want you to overexert yourself."

"Jim, punching in numbers on a phone is not overexertion," Mom said.

I stared at her. Who was this calm creature who had taken over my Jewish mother's Protestant body?

"Natalie's right, dear," Mom continued. "We're what—just a hundred feet away? We can check on her every morning and night and even come home at lunch."

"I have a better idea." Andy snapped his fingers. "Why don't we tag-team it? Since I work at home, I can check on her a couple of times during the day and even bring her lunch if you like."

Dad looked reluctant.

Andy soldiered on. "Meanwhile, if she needs anything, all she has to do is call, and I'm here in two minutes." He slung his arm around Dad's shoulders. "Do you think I'd let anything happen to my little sis? You two can check on her first thing in the morning before you go to work, I'll take midmornings and early afternoons, you can swing by after work, and I'll bet Merritt and Jillian would be only too happy to take turns with the night shift. Right?" He glanced at me.

"Right." I beamed at him. "Sounds great."

"Well . . ." Dad looked from me to Mom to Andy.

"And we can all take turns bringing her dinner," Andy said, closing the deal.

• • •

"Sounds like someone's growing up," Merritt said later that night when I related the story to her.

"And standing up for herself too." Jillian gave me two thumbs-up. "Way to go!"

"Well, I can't stay under my parents' thumb—thumbs—forever."

Merritt tilted her head and gazed up at the ceiling as if she were searching for something.

"What are you doing?" I sent her a puzzled look.

"Looking for the nest you jumped out of."

I tossed a throw pillow at her. And instantly regretted it.

"Ow!"

• • •

My oncologist, Dr. Peterson, a grandfatherly type who reminded me a lot of my dad, has told me that I would definitely lose my hair from the chemotherapy. And for some reason this prospect is harder for me to adjust to than the loss of my breasts.

After all, I've had long hair my whole life.

When I was little, I loved to wear it in Laura Ingalls braids like Melissa Gilbert in *Little House on the Prairie*. When I grew up, I enjoyed changing my hairstyle to go with my mood—a ponytail or French braid when I'm feeling sporty, up in a knot or twist when I'm going for a more glam look, or down and curly for dates.

Jack always liked to play with my hair on our dates. Once he even asked me if he could brush it. "Your hair is so beautiful," he said reverentially as he ran the brush through it. "It's like silk." He captured a section of it in his hand and let it fall between his fingers. "No, I take that back. It's heavier than silk. More like satin. Thick, rich satin."

My eyes blurred when I remembered that. Pretty soon I wouldn't have any hair at all, never mind thick satin.

Almost all the cancer books told me how it would happen. I would wake up one morning with hair on my pillowcase. Or I'd see big clumps of it in my shower. That would be the beginning, and eventually all my hair would fall out. There was nothing I could do about it.

Well, there was one thing. I could *choose* when my hair went. That way I wouldn't give the disease any more control over my body than it already had. And to make the process a little less traumatic, I decided to do it in stages.

But even that was a little problematic.

● ● ●

The stylist at the upscale salon hesitated, scissors in hand. "You have such beautiful hair. Why would you want so much cut?

Most of my clients would kill for hair like yours." She lifted it with her other hand, letting the curtain of hair fall. "It's so thick and gorgeous."

I shot Mom a warning look. I didn't want to play the cancer card everywhere I went. "I just need a change."

Even so, I couldn't watch when she started snipping away.

I shut my eyes and imagined myself in Paris, looking all sophisticated in my little black dress, ankle-strap stilettos, and chic short haircut, walking my poodle down the Champs Élysées. The strains of "La Vie en Rose" would waft from a sidewalk café, and I'd catch the eye of every good-looking Frenchman there, who would watch me pass by and exclaim, "Ooh la la," in my wake.

My French fantasy helped get me through what otherwise could have been a hair breakdown. Because when I first opened my eyes and saw the mass of dark hair on the floor, I began to hyperventilate.

Breathe. In and out. That's it. Keep breathing.

After my haircut—a sleek *Chicago*-style bob—Mom took me shopping for hats. It was the least I could do for her.

My mother, you see, is the absolute queen of headgear. She actually looks a little like the Queen of England with all her varied hats. And for years she'd tried to get me to follow in her, um, headsteps.

But I'd resisted. That's because I suffered from childhood hat trauma.

When I was little, Mom got me a new hat every Christmas and Easter.

Easter hats always had to be some kind of straw. Always. They were sometimes white, sometimes pink, sometimes the natural tan—but if they were tan, then there was always some kind of froufrou ribbon around the base for decoration. At Christmas, the hat was usually something in red, green, or burgundy velvet, or maybe a nice Scotch plaid.

But the year I was seven, I fell in love with a fuzzy white angora cap with fluffy snowballs at the ends of the satin ribbons that tied beneath my chin. I kept bobbing my head in front of the Macy's mirror, utterly captivated by the two bouncing snowballs.

Mom was a little less captivated because, with every energetic bounce of my head, tiny bits of white fuzz would drift down to the dressing room floor. Mom, thinking of her dark green carpet at home and how much she hated to vacuum, vetoed the white angora in favor of a black velvet beret.

That's when my hat hatred began.

And the Easter I was sixteen, when Mom wanted me to wear some ghastly floral concoction with cascading silk flowers down the back, I stomped my foot and laid down the no-hat law—with Dad's full support. Since then, other than the odd baseball cap on a bad hair day, I've gone hatless most of the time.

It's no wonder that today my mother was almost palpitating with excitement.

For twelve long years she'd been deprived of buying me millinery. Now it was full hats ahead.

"I'm not wearing anything polka-dotted or lacy," I warned her as we walked into Macy's.

I forgot to say floral.

Mom immediately grabbed a floaty, flowery, wide-brimmed garden-party monstrosity and handed it to me. But my eye was caught by an Indiana Jones fedora instead. I remembered seeing pictures of Cameron Diaz and Jennifer Lopez wearing similar-looking hats in one of Jillian's celebrity style magazines. Sure, that had been a few years ago, but who cared? Just as long as no one mistook me for Britney Spears, I was a happy camper.

I glanced down at my chest. No danger of anyone making that mistake.

Wanting to make my mother happy, however, I let her buy me two straw hats—a simple tan one with a small brim that turned up, and a dressier, wide-brimmed black one for church. I wore the black one home perched atop my new haircut.

When we pulled into the driveway, Josh, who'd been play-ing catch with his dad, came running over. He stopped short when he saw the huge hat and short hair. "Aunt Natalie?" he said uncertainly.

"Yep." I twirled in the driveway and my head tilted flirta-tiously. "How do you like the new me?"

Andy let loose with a long, low whistle. "Wow. Catherine Zeta-Jones has nothing on you, little sister. Love the new 'do. Very chic and sophisticated."

"I prefer the old Aunt Natalie," Josh grumbled.

Bending down—and losing my new hat in the process—I blew a raspberry on his exposed tummy. "It's still me, silly."

He giggled.

• • •

I feel kicky, oh, so kicky, I hummed as I started experimenting with a little more eye makeup to go with my new hairstyle.

Jillian taught me how to apply eyeliner to the bottom outside corners of my eyes and then smudge it so it looked smoky. She recommended that I use a more upscale mascara from Nordstrom that would lengthen my lashes and not leave clumps like my drugstore brand. She also presented me with a red wool beret for that *je ne sais quois* attitude I was trying to cultivate.

Merritt, on the other hand, gave me a black bowler from one of her thrift stores.

"I say"—I affected an English accent when I tried it on—"all I need are jodhpurs and a riding crop, and I'll be the quintessential English gentlewoman."

"Smashing," Merritt said in as posh a voice as she could muster. Then she added in her regular voice, "Watch out, or we'll start calling you Camilla."

chapter *eleven*

how-and-tell time." A bubbly senior citizen in a pink velour sweat suit bounded to the front of the room and unzipped her hooded sweatshirt with a flourish. Then, to my astonishment, she pulled up the T-shirt underneath.

"Ta-da! Look at my new girls. Aren't they gorgeous? Perky too!"

My jaw dropped. She wasn't wearing a bra.

Someone let loose with a wolf whistle, and everyone else applauded the petite grandma with close-cropped silver hair and perfect, symmetrical breasts. Including me, albeit hesitantly, and with a face as pink as the woman's sweat suit.

"That's wonderful, Pat. They look great." A middle-aged woman in powder-blue scrub pants and a print scrub top stood up from the last chair in the semicircle. "We rejoice in this important moment with you, but"—she inclined her head toward me— "today we have someone new visiting for the first time."

"Oops." The woman named Pat pulled her shirt down and

flashed me again, only this time an apologetic smile. "Sorry. I didn't even see you there. I was too excited about my finally built girls." She blushed and returned to her chair amid more whistles and foot stomping.

"Welcome to the Capital Cancer Center Breast Cancer Support Group." The woman in scrubs moved to the front of the room and sent me a warm smile. "I'm Johnna, the group moderator and breast health nurse. Every woman here has been diagnosed with breast cancer and has been or is now going through treatment." She nodded at the closed door. "Since we want this to be a safe place for you to ask questions and talk openly, we ask that you respect one another's privacy and keep these meetings confidential."

I glanced around the room. Counting Johnna and myself, there were nine women of various shapes, sizes, colors, and ages seated on the metal folding chairs—from a serene, white-haired elderly woman to a tall Tyra Banks type with a red-and-black geometric-patterned scarf wrapped around her head.

"As much as your friends and family love you," Johnna continued, making eye contact with each woman before at last settling her gaze on me, "if they haven't had breast cancer themselves, they can't really understand exactly what you're going through."

I hear ya on that.

"That's why we're here. Within these walls you can scream, cry, kick—not each other, please—rant, rave, laugh . . . even show us your new boobs." She tossed an encouraging smile Pat's way. "So why don't we get started?" Johnna returned to her seat. "Today, since we have a new person, let's go around the room and each person tell a little bit about yourself, including where you are in your treatment. Okay?"

Everyone nodded.

"Good. I'll start," she said to my surprise. "I'm Johnna, and I had a mastectomy almost a decade ago—the day before I turned forty, in fact. Happy birthday to me." The corner of her mouth quirked into an ironic smile. "However, I'm thrilled to say that next month I'll celebrate ten years cancer-free!"

Everyone applauded. "Woo-hoo!" said Flasher Pat. "You go, girl!"

"And can I just say that my fiftieth birthday's gonna be a lot more fun than my fortieth?"

"Preach it, sister!" An attractive thirty-something woman in a white baseball cap with a pink ribbon embroidered on it pumped her fist. Her khaki shorts and T-shirt showed tanned, muscular legs and toned arms.

"I can't wait until I can say ten years too." The not-so-toned Hispanic woman next to Johnna shifted in her chair to face me. "Welcome. I'm Anita. I'm a forty-four-year-old mother, wife, and teacher. I had a lumpectomy four months ago and am going through radiation." Her plump index finger pointed to the red- dened skin above her scoop-necked top, where I could see what looked like blue ink. "X marks the spot." She giggled and then turned to the pale, freckled woman next to her. "Your turn, Jane."

"Hi." The soft-spoken redhead gave me a welcoming smile. "I'm Jane, the proud mother of two beautiful little boys, Luke and Matthew. Matthew will be four weeks old tomorrow, and he's the light of my life." She blushed. "Well, along with Luke and his daddy, that is. My husband, Mitch, is the youth pastor at our church." Jane's proud smile lit up her plain face as she said it. Then the smile vanished, and her voice grew softer. "When I was four and a half months pregnant with Matthew, I found a lump in my neck above the collarbone. The doctor did a needle biopsy, and it was cancer. Then they found a lump in my breast and under my arm." She squared her shoulders. "They wanted me to terminate my pregnancy, but that was never an option." Jane looked down at her slim, freckled piano hands, which were folded in her lap. "I'm thirty-one; I've had a double mastectomy and am going through chemo. And I have stage-four breast cancer."

Stage four? But doesn't that mean . . . ?

The shock must have shown on my face, because Jane said simply, "I know what the statistics say, but I also know that God is in control, and He's much greater than any statistics."

The perfectly made-up blonde in expensive beige sitting between Jane and me grunted. "If God is in control, He's not doing a very good job of it."

"Even the very hairs of my head are all numbered," Jane said quietly.

"Well, that explains it." The fortyish blonde gave a brittle laugh and inclined her head. "There's no more hair left under this wig." She turned to me. "I'm Faye." She shook my hand with her diamond-encrusted one. "I had a lumpectomy two and a half months ago. I'm married, too, but for how long is anyone's guess." She grimaced. "I have one round of chemo left, thank God. Then they can finish my reconstruction, and I can have a matched set again." Faye crossed her perfect legs. "And then maybe my husband will start sleeping with me again."

My face flamed. *TMI.*

A couple of the women expelled nervous giggles and looked at me expectantly.

"My turn? Sorry." I gulped. "Hi. I'm Natalie. I'm twenty-seven and single, and I just had a double mastectomy a few weeks ago."

I took a deep breath and rushed out the rest. "And I'll be starting chemo soon, which freaks me out a little."

Several of them hastened to reassure me.

"I didn't throw up once," Flasher Pat said. "With the anti-nausea drugs available today, most people don't get sick anymore."

Most of the other women nodded in agreement.

"Speak for yourself." Faye scowled. "My chemo sucks. I puke every time afterwards, and not just once." She adjusted the thick gold chain around her slender neck. "But it's not all bad. So far I've lost eleven pounds."

"Everyone responds differently to chemo," Johnna interjected. "There's no way of predicting how each person will react. But I can definitely say we've made huge strides in the past decade. I wish some of these miracle antinausea meds had been around when I had my treatments and was hugging the porcelain god."

"You can say that again." The elegant white-haired woman sitting in the last chair sent Johnna a wry smile.

The Tyra Banks look-alike on my other side patted my arm. "I was scared just like you, but the fear is far worse than the reality." Her silver hoop earrings jangled beneath her scarf-wrapped head as she leaned forward. "I'm Rashida, and I had my third chemo just last week. I admit I felt a little queasy afterward, but I haven't thrown up—at least not yet." She made a face. "By the way, you don't hafta go with that diet plan if you don't want to. Atkins is my preference." Rashida flashed a grin at Jane. "And I'm the proud mama of two boys too. Except mine are teenagers."

"You have teenagers?" I sent her an incredulous glance. "But you look too young."

"Why, thank you." Rashida started to run her hand through her hair, but when her fingers encountered silk, she remembered and brought her hand back down. "I'll take any compliments I can get now that I'm pushing forty." She gave us a Cheshire-cat grin. "Oh, and I'm a lawyer. And I'm on a reduced schedule at work these days. So if anyone wants to sue their surgeon for malpractice, I'm your woman."

A couple of women released nervous titters.

"I'm jus' playin'." Rashida threw back her head and laughed. "You white folks got no sense of humor." She turned to the woman on her left, who was chuckling, and high-fived her. "Except you, girl. You got flavor. Go on now. Your turn."

The attractive woman with the pink ribbon baseball cap lifted her hat and inclined her head to me—a head that bore the faintest signs of light-brown stubble, like Natalie Portman at the last *Star Wars* premiere. "Greetings. Welcome to the boobless wonders. These women rock!" She pumped her fist in the air again to a chorus of "Yeah, we rock."

She returned her hand to her lap. "I'm Zoey, and I work for the state. The lottery, actually. And no, I don't have access to the winning numbers. If I did, I'd have blown this popsicle stand long ago." Zoey touched her flat shirt pocket on the left side of her chest. "I had my breast cut off four months ago. And I'm not married, either, but I live with my partner." She lifted her chin. "We're both thirty-seven."

Oh great. I hope she's not one of those political ones trying to cram her militant agenda down our throats.

"Zoey's got the coolest tattoo on her mastectomy site." Pat bounced up and down in the seat next to her. "A phoenix rising out of the ashes. She'll have to show it to you and the other newbies sometime."

Uh, not in this lifetime.

Pat directed a sheepish giggle my way. "Hi. I'm Pat, as you already know. And no, I'm not a stripper by profession."

This time the whole room erupted in laughter.

"I'm normally not that bold." Pat nodded her head to the front of the room, where she'd given her peep show earlier. "But I had a double mastectomy six months ago, and my girls just got finished yesterday. I was so excited, I couldn't help myself."

"That's okay." I returned her smile. "I may wind up doing the same thing once mine are done."

"Remind me not to bring my husband that day." Faye's eyes narrowed.

My face flushed, and I looked at Johnna. "Um, I didn't know men were allowed. I thought this was for women only?"

Johnna shook her head. "Occasionally, someone will bring their husband or one of their loved ones along, but they have to get permission from the rest of the group first. We want to respect everyone's privacy." She looked around the semicircle. "This group is for people with breast cancer. But that's not just women, by the way. Men can get it too. We had a male member who attended a couple of years ago. Remember, Constance?"

The elegant white-haired woman nodded. "John was a very sweet man."

"Men can get breast cancer?" Jane asked the question everyone else wanted to.

"It's rare." Johnna steepled her fingers. "Only about one percent of breast cancer cases a year are men, but they're definitely not exempt."

"I'll bet that's embarrassing on poker nights." Faye gave a short, hard laugh.

Johnna turned to Pat. "We got a little sidetracked. I'm sorry. Were you finished?"

"Not quite, but I'll be quick." Pat grinned. "I just wanted to add that I'm sixty-three and recently retired from the DMV." She glanced heavenward. "Thank you, God."

We all laughed.

"*And* my husband, Jerry, and I are going on a Caribbean cruise for our fortieth wedding anniversary—a gift from our kids." Pat shot a proud look down at her new chest. "So now that my girls are finished, I'm going to go out and buy the sexiest bathing suit I can find."

Anita giggled. "Don't forget a pretty negligee, too, for those romantic nights."

Rashida winked. "What you need to get yourself is a black lace teddy."

"A red bustier and a thong," Jane offered.

All heads swiveled as one to the quiet pastor's wife, whose cheeks were now as red as her hair.

"What?" She sent us an innocent look. "You think I wear high-necked white cotton or flannel all the time?" Her mouth curved upward in a wicked grin. "We Baptists really know how to get down."

I scraped my chin off the floor.

"Go 'head, girl." Rashida bobbed her chin up and down.

"Who knew we had our own little *Desperate Housewives* right here in Sacramento?" Faye crossed her legs again.

Zoey put her hand over her eyes. "Just don't say anything about fuzzy handcuffs, please."

"Eew," we all shrieked.

"Okay, ladies." Johnna clapped her hands. "Getting a little out of control now. Settle down. We're still not done with the introductions." She nodded to the final woman in the circle.

"Hello, Natalie. Lovely to meet you," the older woman said.

She was straight-backed and elegant, with a lacy network of fine lines on her face. "I'm Constance. What a beautiful tunic. Is that hand-painted?"

"Yes, thanks. My best friend made it for me. She's a wonderful artist."

"I'll say." Constance's faded blue eyes gleamed in appreciation. "Does she have others for sale? Maybe I could commission her to make one for me. Or possibly a vest?" She smiled. "I know vests aren't really in with young people these days, but middle-aged and older women still like them."

Pat raised her hand. "I want a vest too."

"I'll take a tunic," Rashida said.

"Ditto," Zoey chimed in.

"Wow." I shook my head. "Wait'll I tell Merritt what a hit her shirt was. She'll be thrilled."

"Merritt?" Constance gave me a quizzical look. "As in Merritt Chase?"

I nodded, my eyes widening.

"I've seen some of her work around town," Constance said thoughtfully. "She's quite gifted." She stared at my shirt. "I should have recognized her vivid style."

"Constance"— Johnna gave her a fond smile—"could we hold the art discussion 'til later?"

"Of course." She returned the smile. "Excuse me. You know how I get. Back on track now." Constance recited, "I'm seventy-seven and had a mastectomy nearly forty years ago. I was living in the Midwest, and the doctor gave me a hysterectomy at the same time because back then they thought the two were related— both 'female problems,' you know."

I gasped.

Zoey scowled. "Talk about the Dark Ages."

"Every time I hear that, it makes my blood boil." Pat drew her eyebrows together.

Constance waved off our concerns. "It was a different world back then. My doctor had only performed one other mastectomy before mine. Thankfully, I was close to forty and had already had my three kids." She chuckled. "I didn't mind him taking out my plumbing because that way I didn't have to worry about periods any longer." Constance stared off into the distance. "At the time, we thought my cancer was a death sentence, but I've outlived two husbands. You never know what the good Lord has in store."

She directed a reassuring glance to Jane. "I clung to the promise in Jeremiah, where He says He knows the plans He has for me—plans to give me hope and a future." Constance held up her right hand to display a ring with multiple sparkling birthstones. "My future included seeing my children grow up and give me grandbabies. Now those grandbabies have made me a great-grandmother." She winked. "I've got a passel of pictures I'll be only too happy to bore everyone with later."

"Constance is the coleader of the group," Johnna said. "She's one of the founding members from thirty years ago, and she continues to come to encourage other women." She gave the cancer veteran a warm smile. "She's a great encourager and is happy to answer any questions you might have." Johnna shifted in her chair. "Speaking of questions, does anyone have any questions or issues that have come up this past week?"

Anita raised a tentative hand. "A woman at church told me her sister had a friend who was so afraid to lose her breast that she had lumpectomy after lumpectomy but still wound up needing a mastectomy later. Only by that point, the cancer had already spread to her liver and brain." Her voice quavered. "Does that mean my cancer will spread because I had a lumpectomy?"

"No way." Rashida clamped her lips into a thin line.

Faye snorted. "Now we're talking Dark Ages!"

Johnna gave Anita a reassuring look. "A lumpectomy followed by chemo and radiation is just as effective today as a mastectomy. But each cancer is different," she said carefully. "Each woman is different. It's a very personal choice, and you and your doctor have to make the choice that's best for you depending on the kind of cancer you have and what you feel comfortable with. That's why it's so important to educate yourself and learn all you can."

Rashida's eyes blazed. "Do y'all notice that people feel the need to come up and tell you about the worst-case scenario they've ever heard? I mean, everyone has a cousin or a sister-in-law or a friend of a friend who knew somebody that died of cancer, and for some reason, they feel it's their bound duty to tell you about it." Her earrings jangled furiously. "Happened to me, and it was a sistah at my church too. All I have to say to that is 'Get thee behind me, Satan!'" She stabbed the air with her finger. "I'm surrounding myself with only positive people."

Zoey nodded. "You don't need their negative energy."

"Amen to that," Pat said.

Anita raised her hand again, her eyes clouded with pain. "But what about when your husband or boyfriend can't handle it?"

Yeah, what about that?

"Or the woman in your life." Zoey folded her arms across her chest.

"Good question—an important question," Johnna said gently. "Usually the reason your loved ones have difficulty coping is because they're afraid. They're scared, angry, confused, and worried they might lose you. They're also worried how the cancer will affect your life together." She looked around the circle at each woman. "Cancer changes things. It changes *you*. And not just physically. Emotionally. Psychologically. It impacts every area of your life. But that's not a bad thing, ultimately. It can be very empowering." Johnna turned to Anita. "Would the man"—her eyes flicked to Zoey—"or the woman in your life consider going to a support group for caregivers?"

Zoey picked a piece of lint off her shorts. "Maybe. I'll ask."

"Not my husband." Anita sighed. "He's not good about talking about his feelings. It's that whole Latino male thing." Her mouth twisted in an imitation of a smile. "I fell in love with his strong, silent type, but now the silence is deafening." She sighed, and Jane reached over to pat her shoulder with a sympathetic hand.

"Give him time," Johnna said gently. "He may come around. We have fliers at the back listing different caregiver support groups in town—be sure to pick some up on your way out." She looked at her watch. "Okay, that does it for today. See you all next week."

"So, Pat." Rashida linked arms with the older woman as we walked out. "Are you heading to Victoria's Secret from here? You want some help picking out that sexy bathing suit?"

"We could make it a field trip." Constance's eyes twinkled.

Pat blushed.

"I have to get on home." Jane gave a little wave. "But don't forget the thong."

∙ ∙ ∙

"Constance Allen is in your support group?" Merritt's eyes widened.

"Yep. Why? Do you know her?"

"No, but I'd like to. She's a legend in the local arts community and has this fabulous gallery downtown."

I clapped my hand over my mouth. "Oops. They told us the contents of the meetings are confidential. I wonder if that means people's identities too—like in AA." I sent her a beseeching look. "Please don't repeat what I told you. I don't want to get kicked out or anything. There're a lot of cool women I'd like to get to know."

Merritt pouted. "Cooler than me?"

"No one's cooler than you."

"I should think not." She pushed her now-pink-and-turquoise hair behind her ears. "So how'd you find out about this group anyway?"

"There was a notice at the hospital, and Dr. Taggart also recommended it." I glanced at Merritt's C-cups. "She thought it would be good for me to be around other women without breasts—to know I'm not the only one."

"Just so you don't desert your other friends . . ."

"No way. These days I need all the friends I can get."

chapter *twelve*

Who knew a male nurse could be so sexy?

The guy in blue scrubs at the cancer center reminded me of that cute doctor from *Grey's Anatomy*. The one with the great body and fabulous hair. *What's his name again?* He also played the rich New York fiancé Reese Witherspoon left at the altar in *Sweet Home Alabama*.

I'd never leave this guy at the altar. No way.

I was glad I'd worn the loose white camouflage shirt from Merritt and put on some lipstick this morning. I bit my lip, trying to think of the actor's name, as Hunka Nurse bent over my arm and set up my IV.

Behind him, Merritt licked her lips and mouthed the word *wow* to me.

"Patrick Dempsey," I blurted out.

"Sorry?" The nurse looked up at me with deep sea-blue eyes a girl easily could have drowned in.

I reddened. "Uh, I was just trying to think who you reminded me of."

"Who's Patrick Dempsey?"

"A doctor on TV."

A gorgeous doctor, Merritt mouthed behind his back.

"I'm afraid I don't have time to watch much TV," he said. "Although what I want to know is why the gorgeous guys are always doctors. Why can't the leading man ever be a nurse?" He finished up the IV and winked at me.

You can be my leading man any day.

I rushed to fill the gooey-eyed silence. "Hey, thanks for not hurting me with the needle. I'm a bit phobic."

"We aim to please." He smiled.

I felt my eyes going all puppy-dog-like in the smitten silence. Any minute now, my tongue would hang out and I'd start some heavy-duty panting.

"Here you go, sweetie." Mom returned with my 7UP.

Whew. Saved by the mom. Though I never thought I'd use those words in the same sentence.

For my first chemo treatment, I was stretched out on the biggest and baddest leather recliner I'd ever kicked back in. Around me were nine other recliners, each one holding a man, woman, or child—the child being a sweet-looking little bald girl of about seven or eight who kept staring at my hair.

Nurse Drop-Dead Gorgeous, whose name tag read "Paul Gallagher," was explaining the whole procedure and what to expect. "You may feel some nausea later this evening, but hopefully this anti-nausea medication we give you first will stave it off." He offered an encouraging smile, his teeth dazzling white, of course, but the right front one was slightly crooked, which only made him all the more endearing. "There's no way of predicting for sure how you'll react. Many patients feel a little flulike afterwards but never actually throw up."

I thought of Faye's complaints, then pushed those thoughts away and focused instead on the adorable Nurse Paul and his instructions while Merritt took notes. When he looked down to scribble something on my chart, I couldn't help but notice his incredibly long lashes.

Maybe chemo won't be so bad after all.

My mom, Dad, Andy, and Merritt had all volunteered to accompany me to my chemo treatments. We agreed that they'd take turns, especially since there wasn't enough room at the center for everyone. (Jillian had played her get-out-of-hospital-free card, and given her history, I really did understand.)

Merritt won the coin toss for the first treatment. But as we were walking into the chemo room, Mom suddenly appeared beside us with a stack of magazines. "You forgot your reading material, honey."

Yeah, right, Mom.

I sent her down for the 7UP when I saw there was only one visitor's chair next to each recliner. Then she and Merritt took turns sitting with me over the next two and a half hours.

• • •

That first treatment was pretty easy. I stretched out in the comfy recliner and feasted my eyes on Nurse Gorgeous while the chemo did its stuff.

The second treatment, not so much.

The chair was just as comfortable. But Nurse Paul was busy

with another patient, so I had a different, not-so-gorgeous nurse who wasn't as distracting. Nor was Dad, although he tried to take my mind off the toxic chemicals dripping into my body by filling me in on everything that was going on at work.

By the time we left, I was feeling pretty weak and queasy.

Dad had wanted me to move back home for the duration of the weekly treatments, but I'd put my foot down—again. (It got easier each time I did it.) I *needed* to be home in my snug little cottage. And that's where I was, resting on the couch and talking to Merritt and Andy and Josh, when it hit.

"Uh-oh."

Andy and Josh had just delivered Andy's famous spinach lasagna, which I usually adore. Now one whiff stirred up something deep within me—and not in a good way.

I started to run to the bathroom, but no way was I going to make it. Andy grabbed the wastebasket and sprinted to my side, leaping over the hassock on his way and shoving the wastebasket under my chin just in time.

Thankfully the wastebasket was empty. Emphasis on *was*.

I leaned back and closed my eyes, mortified.

"Pretty fast on your feet there, Wonder Man." I could hear the admiration in Merritt's voice.

"Yeah, Dad. Cool!"

"I ran track in high school, remember?" Andy said. "I always won at hurdles."

"That was hurdles, not hurling." I peeked through my fingers, which were still splayed over my red-hot face. "I'm so sorry. Gross."

He waved off my apology and took the wastebasket into the bathroom, where I heard the sounds of flushing and running water. He returned with a glass of water and wiped my face with a cool washcloth. "Don't worry about it. I'm a single dad, remember? I specialize in puke. Right, Josh-man?"

"Right, Dad."

Andy grinned. "Besides, I've seen you toss your cookies before, Miss Moore."

I gave him a blank look.

"The year you were nine, you kept pestering me to take you trick-or-treating, so my folks made me do it, and you ate way too much chocolate."

"Butterfingers." My stomach recoiled at the memory. And that time I actually made it to the bathroom. But the vanilla almond candle on the back of the toilet only made things worse.

Now I understood the reason behind those signs at the center.

At my initial chemo appointment—the one where I first laid eyes on the gorgeous male nursing object of my affection—Merritt had offered to paint my toenails while we waited. But before she even finished one toe, Nurse Paul had appeared by my recliner.

"Sorry." He'd pointed to a sign on the wall: "In deference to our patients, please do not wear perfume, aftershave, or other strong fragrances."

I'd never actually thought of nail polish as a "strong fragrance." Now I did.

It was one of the countless smells I learned I just couldn't tolerate.

Even smells I usually loved became way too much—coffee, candles, body splash, fresh flowers. I'd always liked to keep a Mason jar of fresh-cut roses on my kitchen table and a small vase on the dresser in my bedroom. Now the Mr. Lincolns were just too fragrant. And when I sat outside to get a little fresh air, the star jasmine along the fence was enough to send me running back inside.

Mom had to stop wearing her beloved White Diamonds. I pushed my freesia body splash to the back of my underwear drawer. Even the liquid Ivory soap from the pump dispenser I used to wash my hands was too strong.

It was all very annoying. But most distressing of all was my sudden aversion to chocolate.

Josh and I have always shared a serious addiction to triple-chocolate brownies, which I usually make for us. One day Josh, wanting to make me feel better, had his dad help him bake a batch, which they brought over fresh from the oven.

Just one whiff. That's all it took.

One whiff, and I was puking in the kitchen sink. From then on, the very thought of anything chocolate or sweet made me gag.

Unfortunately, the same held true for Mexican food, Italian food, and most Chinese. There wasn't much that *didn't* set me off. I just wished everyone would quit pushing me to eat.

Mom and Dad tried to coax me with all my preferred foods, but to no avail. "Honey, look, I made your favorite—corned beef and cabbage," Dad said. "And it's not even St. Patrick's Day."

Groan. Another food bit the chemo dust.

What no one seemed to get was I couldn't force it. I wasn't trying to be anorexic or anything—the foods just wouldn't go down, and those that did often came right back up. I got to where my diet consisted of chicken noodle soup, dry toast, tapioca pudding, and Ensure—vanilla only. The chocolate and strawberry flavors were too nauseatingly sweet for my chemo-altered taste buds.

Just like Pop Tarts. And how sad is that—to be unable to tolerate Pop Tarts?

"You're a shadow of your former self." Merritt frowned at me one afternoon.

"Just call me Nicole Richie."

• • •

I decided it was time to start writing in the cancer journal Andy gave me. Maybe it would launch me into a whole new career as a writer. Surely it would make the *New York Times* bestseller list once the scintillating content was revealed.

Monday

5:00 PM—*Another day in chemo paradise. I lie back in the comfy, wide recliner halfway through my two-hour drip of Adriamycin and Cytoxan. Merritt, who's arranged with her work to get off early the days she has chemo duty, distracts me with the latest celebrity gossip from* People.

Today Nurse Paul was busy with another patient, so I got another nurse who didn't know my rolling veins. It took her three painful tries to insert the IV. And people wonder why I don't like needles.

5:32 PM—*Merritt's in the middle of telling me something she read about that new show on Fox when one of the prostate-cancer guys flies past us to the bathroom, pushing his IV pole in front of him. She reads louder to try to drown out his tortured retching sounds, but to no avail.*

My stomach clenches. The little bald girl across the room gives me a sympathetic smile.

8:15 PM—*My tissue expanders are rock-hard and stretching my skin so tightly I feel like they're going to pop out of my chest like giant zits. Discomfort, the doctor said? Can you say understatement of the century?*

11:20 PM—Having a hard time getting comfortable enough to go to sleep. I channel-surf but don't go quickly enough past Fear Factor, and all at once I'm heaving. Something about a woman in a glass enclosure with hundreds of black shiny beetles crawling all—

Back now. Shouldn't have even written about it.

Tuesday

11:55 AM—Got back the results of my blood work and the bone scan that Dr. Peterson ordered. Finally, some good news: the cancer hasn't spread to my bones or organs. Thank you, God! Celebrated with a Snickers bar.

12:22 PM—Threw up my lunch and the Snickers bar.

3:47 PM—Woke up from my nap to throw up again.

5:11 PM—Sucked on some ice chips.

6:13 PM—Threw up.

7:20 PM—Sipped some chicken bouillon on Dad's watch.

8:59 PM—Puked again.

11:17 PM—Too weak to walk. Crawled to the bathroom. Dry heaves. Question of the Day: Will I ever be able to eat chocolate again?

Wednesday

12:59 AM—More dry heaves.

3:32 AM—Ditto.

7:10 AM—Now I'm getting it coming and going. Gross. Okay. Ready to be finished with all this cancer stuff now. Ready for my regular life to return. Now would be good.

10:35 AM—Dr. Peterson said I have an unusually sensitive stomach and he's a little concerned about how often I'm throwing up, so he put me on IV fluids for four hours to hydrate me. He also said he's going to change my chemo treatments to every two weeks instead of *weekly. I don't know if that's good news or bad news. The whole thing will take longer, but I'll have more time to recover in between rounds.*

    7:02 PM—Went nearly eight hours without puking. Yippie!

Thursday

    3:30 AM—Woke up to puke.

    7:16 AM—Threw up again

    11:01 AM—And again.

    12:49 PM—Watched Nana's "story" on TV—the soap opera she watched faithfully for years and years. Just when this season's bad girl announced she was carrying her sister's child in a surrogate pregnancy, I threw up.

    4:30 PM—Napped for most of the afternoon and dreamed of a guy on a white horse. Or was it just a guy in white? Nurse Paul? (Except he wears blue scrubs.) Was enjoying the delicious dream until my rolling stomach woke me up.

    4:33 PM—Threw up again.

    5:10 PM—Josh brought his stuffed Curious George over to keep me company.

    8:01 PM—Shoved Curious George out of the way in my race to the bathroom.

    9:20 PM—Fell into a fitful sleep. Woke up a couple of times in the night with it coming and going from both ends but was too out of it to write down the times. Sucked on some more ice chips since the idea of swallowing anything, even water, is abhorrent.

    If I ever think of bulimia as a way to control my weight, somebody shoot me.

Friday

    Didn't feel like writing much today. Am sick of just writing "Threw up" or "Puked again" all day long. I need a break!

These days I'm sensitive to everything. Noise. Tastes. Smells. My own limitations.

Even the tags on the insides of my shirts.

Those sharp little suckers felt like shards of glass slicing into my skin. In a frenzy, I ripped them out. And when they wouldn't rip, I grabbed the scissors, twisted them around, and cut off the tags.

Leaving holes in every shirt I own.

• • •

On Saturday, Merritt and Jillian brought DVDs over for a Drew Barrymore film fest. Drew's one of my favorite actresses. There's a goofy sweetness to her that's so endearing. I bet she'd make a great friend.

We watched *Ever After* and *Never Been Kissed* for the zillionth time. I sighed as I always do at the end of *Never Been Kissed*, when Michael Vartan strides onto the football field and gives Drew that killer kiss she's been longing for. Mmm, that guy was hot long before *Alias*.

Then it was time for *Charlie's Angels*—just to see three women kick some serious butt. (Although Cameron Diaz shakes hers just a little too much in my opinion.)

Hmm. I didn't remember all the cleavage in this movie. It was one jiggle shot after another. I'd never seen so many tight-fitting costumes and plunging necklines showing the curve of perfect breasts.

I asked Jillian to turn it off.

Then Merritt popped in *Sweet Home Alabama* so Jillian could see what Nurse Gorgeous looks like. She pointed at the screen. "There he is. That's Patrick Dempsey. He looks almost exactly like the nurse Natalie's in love with."

"Yum. If I had that to look forward to, I wouldn't mind going to chemo," Jillian said. Her hand flew to her mouth. "Sorry. That was a stupid thing to say."

"He does make it a little more palatable," I agreed. "Emphasis on *little*."

In the mood for some male eye candy after that taste of my Nurse Gorgeous look-alike, Merritt stuck in *Oceans 11*. And all three of us leaned back and sighed.

"But I can't believe you're into Matt Damon," Jillian said to Merritt. "He's kind of geeky."

"I know. That's what makes him interesting." Merritt crunched on a pretzel. "He's not the typical Hollywood pretty boy. He's smart too."

"Yeah. And you have to admit that he shed the geek factor in *The Bourne Identity*." I took a sip of my banana smoothie, which oddly enough I'd found I could handle. "And *then* some. Oh my."

There was a light rap on the door before it swung open to reveal Andy with a covered dish of steamed chicken (no seasoning), potatoes, and carrots. He set it down on the kitchen counter, then glanced at the TV and our tongues hanging down to the floor. "Oh, it's the lusting-over-Hollywood-hunks film festival again, huh?"

"'Fess up, Andy. I'm sure you have your own little crushes." Jillian nodded at the screen. "Julia Roberts, maybe?"

Merritt shook her head. "Nah. I'm betting he's more an Angelina Jolie kind of guy."

Andy just smiled and grabbed a bottled water from the fridge.

"You're both wrong," I said. "Andy likes the two Kates: Winslet and Blanchett—the latter spelled with a *C*, thank you very much."

Jillian arched her brows at him. "Oh, you have a thing for English accents?"

Andy swigged his water. "Who doesn't? But mostly I like excellent acting and intelligence. And beauty that doesn't try so hard."

Saturday

10:15 PM—Great day! Felt like old times. Laughed loads with Jilly and Merritt and lusted over some movie-star hotties. Didn't feel like cancer-girl for a change. And after several failed culinary attempts, Andy finally brought over a great dinner. Who knew bland chicken and potatoes could taste so scrumptious? I didn't even get sick!

Well, not for a couple of hours at least, and then only once. Hallelujah!

chapter *thirteen*

I was officially on leave from work.

Chemotherapy, at least mine, wasn't conducive to the workplace. Running to the bathroom every few minutes wasn't exactly professional, especially with the thin walls we have.

Can you say *Jurassic Park* in surround sound?

I had really wanted to maintain as much normalcy in my life as possible while going through this whole cancer thing, which meant continuing to work. But after a few embarrassing T-rex barfs in the loo—situated right next to the conference room—during our weekly employee meetings, I began to reconsider. Add to that my general weakness and inability to perform many of my normal office duties, and *everybody* began to reconsider.

So my boss—even if he is my dad, he still has to act like a boss—arranged with the office manager (Mom) for me to take the rest of my sick days at full pay, then a leave of absence at reduced pay for the chemo duration.

And even though all this made me mad at first, the break from

work was good. It gave me time to reevaluate my professional life
and think about what I really wanted to be when I grew up. I
mean, I liked my job. But I was realizing it wasn't my life's ambi-
tion to be executive assistant—or even office manager—in my
dad's office.

But what else could I do? I pulled out my journal to jot down
ideas. But the pages remained blank.

I sighed and looked around my shabby-chic cottage at the
antiques I'd inherited from my grandmother, mixed in with my
"finds" from flea markets and garage sales.

Hey, maybe I could open an antique store. I'd always liked
the idea of owning my own business, and I'd have an excuse to
go on buying trips to Europe and stuff. It would even be a tax
write-off. (Working for a CPA had taught me a few things in that
regard.)

Then that same CPA background reared its practical head.

It costs money to lease the necessary property for a store.
Then there's all the decorating and setup and filling the shop with
antiques people will want to buy. Not to mention hiring help to
cover the register while I'm away on those fabulous trips.

Maybe something that didn't require a shop or so much
money up front might be better. Perhaps I could provide some
sort of service. But what?

Well, I'm really good at keeping things in order. Organization
was one of my strong points at work, and living in such a small
space made me super-organized at home. Maybe I could become
one of those professional organizers and go to people's homes and
workplaces, clear away their clutter and towering stacks of paper,
get them all sorted out. I could do that.

Then again, that's what I already did for Dad at work. I

wanted to try something different. Something a little more exciting. A little more creative, perhaps?

Being a musician was probably out. I love music, even played
the clarinet briefly in fourth grade. But I'm not much of a singer,
and it was a little late to learn another instrument and play it professionally. My chances of becoming the next American Idol were,
well, zero.

What about painting? I dismissed the thought instantly. Merritt
already had that covered, and though I liked to sketch and to
doodle, I'd never be anything like her.

Could I be a writer? I'd actually considered that before. My
seventh-grade teacher had always given me A's on my writing
assignments, and I already owned a laptop and a journal. What
more did I need?

It's not like you need a special degree or anything to be a
writer (unless you want to be a technical writer like Andy, and I
knew there wasn't a chance of that). If Hemingway and Fitzgerald
are any indicators, you just needed lots of angst and booze. I'm
not much of a drinker, but I could definitely call up some angst.
Especially recently.

Turning the page, I resumed my cancer journey entries, keeping in mind that they were now potential publication fodder.

Thursday

No puking today.

Hmm, maybe that was a little too graphic. Perhaps I should
soften it and make it not quite so short. I tried again.

*Today I was so relieved not to throw up again as a result of the
chemotherapy drugs coursing through my body. They do tend to have
a rather negative impact on one's digestive system, even when hardly*

anything has been digested. I believe the medical term for the latter is dry heaves.

I stopped and reread what I had written. Sounded a bit stuffy and clinical. Plus, I'd forgotten a setting. Wasn't it important to always have a setting and lots of description in your writing—or was that just in fiction?

I thought back to something Constance had said at my second support-group meeting: "My life changed for the better as a result of my cancer. It helped me discover my passion."

Her passion, like Merritt's, was art. I made a mental note again to introduce the two of them.

Meanwhile, I wondered, what was my passion? (Nurse Paul and the guys inside my cabinet didn't count.)

Did I even *have* a passion?

• • •

The phone rang. "Hey, girl, you busy?"

"Rashida?"

"The one and only. I'm calling for a favor. I tried a couple of the others, but Constance is out of town, it's Johnna's tae kwan do night, and I can't get ahold of Pat." She expelled a tired sigh. "I promised Jane I'd bring her family some dinner, but my car's in the shop. Could you give me a ride?"

Fifteen minutes later I was knocking on Rashida's front door in one of the newer housing developments in town. Hers was not your basic tract home, not by any stretch. Definitely custom. Which I noticed the moment I stepped into the marble entryway. Soaring cathedral ceilings, a winding cherrywood spindle staircase that led up to the second floor, and a spacious, open living room with floor-to-ceiling windows, a marble fireplace, and burnished cherry hardwood floors beneath plush Oriental carpets and richly colored sofas.

Rashida, in white jeans, a loose tunic, and a black-and-white polka-dot scarf, ushered me into the enormous kitchen. I drank in the granite countertops, slate floor, gleaming stainless-steel appliances, and cooktop island with a full set of Calphalon pots and pans hanging from the pot rack.

She looked at the digital timer on the state-of-the-art convection oven. "That casserole has seven more minutes to bake, so let's sit in the living room and rest while we wait. Don't know about you, but this chemo stuff just wears me out!"

I sat on one of the plush tapestry sofas and picked up a silver-framed photo of a beaming woman in multiple braids and cap and gown, flanked by two smiling young boys. "Is this you?"

Rashida nodded. "That's when I graduated from law school. Those are my babies."

But I wasn't focused on her sons. "Your hair was so long and beautiful. Love all the beads. Did you wear it that way to work?" I stole a surreptitious glance at her now-scarfed head.

She laughed. "Uh-huh. Don't think the partners knew quite what to make of this sistah with the wild hair—though it was mostly extensions. But they'd seen me in the courtroom and knew I was a bulldog who'd do right by my clients."

"Was it hard to lose your hair?" I brushed mine out of my face.

"Oh yeah," she said softly. "At first. But now I'm used to it." She gave me a gentle smile, then slowly unwound her scarf to reveal a perfect milk-chocolate hairless head.

"I hope I look as good as you bald."

"Don't trip. You'll be all right," she said. "'Specially with those gorgeous eyes . . ."

There was a loud clatter from the kitchen and the sound of something hitting the slate floor. Rashida raised her voice. "What'd I tell you 'bout bouncin' that basketball inside my house?"

A couple of disembodied "Sorry, Mamas," wafted into the living room.

"Now get your butts in here and meet my friend."

Two skinny and incredibly tall teens with shaved heads just beginning to stubble appeared in the doorway. Rashida introduced me to fifteen-year-old DeShawn and his younger brother, DeWayne.

They ducked their heads shyly. "Pleased to meet you, ma'am."

"Ma'am?" I looked at Rashida and pouted. "I'm not even thirty yet."

"That's just a sign of respect." She inclined her head to her sons. "Y'all can call her Miss Natalie. Now go on up and shower that flop sweat off you. I'll be leaving soon, but when I come back you both better be nice and clean and doing your homework."

"Yes, ma'am," they said in unison before bounding up the stairs.

Rashida called up after them, "And don't you be playing no computer games until your homework's done, either."

"No, ma'am."

Rashida's fond gaze followed her sons. She cupped her hand and stroked her bald head reflectively. "When I started losing hair on my pillow, my boys shaved my head for me. Then they shaved their own heads too."

My eyes filled. "You have beautiful sons. You must be very proud of them." I looked around. "You've got a beautiful home too."

Her gaze snaked through the living room, which was empty save for the two tapestry couches, one end table, and the silver-framed photo I'd admired earlier. "Thanks. It will be once I get everything in place." She waved her hand to the far end of the room, where a bevy of paintings and pictures leaned against a stack of boxes. "We moved in over two months ago, but between work, my treatments, and just getting food on the table, the last thing I've been worried about is hanging pictures." She sighed. "I planned to hire a decorator, but then I got diagnosed, and I just haven't gotten around to it yet."

A large painting sticking out above the rest of the stack caught my eye. "Mind if I take a closer look?"

"Go'n, girl. It's cool."

I moved aside a couple of basketball posters that were blocking the painting. "Oh, wow."

The painting was a beautiful watercolor of a young woman in a white dress whipped by the wind, shading her eyes and looking out to sea while a little girl played with a rag doll at her feet.

"My mama painted that during one of my daddy's many trips to sea." Rashida got a faraway look in her eyes. "He was in the navy and was always gone more than he was home."

"This is stunning," I breathed. "It deserves a place of honor." Without thinking, I started to lift the heavy canvas.

"Girl, what you doin'?" Rashida hurried over.

Stricken, I stared at her, then slid my eyes to my hands, still clutching the frame. "I'm sorry. How rude. I don't know what I was thinking. I—"

She waved off my apology. "Not that. I just don't want you moving that heavy thing by yourself. That's what kids are for." Rashida strode to the foot of the stairs and called for her sons to come down.

They clattered down the steps. "Yes, ma'am?"

"Natalie, tell them where you want this moved."

I hesitated.

"Go on. I appreciate the help."

Upon my instruction, the boys carefully lifted the family heirloom and set it on top of the mantel, propping it against the wall and centering it according to my direction.

Rashida stared at the painting, her sons flanking her. "I don't know why I didn't think of that. It's the perfect place."

"It's good to see Grandma again," DeWayne (or was it DeShawn?) said.

"You got that right, baby." She hugged him to her. "She's where you boys got your good looks from."

"Aunt Rhonda say we look like our daddy," DeShawn piped up.

Rashida's lips thinned. "Aunt Rhonda talk too much. Now go on back upstairs and finish your homework."

Dying to ask about the boys' father, but knowing it wasn't my place, I returned to the stack of boxes by the pictures, where I'd spotted something else. I pulled out a couple of lighter items and held them up for Rashida's inspection. "Do you mind?"

"Knock yourself out."

I set the tall, red rectangular vase on the mantel to the left side of the painting and a squatty sculpture of a mother and two children dancing next to it. Then I placed the thick, creamy beeswax candle off to the right side.

Stepping back, I looked at it with a critical eye and moved the vase and sculpture a little more to the left. "What do you think?"

Rashida clapped her hands. "I love it! See, that's what I'm talkin' 'bout—you got flavor, girl. I never would have thought of that. That combo is the bomb."

She sniffed the air.

I did too.

She looked at me. "That timer should have gone off by now." Rashida sprinted to the kitchen with me fast on her heels and pulled a blackened casserole from the oven. "I'm going to kill those boys. All that racket they made—I didn't hear the timer go off."

•   •   •

Jane's house, in an older neighborhood that had seen better days, was a far cry from Rashida's. An aging ranch-style sorely in need of a paint job, the small two-bedroom home couldn't have been more than eight hundred square feet. Tops. And every single foot seemed to be filled with clothes, toys, DVDs, glasses with varying levels of liquid in them, and open bags of chips and candy.

Eew. I picked my way carefully through the clutter, all of my fastidious senses inwardly screaming.

Jane lay on the sagging couch, an array of pills and juice and water glasses on the table beside her. "Please excuse the mess." She waved a weak hand. "It usually doesn't look like this, but Mitch isn't home from work yet, and I just haven't had any energy the past few days . . ." Her voice trailed off.

"Girl, cut that," Rashida said. "We ain't trippin' on your house."

Ashamed, I focused on Jane rather than the mess.

Rashida walked over to the bassinet next to the couch. "We came to see you and these beautiful babies." She lifted up the baby, who was starting to fuss, and cradled him in her stronger (away from her mastectomy) right arm. "Hey, Matthew. What's the matter, boo? You hungry?"

"I was just getting ready to feed him." Jane struggled to sit up. "His formula's in the fridge."

Rashida laid a hand on her shoulder. "You stay right there. I'll get it." She smiled. "I think I can remember how to feed a baby." She glanced down at the quiet, carrot-topped boy sitting in front of the couch, stroking the fur of a little white dog. "And maybe Luke here can go help Miss Natalie with dinner. All right, Luke?"

He nodded and scrambled to his feet, the dog scrambling up at the same time and releasing a shower of white hair into the air.

"What a pretty dog." I knelt down to pet the creamy canine with the curved tail—it looked like a little fox. "What's his name?"

"Her. She's Lady."

"Oh, I beg your pardon, Lady. Please excuse me."

The dainty dog wagged its curved tail, wafting more hair into the air.

"What kind of dog is she?" I asked.

"'Merican Eskimo." Luke looked to his mother for confirmation.

"That's right, honey." Jane gave him an encouraging smile and shifted her gaze to me. "She showed up in our backyard a few years ago all scrawny and shivering. Poor little thing." She smiled at the dog, who seemed to know we were talking about her and wagged her tail in response. "We put up signs around the neighborhood and checked with the pound, but nobody claimed her. We think maybe she belonged to the last owner of our house, a little old lady, and when she died, the relatives just let her go." Jane's mouth turned down at the thought. "We thought she was a short-haired dog, but she was just malnourished. Once she got healthy, her coat came in full and fluffy. We usually keep her brushed, but . . ." She made a helpless gesture.

"That's okay. Maybe Luke and I can brush Lady after dinner." I turned my attention to the quiet child. "You hungry, Luke?

He bobbed his head up and down.

I ruffled his hair. "You like macaroni and cheese?"

His hazel eyes grew big, and he bobbed his head up and down again as he followed me into the kitchen.

Rashida picked her way through the trail of toys, retrieved the baby's formula, and headed back to the living room. "Now, Jane, I'm sorry to tell you, but my famous chicken-and-rice casserole is through." She made a cutting motion across her throat.

I began lifting containers of hot food from the grocery deli bag under Luke's watchful eye. "I hope you like rotisserie chicken too. My nephew loves it, and he's about your age." I set the chicken on the counter and smiled at the freckled but too-serious little guy; he was a dead ringer for Opie from Mayberry. "How old are you?"

"Free." He held up three fingers. "But I gonna have a birfday soon."

"You are? Wow. Will you have cake and ice cream?"

"Uh-huh. Choclit."

"Well, maybe we can have a little early birthday celebration tonight." I pulled a tub of vanilla ice cream out of the freezer bag and winked. "Do you like brownies and ice cream?"

His eyes grew even bigger. "With chocolate syrup?"

I yanked open the fridge door, relieved to spot a plastic bottle of Hershey's on the bottom shelf. "Yep. But only if you eat all your green beans and macaroni and cheese."

I poured him a glass of milk and filled his plate, then carried both to the dining room table. Luke followed, silverware in hand, and scrambled into his chair. He slid a shy glance at me. "Do you have a little boy?"

"Not yet. But I do have a nephew, Josh, who's just a little older than you." I handed him a napkin. "Well, he's not really my nephew. He's my next-door neighbor, but he's the nephew of my heart." I smiled. "Josh loves to play with Legos. Would you like to come over and play with him sometime?" I looked over at Jane. "Or maybe I can bring Josh here?"

"Can I, Mom?" Luke's eyes sparked with life.

Jane gave me a grateful smile. "Sure, sweetie."

"Where your husban'?" Luke gave me a thoughtful look.

"Luke . . ."

"That's okay." I sat down next to him. "I don't have a husband yet. Someday, I hope." I nodded to his plate. "Now you'd better eat your dinner before it gets cold."

"Don't forget to say grace," Jane reminded him weakly.

Luke bowed his head and clasped his skinny fingers together. "Sank you, Jesus, for dis food. 'Specially ice cream. An' de nice ladies dat bwought it. An' please make Mommy all better so she don't have to go to heaven. Amen." He picked up his fork and started shoveling in macaroni and cheese.

I turned toward the kitchen so Jane couldn't see the tears flooding my eyes. "What can I get you, Jane? Some chicken maybe?"

"Just a tiny bit of macaroni and cheese, please." She gave an apologetic laugh. "Soft foods are the easiest for me to keep down these days."

"I feel ya on that." Rashida burped the baby. "In fact, I've even been thinking of stocking up on some jars of Gerber. Do they still have those puréed peaches? I always loved those."

Jane nodded. "But stay away from the strained peas. Ick."

My head swiveled from one to the other. "Baby food?"

"Hey, don't knock it 'til you've tried it. Right, Jane?"

"Uh-huh. It's a lot faster and easier than having to blend your own food." Jane giggled. "Baby food is the original smoothie."

"Oh, don't play." Rashida returned a content Matthew to his bassinet. "She keepin' real right there."

We all laughed.

The front door opened, and a giant string bean of a man entered. "Well, if that isn't sweet music to my ears. Hearing my wife laugh again." He strode to the couch and kissed Jane full on the mouth. "Baby, I got you some Jell-O and some of that Gerber oatmeal with pears you like so well."

Jane snorted, and Rashida and I joined in.

"What?" Her husband looked from one of us to the other. "What'd I say?"

· · ·

Outside, I took deep gulps of fresh night air and brushed the dog hair from my pants with one hand and the tears from my eyes with the other.

The car door had barely shut behind her when Rashida said, "We need to lift up that sweet family in prayer. 'Specially that sad little boy."

And we did, all the way back to Rashida's house.

chapter *fourteen*

The biggest problem with wigs, I discovered, is that they itch. When I'd gone to the American Cancer Society for information when I was first diagnosed, I'd also received a voucher toward the purchase of a wig. And Merritt insisted I use it at a wig shop in a nearby strip mall.

"Here's your chance to indulge your wild side, Nat." She grabbed a platinum blonde number that looked like the Dutch boy one Julia Roberts wore in *Pretty Woman* when she first met Richard Gere.

I wrinkled my nose. "A little too wild for me." I picked up a brown, layered shoulder-length model instead. "Oh look, this is kind of like the Rachel. Remember when *Friends* first started, and Jennifer Aniston had that really cool haircut everyone copied?" I fingered the soft wig, then tried it on.

Jennifer Aniston did *not* look back at me from the mirror.

I yanked off the wig, pushed my hair behind my ears, then moved on, quickly bypassing a stash of blonde mops that reminded me of Eva Gabor in *Green Acres*.

"How about red?" Merritt held up a lustrous cascade of auburn curls, complete with cute bangs. "You can be Lindsay Lohan before she went blonde and then brunette."

I looked down at my flat chest. "Not in this lifetime."

Merritt plucked a huge Afro from one of the wig stands. "Now this one is really cool—you could be Nadia from *American Idol*."

"Ah, but for that, I'd need to be able to sing."

At last I settled on a basic, dark brown, just-past-shoulder-length wig with a slight wave that looked like a cross between Monica from *Friends* and Lorelai from *Gilmore Girls*.

I wondered if it would be like that whole transplant thing where people who've gotten a new heart suddenly start craving foods they never liked before—like sushi—then discover their donor liked those foods. I wondered if when I wore my new wig I'd suddenly start spouting witty, rapid-fire remarks to my friends and family à la Lorelai.

I looked in the mirror.

Nah. With your luck, you'll just get all OCD and neat-freakish like Monica.

I yanked off the wig. I just wasn't ready for this.

• • •

On Saturday when I woke up, my head was itching like a bad case of poison ivy. I scratched it, and a clump of hair came away in my hand. And when I lifted my head from the pillow, my white pillowcase was black with hair.

I immediately called Merritt and Jillian.

"It's time," I said to Jillian. "Bring the clippers."

Before Jillian decided to become a personal shopper, she had tried a variety of career paths: model, massage therapist, and hair stylist. She said the model thing was too boring. She had freaked the first time she had to massage an old guy with a hairy gray back. And she had attended cosmetology school just long enough to know she didn't want to do it for a living—but also long enough to learn how to wield a set of hair scissors and clippers.

She showed up at my house with them half an hour later. Along with Merritt, who brought a basket of CDs.

Merritt shuffled through the CDs until she found the one she was looking for and blasted the *South Pacific* soundtrack through my kitchen, playing "I'm Gonna Wash That Man Right Outta My Hair" again and again. Of all the people my age I know, *only* Merritt would have ever heard of that song, let alone own the soundtrack. But now they both were singing, "We're gonna shave that hair right offa your head!"

Jillian pointed to the seat of the stepstool. "Sit," she said. When I did, she tucked the towel around my neck, held up the Texas chain saw formerly known as electric clippers, and asked, "Ready?"

I squeezed my eyes shut. "Ready."

Merritt changed the CD and turned up the volume to drown out the hair chain saw, and we rocked out to Bo Bice's "Vehicle" single. We'd all been mesmerized by this humble, true-to-himself growly Southern rocker on *American Idol*.

The chain saw stopped, but I kept my eyes closed.

"Hey, Nat, you look really hip," Jillian said.

"I'll say." Merritt whistled. "Very Demi Moore in *GI Jane*. Or Melissa Etheridge. Remember when she performed at the Grammys? She was totally bald, and she rocked the house! Very cool."

I opened my eyes and slowly made my way to the bathroom, keeping my eyes downcast the whole time until I stood before the sink. Then I took a deep breath, gingerly lifted my head, and looked in the mirror.

And freaked.

"Yeah, I'm hip all right. For a concentration camp survivor."

"You got part of that right, Nat. You are a survivor." Jillian slung her arm around my shoulders and met my swimming eyes in the mirror. "A survivor," she repeated firmly. "That's the important thing."

Survivor. The word took on new meaning for me.

"You're right. I'm sorry." I took another look in the mirror, but this time I didn't stop at my buzzed head. My eyes started there, traveled down my neck, and finally came to rest on my flat chest. I met Jillian's eyes in the mirror again. "I think I definitely ought to try out for prom queen, don't you? Or maybe I can get them to revive *Baywatch*. I think America's tired of the same-old, same-old, don't you? I mean, how many busty, long-haired blondes can one audience stand?"

Turning sideways, I examined my profile. "One look at me, and all those guys will be falling over each other to be running in slow motion next to me on the beach."

"I hear that," Jillian said.

When Gloria Gaynor's "I Will Survive" blasted from the kitchen, I scrabbled beneath the bathroom sink until I found what I was looking for. I handed Jillian the curling iron and kept the flatiron for myself. We karaoked our way into the living room, singing into our pretend microphones.

Merritt excused herself. "I'll be right back."

"Was it something we sang?" I giggled again.

Just then we could hear a frenzied knocking. I peeked out the side curtain and spied Josh and Andy on my front stoop. I yanked my head back before they saw me. "Quick, get me a hat or something."

Jillian tossed me the black bowler, and I jammed it onto my newly shorn head as she went to answer the door.

Seconds later Andy and Josh appeared, both wearing over-sized cowboy hats.

Cowboy hats?

Josh's eyes danced. "Aunt Natalie, we have a surprise for you." He looked over at his father. "Ready, Dad?"

Andy winked. "Ready, pardner."

"You didn't . . ."

Father and son removed their hats in unison and shook their heads to reveal . . . a pair of cheesy-looking long black wigs.

My mouth did a *Finding Nemo* thing. Then I bent over laughing.

Leave it to Andy and Josh to do the unexpected. From what I'd heard, it was almost a standard thing for family and friends of cancer patients to shave their heads in solidarity. But this . . . this was just *inspired*.

"Did we fool you, Aunt Nat?"

"Oh yes," I admitted. "You got me good."

"Cool," he said. "But look!" He caught Andy's eye, and they both pulled off the wigs to show their matching buzz cuts.

"Do you like it?" Josh jumped up and down. "We wanted to be just like you."

"I love it." My eyes were swimming again, and I had to blink to clear them. "What a couple of handsome guys. You're going to have to beat the girls off with a stick." I squatted down and opened my arms to Josh, mouthing *Thank you* to Andy as I did.

Josh scampered in for a hug. "We're the Three Musketeers, huh, Aunt Natalie?"

"Make that four." Merritt rejoined us, removing her favorite felt fedora as she did so to reveal her also-shaved head.

"Sweet!" Josh said.

I put my hand to my mouth. "Mer, what did you *do*?"

"No big deal." Merritt rubbed her hand over the top of her head. "I damaged my hair anyway with all those different dyes I've been putting on, so I decided it was time to start fresh."

"Well then, guess I'd better make it unanimous." I pulled off the bowler. "Ta-da!"

"Cool, Aunt Nat. Can I feel your head?"

"Only if I can feel yours." We took turns rubbing each other's scalp stubble and giggling. Then Josh caught sight of Jillian's long blonde hair. "Hey, you need to cut your hair too."

Jillian blanched and backed up to the kitchen counter. "It's not that I don't love you, Nat, but—"

"But you have to work with the public, and you don't want to look like the Bride of Frankenstein. Not to worry, Jilly." I looked around at our four shorn heads and grinned. "Although . . . I think you need to hire us as the band for your wedding reception: The Buzzheads."

Andy riffed on his air guitar, dropping to the floor in a Mick Jagger frenzy. "Nah, I think we should be the Cueballs."

"The Bowling Balls," Merritt threw into the mix. "Just don't call us pinheads."

"No, no." Josh jumped up and down, his eyes dancing with delight. "I got the best one. The Skinheads!"

After a long, pregnant silence interrupted only by a fit of coughing from Jillian, Andy said gently, "Uh, that one wouldn't work so good, buddy."

"How come?"

"And that would be why you're a parent and I'm not," Merritt muttered under her breath.

• • •

Sunday

9:00 AM— I've discovered there's something good to be said for not having any hair.

Time.

It used to take me an hour from start to finish to wash, dry, and style my hair. But these days I just wash my head along with the rest of my body in the shower, using my favorite (unscented) body wash. No shampoo. No conditioner. No blow drying. And no curling iron. Or flat-iron, barrettes, scrunchies, clips, or headbands.

Nothing. Nada. Zip. Just me and my low-maintenance bowling-ball head.

Freedom! I feel like Mel Gibson in Braveheart.

Except he had long hair.

chapter *fifteen*

Andy took me to chemo the next day.

Eager to see my Paul Gallagher again, I'd donned my prettiest hat for the occasion. Andy dressed up too. He wore his least-rumpled pair of shorts, a black T-shirt, and his favorite Birkenstocks.

I'd told Andy all about Paul. He was always great about giving me that objective male perspective. He was really looking forward to meeting this "Florenz Nightingale" in the flesh.

But Paul had the day off.

I was disappointed but also a little relieved. Andy loved to tease me, and there was no telling what he might have said to embarrass me in front of the new object of my affection. He can be a little intimidating when he goes into his protective big-brother mode. And I didn't want to scare Paul away.

I lounged back in my chemo recliner. *Not when we're just starting to get to know each other.*

"How's work?" I asked Andy.

"Going well. Just started on a new user guide."

Andy is a technical writer for one of the high-tech firms in the area. After Sheila left him and he became a single dad, he worked out a deal with his boss to telecommute so he could be home with Josh as much as possible.

"So how's the writing going? Tell me about it."

"Please!" He rolled his eyes. "You're the least technical person I know."

"Maybe." I lifted my chin. "But I'm toying with the idea of becoming a writer."

"Well, if I were you, I'd stick to romance novels."

"Hey!" I glowered at him. "Sexist much?"

"Not at all." Andy smirked. "I just know you, O lover of chick flicks and sappy love stories like *When Harry Met Sally* and *Never Been Kissed*." He shifted in the uncomfortable hospital chair. "Technical writing is a totally different animal."

"Speaking of animals, been to visit your relatives in the baboon compound lately?" I batted my eyes and gave him a sweet smile, which quickly morphed into something else as someone walked by with a cup of strong coffee.

Mom, who couldn't grasp the concept of not being there for every treatment, chose that auspicious moment to return from the cafeteria. "What happened?" she asked, looking at my messy shirt.

"She got sick," Andy said, stating the obvious. He was trying to blot up the barf while I held my non-IV hand over my mouth and nose, trying in vain not to gag.

"Oh, honey, I'm so sorry. Maybe we can get them to bring you a hospital gown." Mom looked around for a nurse. "Wait. I just remembered. I have some dry cleaning in the car. Andy, would you run down and grab a blouse for Natalie?"

A plump middle-aged nurse bustled over with a towel, clucking sympathetically. "Did we get sick? Let's get you out of that wet shirt, sweetie."

Andy backed away to give her room, and Mom handed him her car keys.

"Thanks," I said to him through my still-plugged nose.

"No problem." He winked. "Anytime you need to upchuck, I'm your man." He left to get the blouse.

"What a sweet husband." The nurse drew the modesty curtain around my recliner and helped me out of the foul-smelling shirt. "Most men aren't good in the sickroom."

"He's not my husband." I snorted with laughter. "He's just my friend."

"Well, that's what I call a nice friend."

• • •

Tuesday

I've decided that Faye's right: losing weight is the only good thing about chemo.

No, I take that back. As awful as I feel afterward, I console myself with the thought that this toxic medicine that wipes me out and ruins my appetite is also wiping out every deadly cancer cell in its relentless path. That's the only thing that keeps me going back for each treatment.

That and Paul Gallagher, of course. Unfortunately, he wasn't even here today. But I'm beginning to think he just might be the perfect man. Not only is he heart-stoppingly handsome; he's also kind and gentle. Funny too—he makes me laugh. Sort of like Patch Adams in the movie, only not as hairy as Robin Williams.

And Paul would never dump a woman because she got cancer.

• • •

"How can you raise your eyebrows when they're gone?"

"Huh?" Merritt said from the living room.

I raised my voice. "Everyone warned me I would lose my hair, but no one said a word about eyebrows. Or eyelashes." I peered in the bathroom mirror. "Yep, definitely gone. So much for my new mascara and all the makeup tips Jillian gave me."

I looked in the mirror again. Now I really looked like a cancer patient.

Or a peeled kiwi—only I'm not green. Except when I puke.

"I've lost every single blasted hair on my body." I rubbed my smooth arms. "I'm like that expensive furless cat Rachel got stuck with on that one *Friends* episode."

"Nah. You look much better than that cat," Merritt said, coming up behind me. "That cat was seriously ugly."

• • •

Friday

11:17 AM—Another upside of not having any hair is I don't have to shave my legs anymore.

That's me, putting a positive spin on the cancer. I've been spinning this whole thing ever since I began this cancer journey—a journey I never wanted to take.

And I have to say, I'm a little dizzy.

By nature, I consider myself a pretty positive, go-with-the-flow kind of person. So although I was shocked and scared when I first got my diagnosis, the last thing I wanted to do was be around doom-and-gloom, negative people. Not me. I want encouragement, cheerleading, and a can-do attitude.

But if one more person says to me, "Think positive," or "Look for the positive," I'm going to tell them, "You look for the positive. I'm tired!"

• • •

I couldn't make my bed on Monday.

I always made it first thing every morning as soon as my feet touched the floor. I got that from my nana—definitely not my mother. When I was little, Nana taught me how to make a bed properly—pull the sheets taut and make hospital corners, then pull the blanket up two inches from the top of the bed so the top sheet can be folded over neatly to form a nice three-inch trim. Finally, pull up the quilt or bedspread and align the pillow shams just so, making sure the flowers on the shams are always facing up. (Never ever upside down.)

Even as a child, I felt better when the bed was made. Living in a tiny house where the bed was in plain sight (to use the bathroom, you had to go through my bedroom) reinforced the habit. And since I got cancer, making the bed was especially important to me because an unmade bed screams out, *A sick person lives here!*

But the thing is, I just couldn't do it. I didn't have the strength.

Pulling up the top sheet wasn't too difficult. But the heirloom crazy quilt from my great-grandmother was another story. Why'd she have to make it so heavy? It was like she had sewn rocks in the batting or something. I mean, I know times were tough and they had to make do with the materials on hand, but c'mon. Why not a couple of empty flour sacks instead?

I tried once again to pull it up, but I couldn't manage. I collapsed on the bed, panting from the exertion.

I knew Dr. Peterson had said not to "do anything," but I hadn't realized he meant *anything*. It had something to do with the chemo wiping out not only cancer cells, but also my healthy white and red blood cells—important bodily things that I need to function. One of them, I can't remember which right now, white or red (chemo also wipes out brain cells, so that's going to be my excuse from here on out), carries oxygen, which the body needs to do the normal everyday things it does.

Like making the bed.

Without enough oxygen, I was pretty much as helpless as a baby. The simple act of brushing my teeth wore me out. After rinsing out my mouth, I staggered back to my room and fell on my bed, shivering. Then, with every ounce of strength I possessed, I pulled the concrete quilt over me.

• • •

Mom had the early shift that morning. Before leaving for work, she brought me breakfast—vanilla Ensure and a cup of applesauce. Then she got me situated on the couch, handed me the remote, and popped in one of my *Friends* DVDs before she headed to the kitchen to stock the cupboard with more Ensure.

Immediately I fast-forwarded to the episode in the second season when Ross realizes how Rachel feels for him and he shows up at Central Perk just as she's closing up for the night. They look at each other with such yearning through the glass—he's standing out in the rain, and she unlocks all the locks one by one, struggling with one. Then he's inside, and they're in each other's arms, kissing like mad.

Oh, to be adored like that.

As the screen faded to black, I caught sight of my reflection.

Not likely anytime soon, O hairless one. Just imagine if Jack could see you now.

I threw the remote on the floor. It bounced and cracked a CD case that was propped against the armoire.

Mom looked in from the kitchen. "Are you okay?" She noticed the remote and the cracked CD case. "What's wrong, honey?"

"What's wrong? What's wrong?" I shrieked. "I have cancer! I look like Mr. Giant Freakin' Potato Head or something. I don't even have any eyelashes anymore! I'm just this ugly sexless thing who doesn't even look like a woman." I started to wail. "I'm never going to get kissed again."

"Of course you will, honey. You're just having a bad day," she soothed, tucking the chenille throw around me. "This is all temporary. It will pass, and soon you'll have your beautiful hair again and be back to your old self."

"No, I won't! I'll never be my old self again. How can I be?" I looked down at my chest. "My breasts got cut off, remember?"

Mom sucked in a sharp breath.

I flung off the throw, breathing hard. "I can't do anything— even make my bed. I'm sick of being helpless and having to depend on everyone for every little thing."

Who are you and what have you done with my sweet, compliant, never-make-a-fuss daughter? Mom's shocked face read.

She moved to tuck the throw back around me as I started shivering.

"Just leave it! I'm tired of being fussed over. Just leave me alone." I began to cry in earnest now. "Why can't everyone just leave me alone?" I closed my eyes, the tears leaking into my ears.

A moment later I heard the soft *click* as the front door shut, but I was too exhausted to even care.

● ● ●

When I opened one eye a couple of hours later, Jillian had her back to me and was busy dusting off my bookshelves with a feather duster.

I coughed, and she whirled around, startled.

"What *are* you doing, Susie Homemaker?"

"I'm sorry," Jillian said. "Did I wake you? I was trying to be really quiet."

I swung my legs off the couch. "That's okay. I need to go to the bathroom anyway." Swaying a little when I stood, I grabbed the armrest.

Jillian dropped the feather duster and rushed to help me.

"That's okay. I got it." I waved her away impatiently. "But I think something else could use a little help." I nodded in the direction of the feather duster, which had rained dust all over my pristine end table.

Jillian gave a helpless lift of her shoulders. "What can I say? I never was very domestic."

"That's for sure. You or my mom." I grunted and began the laborious trek to the bathroom.

While washing my hands, I glanced in the bathroom mirror. *That's another good thing about being bald—you don't have to worry about bed-head.* I shuffled back to the living room, but Jillian was no longer there. "Jilly?"

"In here." I followed the sound of her muffled voice to the kitchen, just in time to see her hit her head on the freezer door as she straightened up. "Ouch!"

She rubbed her head. "I'm here on my lunch break, so I thought I'd make some lunch. What would you like?"

I considered. It had been seven days since my latest chemo treatment, so I figured the worst should be behind me barfwise. I ran through all the food options in my head, testing each one in consideration of my tender stomach. "How about chicken noodle soup and grilled cheese sandwiches?"

"You got it." Jillian started opening cupboard doors, looking for soup cans. "Well, well, what have we here?" She released a long, appreciative whistle. "Like your collection of hotties, Nat." Then she did a double take and tapped her French-manicured nail against one of the pictures. "Clay Aiken? Can you say 'one of these is not like the others'?"

"Oh yes, he is." I lifted my chin and eased into one of the metal bistro chairs to which I'd recently added cushions to provide some extra padding for my too-tender body. "His voice is totally hot. And I think he's cute. He's down-to-earth and humble and used to teach special-ed kids."

"Whatever." She scrutinized the rest of my collection. "So where's Brad Pitt?"

"Patrick Dempsey replaced him." My stomach rumbled. "Uh, weren't you going to fix some lunch?"

"Of course. Just looking for the soup."

I pointed to the end cupboard.

She retrieved the soup, then started yanking open all the drawers.

"Can opener's in the top utensil drawer." I pointed. "Same as yours and Merritt's."

"You can tell I don't eat at home much." Jillian dumped the soup in a pan with water and started buttering bread for our sandwiches.

"Um, Jillian?"

"Yes?"

"Have you ever made grilled cheese before?"

"No. Merritt usually makes them, but I've watched her."

"How closely?"

"Why?"

"The butter usually goes on the outside of the bread, not inside with the cheese."

"Oh." She giggled and started peeling the bread apart. "Good thing Bill plans to do most of the cooking once we're married."

"I'll say. Otherwise you guys would starve."

She tossed her hair. "Not as long as there's takeout. Besides, your mom's not much of a cook, and your family's always done okay, hasn't it?"

Thinking of my mom, I felt a wave of guilt wash over me. I confessed to Jillian about my earlier outburst. "I've never yelled at my mom like that before in my entire life."

"Really? Even when you were a teenager?" She gave me an incredulous look. "I yelled at my stepmom plenty of times. Even told her I hated her once or twice."

"You did?"

"Sure. Every teenager does. Surely you did too?"

I shook my head.

"Oh, that's right—I forgot. You don't like conflict." She set my soup and sandwich before me. "My family's part Italian, remember? We're very expressive, so yelling doesn't bother me. Sometimes you just need to let off a little steam." Jillian grunted. "With everything you've been through lately, I think you're entitled."

"Maybe. But that still doesn't give me license to go and yell at people. Especially my mother, who was only trying to help."

"So apologize." She took a bite of her sandwich. "Then let it go. It's not the end of the world—trust me."

• • •

After Jillian left, I was feeling much stronger. In fact, I had a sudden craving for Sara Lee cheesecake and decided to run down to the store to pick some up.

I know that sounds crazy—thinking I could drive when that morning I couldn't even make my bed. But the store was only a couple of blocks away. And I just needed to dash in and out. And as I said, I was feeling stronger.

Scratch that.

Dashing wasn't exactly doable these days. And walking through the entire grocery store to get to the frozen-food cases at the back felt like crossing the Sahara. By the time I made it to the register, Sara Lee in hand, I was totally wiped.

Driving home, I noticed that my gas gauge was on empty, so I pulled into the convenience store to fill up. I slid my ATM card through the machine and removed the nozzle. Or tried to. I staggered under the weight and to my utter surprise found that I couldn't move it over to my car to fill my tank—even with both hands.

I thought back to those 1950s TV shows when gas station attendants in creased uniforms and crisp hats would ask, "Fill her up, ma'am? Regular or Ethyl?"

"I'll take Lucy instead," I'd always shouted at the screen whenever the question was asked. Funny—but it wouldn't help a bit with my current gas-pumping dilemma.

A slow-moving white-haired man who had to be pushing

eighty shuffled over from the pump on the other side of mine. "Can I help you with that, young lady?"

"Thank you." I shot him a grateful smile. "Usually this is no problem. It's just that—"

He patted my shoulder. "I understand. My wife had cancer."

chapter *sixteen*

I always had the best boobs around. Even in high school."
Faye took a sip of coffee from her Styrofoam cup, leaving a bright pink lip print on the rim. She shot a defiant look at all of us in the circle. "Everyone was jealous of me." She patted her chest. "These babies have gotten me far. I won poise and appearance at our local Junior Miss pageant."

I stole a glance at Rashida and rolled my eyes, but Constance was listening very intently to Faye's monologue. Johnna was out sick that day, so Constance was running the meeting.

She had posed the probing question, how important are breasts?

And Faye had been first to reply, launching into the story of her life. "After modeling for a while, I became a flight attendant. That's where I met my husband, Steve." She drained the rest of her coffee and started playing with her empty cup. "But Steve was jealous of me flying with all those good-looking pilots, so after we got married, I stayed home and did the whole Junior League, country-club thing."

She ripped off a piece of Styrofoam. "Everything was going great until this stupid cancer interfered."

She ripped off another piece and furiously began shredding her cup. "It's really wreaking havoc on my sex life."

Thanks so much for sharing.

Constance laid her hand on Faye's arm and said gently, "How does—"

Faye shook off Constance's hand. "Don't try your psycho-babble on me. You want to know how it makes me feel?" She crumpled what remained of her cup. "Pissed off. That's how I feel."

"Me too," Jane said softly. "I get pi—" She couldn't bring herself to say the *P*-word. "I get angry a lot."

I shot Jane a surprised look.

"*You* angry?" Faye dumped the shredded pile of Styrofoam from her skirt into the trash can next to her. "That's rich. Tell us another one."

Jane flushed. "I've never been pretty or popular like you, Faye." She closed her eyes for a moment, her pale lids looking translucent in the light. "Most guys never gave me a second look in high school or college, so I'd pretty much decided I'd never get married." She opened her eyes, and a sweet smile lit up her plain face. "And then—"

"And then you met the great love of your life, who swept you off your feet." Faye snorted. "Spare me. I've seen it before on the Hallmark channel."

Zoey and Rashida both gave Faye dirty looks. And I barely refrained from jumping up and slapping her silly.

"Shh," Pat said. "We want to hear."

Jane looked uncertainly at Constance. "Are you sure? I don't want to take up the whole time . . . ."

"Please." Constance gave her an encouraging smile.

Jane took a deep breath. "Well, as I was saying . . . then one day I met Mitch, and to him I was beautiful. But it was never about my breasts." She looked down at her slightly concave chest and thin, freckled arms and legs. "Or any part of my body, for that matter." She said simply, "Loving Mitch made me beautiful."

Anita sniffled.

"And this makes you pissed off—I mean, angry—exactly *why?*" Faye crossed her arms over her twin babies and raised her chin.

Jane locked eyes with her. "Because I've been married for only five years to the most precious man in the world, and we have two little boys I probably won't get to see grow up."

Thursday

8:45 PM—After Jane's revelation in group today, my lack of eyebrows and eyelashes seems suddenly insignificant.

Lord, please don't take that sweet woman home. Her family needs her.

Now Faye, on the other hand . . .

That woman is so angry and arrogant. What a whiner. She can run whining circles around everyone. And speaking of whiners, I hate that I've turned into one. I've always been more of the pull-yourself-up-by-your-bootstraps kind of girl. If something's broken, fix it. If you don't like something, change it. But don't whine about it. Shut up or put up! And now I've become the biggest whiner in the world.

Why can't I be more like Jane or Constance? Or even Zoey? They may be coming from totally different places, but overall they still have a good attitude. Rashida too. And Jane's the quintessential quiet, gentle spirit. She could be the poster child for how all Christians should be.

She's not the least bit judgmental, even to Zoey, and is always asking after everyone else and their families and telling them she'll pray for them.

Best of all, when she says it, you know she means it.

"I'll be praying for you," or "You're in my prayers," has become the Christian equivalent of "Have a nice day." We toss those prayer promises around so easily, but how many of us actually follow through on them?

Hard swallow. I'm so talking to myself here.

Promising to pray sounds good, and I used to mean it when I said it. But now it's become one of those standard Christianese expressions I just say out of habit.

I'm pretty sure Constance is a praying woman like Jane—or "prayer warrior," as we say in Christianese. She has that wise old sage role down pat, dispensing wisdom and kindness at every meeting. Of course, it's been more than thirty years since she had to go through all this, so maybe it's easy for her to be all wise and understanding. I would be, too, if I was thirty years cancer-free.

I really hope I make it to the thirty-year mark.

And Zoey? I don't have a clue where she's coming from spiritually— probably something New Agey since she's always recommending herbs and supplements to everyone. And recently she told us about a massage therapist who works primarily with cancer patients and uses holistic oils and stuff. But the thing about Zoey is she doesn't throw a pity party for herself. She's a fighter who stays on top of all the latest treatment news and takes charge of her health. She's always telling us, "You need to stand up for yourself. This is your body and your life!"

Rashida says stuff like that too. "As wonderful as your doctors and nurses may be, they're not God, and they don't have all the answers. They can make mistakes. You're not their only patient, you know. That's why you have to become your own health-care advocate.

Nobody knows your body better than you. You know when something's wrong. And if you have a doctor who doesn't listen to you or who you feel uncomfortable with, then change your doctor! Stand up for yourself. You only get one life."

Rashida's my girl. I just love her. And maybe if I hang around with her enough, some of her good sense will rub off on me.

• • •

"I'm not going to church today, Mom."

She set her purse down on my kitchen counter. "Is it another one of your bad days, honey? I thought you were feeling better."

"I am. I just need a little break."

"A break?" Her eyebrows disappeared into her hairline. "From church?"

"From everyone knowing." I sighed. "And asking. And looking. Or doing their best not to look." I rubbed my hands over my nonexistent eyebrows. "I'm just tired of all the platitudes and sympathy. Tired of being 'poor Natalie Moore with cancer.' I just want to be plain old Natalie." I licked my lips. "And I can't be that there."

She stared at me. "But you've gone to that church since you were a baby. Why, you were baptized there." Her eyebrows settled back into place and met in the middle as she squared her shoulders. "You're *going* to church, young lady."

"No, I'm not." I squared my shoulders right back. "I'm twenty-seven years old, Mother. Old enough to make my own decisions."

"Everyone ready?" Dad poked his head in the front door. "Don't want to be late."

"Good. I'm glad you're here." Mom picked up her purse. "You can talk sense into your daughter." Her lips tightened. "Natalie's decided she's not going to church. She needs a *break*."

Dad looked from me to my thin-lipped mother. Then he looked at his watch. "Come on, Ruth, let's go. Natalie's a big girl." He sent me a little smile. "If she doesn't want to go to church, she doesn't have to go to church."

And he led my protesting mother away.

· · ·

Sunday morning

I grew up with God.

He's been part of my life ever since I can remember. I asked Jesus into my heart when I was four, got gold stars in Sunday school for always having my Bible-verse-of-the-week memorized, tried to convert half my kindergarten class, went away to church camp every summer, and became a Christian camp counselor in high school.

I also wore one of those purity rings all through high school and into college.

The past couple of years, though, everything's become more or less rote. I continued to do what I always had and what was expected of me. I mean, I taught Sunday school and Vacation Bible School, went to mid-week Bible study, decorated the fellowship hall for women's events, and fed the homeless at Thanksgiving.

But I just wasn't feeling Jesus the way I used to. You know what I'm saying?

It's like somewhere along the way He lost me. Or maybe I lost Him. I don't know. But I do know it's tied up with going to the same old church my whole life.

The thing is, I'm really ready to seek God out.

More than ever, I know I need Him.

Maybe I just need to branch out and find a better place to spend time with Him.

• • •

After my parents left, I sat down on the couch and expelled a huge breath I didn't realize I'd been holding. I called Merritt and asked her if she wanted to go to the movies. There was a romantic comedy we'd both been waiting to see.

"You want to go to the movies *now*? Shouldn't you be at church?"

"I decided not to go today. So do you want to go to the movies or not?"

"Sure. Just hope God doesn't send an earthquake to demolish the theater while you're sinning." She chuckled.

Merritt had gone to church with me a few times in high school and still occasionally attended a Christmas pageant or special concert when the mood struck. But in general, church just wasn't her thing. And I didn't push her. I figured God didn't need me getting in His way and messing things up.

It felt strange to be in a movie theater munching on unsalted popcorn—no butter—instead of singing worship songs. But I liked it—in the darkened theater, no one could see my hairless cancer self. I felt only a little guilty.

The next Sunday I called Jillian and asked if I could go to church with her and Bill. They attended one of those razzle-dazzle megachurches with thousands of members, so I knew I could go there and just be anonymous.

And who knew? Maybe I could even meet someone who'd step in romantically in case Paul Gallagher didn't work out.

The prospect of romance, of course, called for the wig.

Once I'd had my head shaved, I'd actually gone back to the wig shop and used my coupon on the wavy brunette number that looked a lot like my long-lost hair, only shorter. I rarely wore it because it was too hot and itchy. But today I wanted to look as normal as possible. So I brushed the wig thoroughly, taking special care with the bangs. Then I penciled in eyebrows, smudged a little liner beneath my bottom lid in an effort to hide the fact that I no longer had eyelashes, added a little blush and lipstick for color, and surveyed the results in the mirror.

Not bad. I actually looked human again.

Or so I thought.

Jillian and Bill picked me up, and when we walked into the lobby a few minutes before the service, a tall, wavy-haired guy strode over. His suit was gray silk, obviously expensive. So were his shoes and his sprayed-into-submission, nothing-moving haircut. He and Bill did the brotherly church-hug thing, clapping each other on the back when they released. Then he gave Jillian a quick hug.

She started to introduce us. "Justin, this is my friend—"

"Natalie, right?" He swooped in to give me a welcoming hug, and his expensive cologne made me glad I hadn't had chemo that week. "It's so good to see you up and about." He nodded to Bill. "We've been praying for you in our men's study." Justin held out his arm. "You look a little pale. May I escort you into the sanctuary?"

Behind him, Jillian mouthed *Sorry* and jabbed Bill with her elbow.

Not wanting to make a scene, I acquiesced.

Justin of the unmoving hair sat with us and sang out loud and enthusiastically during worship time. He raised his hands with their buffed nails high into the air. And as the pastor approached the podium, he leaned over and whispered into my ear, "You're in for a special treat." He patted my arm and whispered again, his eyes all shiny. "It's a total God thing that you came today."

A little flutter started in my stomach. Justin wasn't my normal type—a little too polished and slickly put together for my taste. But it did feel nice to have a man's attention again. And a good-looking man's attention to boot.

Then a man got up and announced that a visiting preacher would conduct a special service that day.

A healing service.

With a call for people to come forward and be healed. And the promise that it would happen—just as long as they truly believed.

Really? What about Joni Eareckson Tada?

I glanced over at Jillian, who just widened her eyes and shrugged. Apparently all this was news to her.

But not to Justin.

He leaned over and whispered to me again. "See what I mean? A total God thing that you came today!" He leapt up from his seat, bumping my wig a little askew as he did. "Here, let me help you down to the front."

• • •

Sunday afternoon

What was I thinking? That guy Justin looked good at first, but he was just . . . too much. I wonder how long it takes him to do his hair in the morning. Definitely longer than me—probably even when I had hair. Important Dating Rule: Never trust a man who spends more time on his grooming than you.

Paul Gallagher, on the other hand, has natural good looks. I'll bet he doesn't even own any hair spray. I love the way his hair flops over his forehead when he leans over to insert my IV. He's so—

"Natalie? Is that you?"

I slapped my journal shut and looked up from the picnic table at a pair of faded jeans and a deliciously torn T-shirt flecked with sweat. "Paul. Uh, what are you doing here?"

He smiled and nodded to the panting golden retriever at his side. "Taking Radar for his Sunday run. But I need a break—he's got more energy than I do. Mind if we join you?"

Anytime.

"Sure."

Paul tied the leash to one of the table legs, then removed a bottle of water and a folding nylon bowl from his fanny pack. He poured some water into the bowl. The dog lapped noisily.

"Gorgeous dog." I grinned. "Kind of an odd name—Radar."

Paul gave me a heart-stopping smile. "It's really Radar O'Reilly."

"As in *M*A*S*H*?"

"You got it. One of my favorite old TV shows." He reached down to scratch the back of his dog's neck. "And my Radar's just as loyal and dependable as his namesake, aren't you, boy?"

Radar wagged his tail, then dropped to the ground and rolled in the grass.

Paul sat down across from me. "So what are you doing all dressed up in the park on a Sunday? By the way, you look very nice." He tilted his head. "That hairstyle really suits you."

He's tactful too. He didn't even mention that he knows it's a wig.

I blushed. "Thanks. I was driving home from church and it was such a gorgeous day, I thought I'd make a slight detour."

He glanced at the closed book. "Catching up on your reading?"

I blushed again. "Uh, no. I'm keeping a cancer journal."

His eyes lit up. "Great idea! I should recommend that to some of my other patients. Do you find it therapeutic?"

Do I? I hadn't really thought about it.

"Yeah, I think so." I gave him a wry grin. "If nothing else, it's a safe place to vent."

Paul rubbed the back of my hand. "I'm sorry your chemo has been so rough. Wish there was something I could do to make it less yucky."

Asking me out would help.

Radar barked and nudged against Paul's legs.

"Okay, fella. I know." He grinned and stood up. "He'll just keep pestering me 'til we finish his run." He packed the bowl into his fanny pack, then gave a chivalrous bow. "May we escort you to your car, my lady?"

"Thanks, but I'm going to hang out here a little longer."

Paul pretended to tip an imaginary hat. "Well then, great to see you. Happy journaling." He grinned. "Hope you say nice things about me."

If you only knew. "Of course," I said with a flirtatious gleam in my eye. "No one takes care of my rolling veins like you."

Radar strained at his leash. "Okay, okay, we're going." He gave me a loopy grin. "See you soon."

Can't wait. I stared at his retreating form, which I appreciated all the more in jeans rather than baggy hospital scrubs.

I opened my journal again.

Well, ask and ye shall receive . . . Paul Gallagher actually showed up in the park as I was writing. He was running with his dog. And he's twice as adorable outside the hospital setting. There's nothing more attractive than a man who loves animals (although it doesn't hurt that he looks absolutely delicious too).

I'm beginning to think I really have met the man of my dreams. And I really think there's some kind of spark. I'm definitely going after that guy—as soon as I get my hair and my boobs, that is.

How's that for a positive attitude?

chapter seventeen

Both Jane and Faye were missing from group the next week.

"Jane's white counts are really low." Johnna took a sip of coffee from her Styrofoam cup and grimaced. "Her husband called and said she's feeling pretty weak. So she's resting today, but she said to send you all her love."

"We should go see her." Rashida looked at me. "Take her some soup. That girl needs some protein. And not to brag, but my boys say my chicken gumbo works better than any medicine."

Johnna shook her head. "She's not having visitors right now. The risk of infection is too great. But Mitch said he'd call me in a few days and let me know when it's safe for people to come by." She shifted in her chair. "He also said that they'd appreciate your prayers."

Anita crossed herself.

"Why don't we pray right now?" Pat asked.

"This isn't a religious group," Johnna reminded her. "Not everyone shares the same beliefs, and we don't want to force anything on anyone or make them uncomfortable."

Zoey glanced around the circle. "I can't imagine that any of us here wouldn't want to pray for Jane. Am I right?"

Everyone nodded.

"I understand Johnna's hesitation." Rashida had donned her lawyer hat. "If we were in church or someone's living room or even outside in a park or something, it wouldn't be a problem. But because we're on hospital property and this is an official cancer center–affiliated group as opposed to a religious one, she'd be opening the center up to all sorts of legal hassles."

Johnna sent her a look of gratitude.

"How about a compromise?" Rashida offered. "What if we just take a minute or so—you know, like those moments of silence they always do in public places—and anyone who wants to can pray silently for Jane. Would that be okay?"

Johnna hesitated.

Constance smiled at her. "Didn't you say you needed to run to the bathroom for a minute? I'll be happy to take over the group while you're gone."

"Thanks, Constance." Johnna returned the smile and headed to the door. "I'll be back in a couple of minutes."

The second the door shut behind her, Constance said, "Okay, ready, set, pray! And remember—silently."

All six remaining heads bowed as one.

When Johnna returned, we all attacked the coffee-and-tea cart. Zoey had contributed a basket of different herbal teas so we'd have an alternative to the sorry packets of Lipton. She went for lemon zest while I selected mint.

I dunked my tea bag. "So where's Faye and her fabulous, famous breasts tonight? It's so quiet without her."

Zoey grunted. "I hear ya on that."

Johnna and Constance exchanged a look. "Faye's husband left her," Johnna said softly.

"Oh, *madre mia*." Anita crossed herself.

"Jerk!" Pat's face flushed.

Zoey didn't say anything. Just clenched and unclenched her fists.

My face flooded with heat. *Want a little salt with that shoe leather?*

Constance's lips set in a thin line. "Apparently he already has wife number three lined up. Oldest story in the book—his twenty-five-year-old secretary."

That explained why she'd been so nasty to me the other day.

"Poor Faye." Rashida sighed and looked down at her hands. "The more things change, the more they stay the same."

I gave her a questioning look.

"My husband left me for his secretary when I was pregnant with DeWayne." She rubbed her scarf over her growing-in stubble. "Skipped the state so he wouldn't have to pay child support. That's why I put myself through law school."

I stared at her. "I never knew you were married. You never said."

Pat nodded in surprised agreement.

"What?" Rashida looked from me to Pat. "You just assumed I was another one of them unwed black mothers?"

We flushed.

Rashida slapped her thigh. "I'm just playin' with you." Her tone turned serious. "I can understand how you'd think that since I never mentioned a husband." She waved her hand. "But that was a lifetime ago. My sons' father hasn't seen fit to communicate with his own flesh and blood, so I don't waste energy thinking about him. It's his loss, after all." She looked around the circle. "Besides, DeWayne and DeShawn got their heavenly Father lookin' after them. What could be better than that?"

"Amen," Pat and Constance said in unison.

• • •

After group, most of us went out for fruit smoothies. Pat and Anita both had plans with their husbands, but Pat decided to come along, "just for a minute." She called her husband and asked him to pick her up at the smoothie shop.

"Men can be such pigs." I jabbed my straw in my banana-with-protein concoction and thought of Jack.

"Ain't that the truth." Rashida placed her napkin in her lap. "Girl's gon' need her a good lawyer."

Zoey was strangely silent.

I sent her a curious look. "Why so quiet? I figured you of all people would be ready to lead the male-bashing charge."

"Why? Because I'm gay? Contrary to popular belief, not all lesbians hate men." Zoey slid me an impish grin. "In fact, some of my best friends are men. Besides"—she took a sip of her smoothie and gave a sad little smile—"it's not just men who leave."

I flushed for the third time that night. "I'm sorry."

Constance patted Zoey's hand. "Want to talk about it, dear?" She shook her head.

"I think we need to talk about the best way to get back at Faye's husband." Rashida's eyes gleamed. "Anyone up for a good ol'-fashioned lynching? My people have a lot of experience with that."

Johnna and I both choked on our smoothies.

"Or maybe we can get one of our doctors to perform some kind of ectomy on him?" Rashida suggested.

"How about a prostate-ectomy?" the elegant Constance said.

Pat's suggestion was a little less elegant.

My face reddened while everyone else giggled.

"Oh sorry, Natalie." Pat was instantly contrite. "I forgot about your tender ears."

"They're not that tender. Just burning a little at the moment."

Rashida looked around the table. "Well, since lynchings and ectomies are out, guess we'll just have to find Faye a good divorce lawyer."

Thursday

I really put my foot into it at group today. Three times, no less. I need to be less judgmental and less quick about assuming. Hope I didn't hurt Rashida's feelings. And as much as Faye gets on my nerves, I do feel bad for her.

I'm going to church with Anita tomorrow evening—more of the old church-hop two-step. Anita says they have Mass (services) at her church every day, and she goes to as many as she can. That's really kind of nice when you think of it—sort of a daily reminder. Anyway, it will be interesting to try out a church that's really different from mine. (With my attitude lately, maybe I need to go visit one of those confession booths.)

One fun thing: Pat and her husband, Jerry, are going on another cruise. They had such a blast on their anniversary cruise, they've decided to do another one as soon as possible. Pat went with us to get smoothies tonight, and Jerry met her there with a handful of brochures—he'd just been to the travel agent on the corner. Then they walked off holding hands. They're so cute together—I hope I can have

a marriage like that someday. And it's really good to know that every-
thing has worked out so well for her. Gives me hope to know it can
happen.

I'm sort of worried about Jane, though. Her counts are so low we're
not even supposed to visit. I'm not sure she has much time left. I hate
even writing that down—it makes it real, and that's scary. I'm afraid I
won't handle her death very well. And I'm embarrassed to write that,
but it's the truth. I mean, I know this isn't all about me. But she's only
three years older than me! And this is my journal, so I have to be hon-
est. Right?

Anyway, God, please be with Jane and her family. And help me be
supportive in the right way. And not be a jerk about it.

• • •

I'd never been to a Catholic church before aside from a wedding
of one of my dad's friends. It had always been one of those stal-
wart Protestant off-limits kind of things. ("They worship *Mary*,
you know.") But as a child I'd been fascinated by what I'd seen
of Catholicism in movies or on TV. It all seemed so foreign and
mysterious.

When I was little I thought it would be cool to go into the
confessional cubicle with the curtains pulled shut—and no chintzy
half-curtains like in those cheesy photo booths that just cover the
top of you, but curtains all the way down to the ground. You
could sit in this dark little cocoon where no one could see you
and only the priest heard you, and you could tell him everything
you did wrong. Then you'd just have to count some beads afterward or something like that, and you'd be off the hook.

At least that's how I understood it at the time.

But the truth is, I had no idea what to expect in a real Catholic church.

Anita's church was very traditional. The entire service—I mean Mass—was in Latin. Anita told me that was kind of unusual now, that most services were in English or Spanish or whatever. But she liked the Latin, which was what she grew up with.

The congregation kept standing and sitting and murmuring along with the priest and sometimes crossing themselves. And although I didn't understand a word of it, there was something beautiful and mystical about the whole thing.

Only thing was, I kept looking around for Whoopi Goldberg and her *Sister Act* choir. And was a little disappointed when they never showed. Guess they had other Friday night plans.

I went away thinking that the Catholic service was interesting and beautiful, but not really for me. I'd try somewhere else on Sunday.

• • •

I spent most of Saturday afternoon puttering around my little house. Or alternating between puttering and resting. But it had been a long time since I felt strong enough to do *anything*, so I was thrilled with my accomplishments.

I cleaned out my spice shelf. That paprika was way past its expiration date, and I tossed out the garlic salt and onion salt too. Time to get a little healthier.

Then I rested awhile and tried my new "be still" strategy.

I piled all my dirty linens in a basket for Mom to take back to the house and wash.

And took a nap.

I measured the edges of my bedroom valances so I could perk them up with some braid or fringe. (I'd gotten the idea during all those hours of lying in bed—staring at the drapes. They were good, but they could be better. And later I could pull out the left-over fabric and make some matching pillows for the bed.)

Another nap. And an hour or so thumbing through a new decorating magazine and an "anticancer" cookbook that Andy had brought over. A lot of the recipes sounded awful, but a few had possibilities. And the idea of "healthy living" was a lot more appealing to me than it ever had been before.

All through that day, for some reason, I kept thinking about Jane. I was worried about her. I tried to call, but the answering machine picked up immediately, so I realized they were probably screening calls so she could rest. I decided I'd try again tomorrow after church.

I was already in bed when the phone rang about nine that night—a little late for me these days, but Merritt was a night owl and sometimes forgot that other people weren't—especially people who were doing chemo. And this time I happened to be awake, though tired, and feeling pretty good.

I reached for the phone. It would be fun to get in a little girl-friend time.

But it wasn't Merritt. And the somber sound of Rashida's hello made me sink back against my pillows.

"Uh, listen, I hate to call this late, but . . . I thought you'd want to know."

My fingers gripped the phone. I closed my eyes.

I'd known it was coming. We all had. But I still wasn't ready.

Would I ever be ready for something like this?

chapter *eighteen*

It wasn't the cancer," Rashida explained. "She fell in the kitchen."
And it wasn't Jane. It was Pat.

The fun-loving, effervescent woman who had so proudly
flashed her new breast set at my first support-group meeting had
died of a fall. A stupid household accident.

"She and her Jerry were going over all those brochures for
their next cruise." Rashida relayed to me what Johnna had told
her. "Then Jerry had to run to the hardware store. And when he
came home, he found Pat lying there on the floor by a stepstool.
She'd slipped and hit her head on the counter."

"How awful." I clenched the phone with numb fingers.

"I know." Rashida released a heavy sigh. "Poor Jerry's just
devastated."

"I can imagine," I murmured automatically, but my mind was
elsewhere. I was thinking how quickly a life can end. Without any
warning. One minute you're there making romantic travel plans
with your husband. And the next you're just lying on the floor.

It all seemed so . . . pointless.

". . . funeral will be Tuesday," Rashida was saying. "Johnna thought it would be nice if the whole group went together."

• • •

After hearing about Pat, I wasn't really in the mood for church-hopping the next day. But I had already made plans, so I went. Maybe it would help.

I'd heard this was a "cool church"—a small, nondenominational congregation that met in a warehouse downtown—so I thought it might be interesting. And the news about Pat's death had shaken me up—I needed the comfort of a congregation.

This church turned out to be a little more cutting edge—okay, a *lot* more cutting edge—than I was used to. And not exactly comforting, but definitely interesting. Instead of mellow praise songs and hymns, they had a heavy metal band, and there was an artist up front doing an interpretive painting to the sermon. *Sure beats the heck out of flannel graphs.*

The pastor wore flip-flops, cut-offs, and a Hawaiian shirt that I really liked. And he invited others to the front (no pulpit, just a cordless mike) to preach after his brief sermon—including a couple of women.

I appreciated what they had to say and thought it was actually pretty cool to hear women share the gospel in a venue other than a ladies' afternoon tea or a stadium packed with thousands of other women.

That is, until I heard the language that came out of their mouths. They actually cussed in the pulpit—except there wasn't one. And this wasn't about going to hell, either. This was your standard, garden-variety kind of cussing heard on the street or at football games.

A little too edgy for yours truly.

Plus, I kept waiting for them to dismiss the kids to Sunday school or the nursery, but they never did. At this church, children were considered a normal part of the worship service. Which I also thought was pretty cool—until they screamed in my ear and started running up and down the aisles, shrieking and laughing and throwing Silly Putty.

Some comfort. I couldn't even hear myself think, let alone the edgy words up front or the still, small voice of God.

So what was a good Christian girl like me supposed to do?

Time for a little church break, I decided.

A real break, not more church-hopping. I just didn't have the heart for any more Sundays like that.

For the present, at least, I'd try worshiping in the sanctuary of my own four walls.

• • •

I didn't go to Pat's funeral.

I'd just had chemo the day before, so I wasn't feeling great. And it wasn't as if I'd really known Pat all that well. I mean, I liked her, but we weren't exactly friends or anything—just fellow cancer travelers in the same support group.

Now Pat's journey had ended. And I just couldn't work up the energy to see her off.

I skipped group that week too.

Afterward, Rashida's courtroom voice punctured the speakers on my new answering machine. "Girl, where you been?" Her

voice softened. "The service was beautiful—a wonderful celebration of Pat's life. The pastor preached a nice come-to-Jesus message too." She let loose a low, throaty chuckle mixed with a sniffle.
"And you won't believe what her Jerry put inside the casket! Pat
was holding a Bible and a red rose. And alongside her, he put that
black-and-pink swimsuit she'd gotten special for their anniversary cruise. Said he knew it was unorthodox, but she was so
proud to wear that suit, and she looked so beautiful in it, that he
didn't think the good Lord would mind. I said amen to that!" She
giggled. "Call me."

The next message came from Johnna. "Hi, Natalie. Just wanted
to say we missed you at group tonight and at Pat's service, and I
wanted to check and see how you're doing. Hope to see you back
next week. Take care."

I shuffled over to my hottie cupboard to make a cup of tea.

Sigh. *That Patrick Dempsey is pretty yummy, but he's married.
Too bad. Maybe next chemo treatment I can get Merritt to take a picture of Paul Gallagher with her camera phone so I can have the real
thing instead of a movie star imitation.*

The phone rang again. And again I let the machine pick up.

"Natalie?" Jane's soft, tentative voice hovered in the kitchen
air. "I just want you to know that I understand, and if you'd like
to talk, I'm here. Take care, and I hope to see you soon."

Eager to escape the guilt grenades coming fast and furiously
from my answering machine, I turned down the volume and
decided to veg out in front of the TV.

I picked up the remote and channel-surfed, quickly bypassing all the football and boxing. I've never gotten into football—all
that running and hitting and tackling. So aggressive. But at least
it's better than boxing. Not as much noticeable blood and sweat.

There was nothing on TV I cared to watch, so I clicked off the set and picked up my worn copy of *The Lion, the Witch and the Wardrobe* instead, happy to lose myself in the land of Narnia. I'd read that story over and over since childhood, and it never failed to carry me away.

Trouble is, it got me a little *too* carried away—because reading about Turkish Delight gave me a sudden craving.

An intense craving. For something sweet. But not Turkish Delight. Chocolate.

And not just any chocolate, but my favorite: brownies. Rich, triple-chocolate brownies and a nice cold glass of milk.

Taking this as a positive sign in the war on puke—my stomach didn't clench once at the sweet thought—I bounded off the couch and began rummaging through the cupboard for some brownie mix.

Good—there was one box left.

I poured the taupe powder into a bowl; added an egg, some vegetable oil, and water; and lifted my hand mixer.

Correction. Tried to lift the mixer. That little sucker was heavy. It took both hands just to stick the beaters in the bowl. Whew.

I rested for a moment before turning it on. Then I stared transfixed as that familiar, beloved concoction of thick chocolate lava studded with tiny lumps formed beneath the whirring beaters. Removing one hand from the mixer to sneak the obligatory lick from the side of the bowl, I sucked on my chocolate-coated finger.

Rapture. And major tactical error.

The still-rotating mixer was now a two-ton anchor in my weak left hand. An anchor that needed to be dropped. Immediately.

Falling from my useless hand, the beaters-gone-wild splattered batter everywhere, and the heavy, still-whirring mixer dropped into the glass bowl, cracking the bottom and causing the fudgy mass to erupt like a volcano.

It all happened so fast I had no time to react. Afraid the monster beater might slice off one of my fingers if I tried to reach in the bowl and shut it off, I yanked the cord from the wall. Staring at the chocolate mess that had once been my clean kitchen, I slid down, sniffling, to the sticky vinyl floor.

Then the sniffling gave way to sobs. Deep, gut-wrenching sobs. I couldn't do this. It was just too hard.

God, I don't know how much more I can take. Why don't You just take me home now and put me out of my misery?

Spent and hot from crying, I wiped my nose across my sleeve, leaving a snail-trail of snot behind. I leaned over and laid my head on the cool vinyl.

And closed my eyes.

And then I was floating over what looked like my high school football field. Ugh. The stands on both sides were packed, and as I floated down closer, I recognized Jillian in her high school cheerleading outfit in front of the crowd. Then I spotted Merritt— also in a cheerleading outfit.

Now I knew I was dreaming. Merritt wouldn't be caught dead at a football game or in a cheerleading outfit. But she was—only her uniform was tie-dyed and her hair was in purple pigtails. Constance and Johnna from group were there, too, holding pompoms, but Constance wore a silk hand-painted vest, and Johnna's outfit looked a lot like hospital scrubs. There were a few more cheerleaders off to the far end, but I couldn't quite make them out. Then they came into focus, and I recognized my parents— Dad in his polo shirt and plaid golf shorts, Mom in a twinset with pearls, nylons, and pumps. And Andy. And Josh. And someone else who looked suspiciously like my junior high science teacher, Mrs. Vogt.

"What are you doing here?" I started to ask. But the fans were growing impatient. They all started stomping their feet and throwing triple-chocolate brownies onto the field. The crowd grew wild as a mascot appeared on the field dressed in a lion's outfit. But it wasn't a mascot exactly, but the Cowardly Lion from *The Wizard of Oz*, all primped and coiffed like in the movie when he visited the Emerald City, with his long mane in ringlets and a bow. The lion did a double backflip, and as he tumbled past, I recognized a familiar face. Jack.

"Somebody stop him," I was yelling. "He's not allowed!" But Mrs. Vogt had raised a megaphone up to her mouth, and the rest of the cheerleaders formed a human pyramid behind her. She yelled to the crowd, her voice distorted from the megaphone. "Give me a *C*!"

"*C*!" They roared back, pounding their feet.

"Give me an *A*!"

"*A*!"

"Give me an *N*!"

"*N*!"

"Give me a *C*!"

"*C*!"

"Give me an *E*!"

Even in the dream, I saw where they were going with this, and I was yelling right along with the crowd.

"*E*!"

"Give me an *R*!"

"*R*!"

"What's that spell?"

"Cancer!"

"What's it mean?"

"Fight it!"

"Are we gonna win?"

"Yeah!"

Merritt, the top of the pyramid, somersaulted off, purple pig-tails flying. And the crowd surged to its feet as the two teams ran onto the field.

But these weren't your normal high school football teams. One side was a giant, beefy mass of Incredible Hulk clones, snarling and crushing everything in their way. The other team was a cluster of pale hairless women in hospital gowns, clutching IV poles, glugging down Ensures, and, I was startled to realize, led by yours truly! We lurched jerkily down the field as the Hulk clones advanced steadily in our direction.

All at once the Hulks morphed into a writhing mass of red octopi, their tentacles snaking toward us.

Hurry. Move. They're gaining on us. Run. Faster. Faster.

One of the women tripped on her IV pole and was instantly engulfed by a mass of red sucking arms. Then another one went under. I fell, too, and everything went blurry. When the scene came back into focus, the football field had transformed some-how into a boxing ring. And now it was just me with one of the massive Hulks inside the ring with a sea of swirling octopi beneath our fancy footwork.

I backed into a corner, arms crossed protectively across my hospital-gowned chest, the ropes of the ring cutting into the flesh on my exposed back. The tentacles wrapped around my legs, pulling me down as the Hulk towered over me and began battering me with powerful fists. Just as I was about to go down for the count, there was a powerful roar. The Cowardly Lion mascot had pounced on the Hulk's back.

Only now it wasn't the Cowardly Lion anymore. It was Aslan, the lion from Narnia. The lion and the Hulk fell away from me, locked in violent combat, and I slumped against the ropes, exhausted, relieved not to be fighting but anxious about the outcome.

Because I had caught a glimpse of the lion's bloodied face.

And I still wasn't sure who would win.

● ● ●

"Aslan?"

I woke up drenched in sweat, still on the vinyl floor, to see Andy hovering over me, his brow puckered with concern.

"Are we talking C. S. Lewis?" He gave a low whistle. "Where *have* you been?" He helped me to a sitting position and placed my damp head on his shoulder. Then he looked around. "Looks like there was a chocolate explosion in here. Maybe two?"

I gave a weary nod. "I'm so tired of all this. I just want it to be over."

"It will be. Soon." He knuckled my bald head in a gentle, affectionate noogie. "You need to just take it moment by moment, one day at a time."

I twisted my head to look up at him. "Since when did you start going to AA?"

"I didn't, but the principles work in all situations."

"And you'd know that exactly *how*?" I wrenched away from him, my voice rising. "Have *you* ever had cancer?"

"No." His eyes clouded. "Look, Nattie, I know this is awful

and crappy and scary." He took a deep breath. "But the cancer isn't just hard on you. It's really hard on all the people who love you too."

"Oh yeah?" I sneered. "I'm sure it's really hard when they're barfing their guts out. I'll be only too happy to trade places with any one of them. Anytime."

Andy's eyes widened, and I lowered my head. "I'm sorry. I don't mean to be such a brat." I lifted my head back up and batted my eyelashes at him. "The chemo made me do it."

Then I remembered I didn't *have* any eyelashes.

But Andy wasn't looking at my eyes anyway. Instead, he'd lasered in on the side of my head.

"What?" I asked irritably.

He grinned and reached over to remove a clump of brownie batter, which he popped into his mouth.

"Yum, I don't think I've ever had chocolate *pate* before." He rhymed it with *late*. "Goose liver, yes. But not chocolate."

I crossed my eyes at him. "That's pâté, goofball."

• • •

I skipped group again that week.

After my brownie debacle, I told myself (though I knew better) that it was more important to spend time with my family and longtime friends like Andy and Josh and Merritt and Jillian.

So one night that week I invited Josh and Andy over to play Candyland and checkers. Andy brought brownies and presented them to me with a grin. Unfortunately, my stomach lurched when I saw them.

Sigh. One step forward, three steps back.

The next night, Mom and Dad brought a bland dinner and some old movie musicals. We watched them together with our feet up, and I felt almost like a little kid again. Almost.

Another night that week, Merritt, Jilly, and I just vegged out with our movies and *Friends* DVDs. I wished I could handle pizza, but we made do with chicken noodle soup and grilled cheese sandwiches. Actually, they had the grilled cheese. I was feeling queasy again, so I settled for a piece of dry toast that I dunked in the soup for flavor.

Rashida called that night, and Merritt looked at me funny when I let the machine pick up.

"That's your friend from group, isn't it? Aren't you going to answer it?"

"I'll call her later," I said.

But I didn't.

Rashida called a couple of more times after that, as did Johnna, Constance, and Jane. But somehow I didn't get around to returning their calls.

• • •

Saturday morning, there was a light knock on my door. I opened it expecting to see Andy, but instead Jane was standing on my doorstep, leaning heavily on a cane and looking pale but determined. I hadn't seen her since . . . since before . . .

"Hi, Natalie," she said softly. "May I come in?"

"Uh, sure . . ." My voice trailed off.

"What a darling little cottage," Jane said. "I love the way it's decorated. So cheery. And tidy! Did you do all this?"

I looked around, feeling the familiar surge of satisfaction at my handiwork. "Yeah. I'm big on neat after growing up in my mom's messy home. Housekeeping wasn't her thing." I waved Jane over to the club chair. "You want some tea or water or something?"

"Water would be great." She sank gratefully into the chair. "Thanks."

I took my time in the kitchen, dreading the encounter that awaited me in the living room. I put two waters on a tray along with another item that I hoped would delay the chastising I deserved.

Jane giggled when she saw the jar of puréed baby peaches. "I see you've come over to the mommy side with Rashida and me."

I shrugged my shoulders. "If you can't beat 'em, join 'em."

"Speaking of joining . . ." Her eyes bored into mine. "I get the distinct feeling that you're avoiding me. Actually, *all* of us at group, but especially me."

"Of course I'm not." I picked a fleck of lint off my flannel pants. "I've just been . . . really busy with my family and stuff."

Jane took a sip of her water and gave me a look that was both gentle and no-nonsense. "Natalie, Pat's death was a terrible shock to all of us."

"It's so unfair! She beat this awful disease, and then she dies from a fall."

"You're right. It's not fair at all," she said sadly. "But aren't we a little bit beyond fair these days? I mean, is it fair that you, a young single woman, had to have both breasts removed? Or that Faye's husband left her? Or that Pat actually beat cancer and was doing great and then died so suddenly and unexpectedly? Sure it's unfair. It's awful. Death is awful."

I shook my head miserably, wondering where she was going with this.

"Look, I know that life is fragile and fleeting. Tell the truth, I've been thinking about that a lot these—"

"Jane—"

"But the thing is, Natalie, hiding doesn't make it any less awful. The only thing that helps with stuff like this is the truth. And this is the truth." She quoted softly, "'We know that if the earthly tent we live in is destroyed, we have a building from God, an eternal house in heaven, not built by human hands.'" She looked off into the distance. "Pat knew that, and so do I." She added softly, "And so do you."

I didn't know what to say, so I just sat there and drank my water. Finally, I said, "The thing is . . . I'm just not ready to go there yet." That sounded lame even to me.

"Which is why you've been staying away." She sighed. "Seeing the others—especially me—makes it all real, and that's scary. So it's just easier to stay away."

Stay away. When Jane said that, I thought of Jack. And Lynn from the office next to mine. And even Jillian—and how they'd all responded to my cancer.

The difference was that Jillian had come around. And I . . .

"Natalie, sweetie, it's all right," Jane was saying. "It really is."

And only then did I realize that tears were streaming down my cheeks.

chapter nineteen

T his bra is *buggin'* me. It gets so heavy." Rashida reached under her blouse and in one discreet, fluid motion unhooked the cumbersome bra, yanked it from beneath her shirt, and dropped it on the couch.

I giggled. "I know they say we're a sisterhood of breast cancer survivors, but that proves we really are sisters." I nodded toward her couch bra. "At home I do the exact same thing."

Slowly, her prosthesis slipped from the bra and fell to the floor with a gentle *plop*.

"Well, maybe not the exact same thing." My eyes widened. "Hey! I didn't know they came in different colors."

Rashida scooped up the mocha breast form and shoved it back inside the bra. "Oh yeah. But you got to ask. When I went to get fitted for my prosthesis, Miss Thang tried to give me this standard pink issue." She rolled her eyes, pointing at her face. "Does this beautiful chocolate skin look like it rolls with pink anythang? I don't think so. I asked if they had any other colors."

Her earrings jangled. "Girl, she looked at me and said, 'Yes, but no one's going to see it.' Can you even *believe* that?" Rashida jutted out her chin. "I told her, 'Well *I* am.'"

She glanced at me from beneath her scarf. "Unlike some of my sistahs—and here I'm talking about the kind that don't end in *-er*—I never wanted to be nothin' other than who I am—a strong chocolate sistah with much attitude. You feel me?"

"Preach it, sister! I mean, sistah." I grinned over at her from my perch on the sturdy stepstool. "Now hand me that little hammer, please, so I can finish hanging this picture." I clambered down and stepped back to look at my handiwork. "What do you think?"

"Girl, you got the touch."

After talking with Jane, I'd gone over to Rashida's to apologize for my absence and to help her get settled into her new home. With the muscular assistance of DeWayne and DeShawn, we'd rearranged the couches and other furniture to make the living room warmer and cozier.

Hands on her hips, Rashida surveyed the room, a pleased smile stealing over her gorgeous features. "I should hire you."

"To do what?"

"Decorate my house."

"Nah." I fluffed a throw pillow on the couch. "This is fun, not work."

"So who says work can't be fun?"

"Right."

"Sounds like you've been in the wrong job." She sent me a knowing look. "To love what you do and feel that it matters—how could anything be more fun?"

"Pretty profound."

"I know. Too bad I didn't say it." Rashida gave me a playful smile. "Katharine Graham, publisher of the *Washington Post*, did."

I raised my eyebrow indentations.

She shrugged. "I love quotes. I collect them." She walked over to the fireplace, lost in thought, then gave me a speculative look. "So what kind of quote could you give me to decorate my whole house?"

"What?"

She nodded at the painting above the mantel. "Every morning I sit in here with my coffee and my Bible having my quiet time, and when I look up at that picture, it reminds me that Mama is looking down on me." She wiped at her eyes. "*You* did that. Like I said, you got the gift. So what would you charge to decorate the rest of my house?"

"Nothing. I love doing stuff like this." I adjusted a throw on the armrest of her easy chair. "I'd love to help you with the rest of your house, but there's no way I'd charge you for it."

"A workman is worth his wages." Rashida wagged her finger at me.

"I'm not a workman." I gave her an impish smile. "Or a workwoman. I just do this for fun."

"But you're good at it. And didn't you say you were thinking of making a career change? Wouldn't it be fun if you could make money doing something you love?" She picked up a copy of *O Magazine* from her coffee table and waved it under my nose. "Like Nate, that designer Oprah always has on her show."

"Ooh, I *love* Nate. He's too cute. I'll never forget when Oprah had the ugliest-room-in-America contest, and he transformed this hideous monstrosity into a thing of beauty." I sighed. "He does that all the time. And magnificently. The boy's a genius." I gave her a wry look. "But he's also a professional. I'm not."

"He had to start somewhere. And so do you. Why not start with me?" She cupped her scarf-clad head and made her face all plaintive. "Do it for the cancer sisterhood. *Please*?"

"Whoa. Good closing argument, counselor." I lifted my shoulders in a helpless shrug. "But I wouldn't even have a clue what to charge."

Rashida's eyes gleamed. "I think I've still got some bids from a couple of decorators in my office. I'll go get them." She returned in seconds and handed me an open folder.

The numbers on the page swam before my eyes. Those firms were asking for more money than I made in an entire year. For moving plants and furniture, choosing rugs and window treatments, and painting a few walls?

I was definitely in the wrong line of work.

• • •

"You'd make a good wife and mother."

"Excuse me?" I looked up from the stack of CDs and DVDs I was putting back in their proper cases in Jane's living room. "Sorry. I was reading the back of this DVD. What'd you say?"

Her pale face flushed. "I said I think you'd make a good wife and mother." She shifted on the couch, trying to get comfortable. "You're wonderful with my Luke, and it's obvious that you adore Josh."

"What's not to adore?"

With Andy's and Mitch's permission, I'd brought Josh over to play with Luke. The two had bonded over Legos but were now at the park with Mitch, so Jane and I could have a little girl time while little Matthew took a nap. "I've known Josh since he was a baby, and I love him to bits." I popped another DVD case shut. "Since I'm an only child, he's the nephew I'll never have."

"How'd you like to have two sons?"

"Sorry?"

Jane took a deep breath, and the words tumbled out. "I'm trying to find a replacement wife for Mitch for when I'm gone. He can't take care of two small boys all by himself." She rushed on before I could form words from my gaping mouth. "She needs to love children, share the same faith, and be a partner in his ministry. I think you'd be perfect."

My hands shook as I set down the DVD case and tried to come up with a coherent response. "No one can replace you, Jane," I said gently. I started to add, "And you're not going anywhere," but I stopped myself. We both knew better.

She gave me a resigned smile, her freckles standing out in stark relief against her chalk-white face. "I'm not trying to be morbid. I'm not afraid to die. I get to go home and be with the Lord"—she glanced down at the PICC line the doctors had inserted in her left arm after all her veins collapsed—"and leave this broken body behind. What could be better than that?" Her eyes shone. Then the slightest trace of a shadow flitted across her face. "I just want to make sure my family will be taken care of."

Jane looked around the messy room. "Mitch is kind of helpless with all the house stuff, and you're a natural. Plus, Luke adores you. You're wonderful with kids." She gave me an anxious look. "But maybe you don't want a ready-made family?"

"It's not that; it's just—"

"Got the vacuum cleaner bags." The front door slammed shut behind Rashida, who held up a plastic sack from Target. She looked from Jane to me. "What'd I miss?"

My face reddened.

"Not much." The corners of Jane's mouth curved up. "I was just trying to recruit Natalie to take my place as wife and mother when I'm gone. But she seems a little shocked by the idea."

"Imagine that." Rashida set the bag down on the coffee table. "Now you hush your mouth, girl. It's not up to you to be makin' those plans. That's in the Lord's hands." She stroked Jane's thin arm—the one without the two plastic tubes sticking from it. "And if He takes you home early, He'll provide for your family—don't you fret. Besides"—she shot a devilish look my way—"I think Miss Natalie here is already sweet on someone else."

"Really?" A spark flickered in Jane's eyes. "That's great! Who?"

I folded my arms across my tissue-expanded chest. "I'd like to know the answer to that too." How could she have found out about Paul Gallagher? Only three people knew of my crush—Andy, Merritt, and Jillian—and I was *not* ready for the news to spread.

Rashida smiled. "Your next-door neighbor."

"Andy?" Relieved, I rolled my eyes. "Andy's just a friend. He's like my big brother."

"Uh-huh. I've heard that before." Rashida winked at Jane. "You talk about him all the time. Andy this and Andy that."

"That's because we're good *friends*—best friends, really. We've known each other forever."

A dreamy smile lit up Jane's face. "Mitch and I started out as friends . . ." Her voice trailed off.

Rashida frowned. "Maybe if my husband and I had started out as friends, we'd still be together." She sighed. "But with us, it was pure lust from the moment we met. Not the best foundation for marriage."

"Maybe not, but a little lust is an important part of the package,"

Jane said knowingly. She recited from the Song of Solomon. "'Let him kiss me with the kisses of his mouth—for your love is more delightful than wine . . . Take me away with you—let us hurry! Let the king bring me into his chambers.'"

I flapped my hand furiously in front of my face. "Whew, is it hot in here?" Sticking the last DVD in its case, I removed a dog hair and returned the case to the wobbly entertainment center. I turned to Rashida. "Hey, lust-woman, how's your arm these days?"

She lifted her left arm and flexed it. "Pretty good. I've almost got my full range of motion back now."

"Good." I nodded to the upright vacuum cleaner with its gaping insides exposed. "Then could you bring that vacuum cleaner bag over here, please, and vacuum this carpet for me?"

Josh was a decoy. The real reason for our coming over was so that Rashida and I could visit Jane and also straighten up her house a little for her—which we did against her protests.

"If the flip-flop was on the other foot, you'd do the same for us, right?" I wiggled my pink sparkly flip-flops at her.

Jane nodded weakly. "I suppose." Then she stuck her tongue out at me. "Even though you won't do that one teeny-tiny favor I asked of you."

chapter *twenty*

There's nothing like the wind in your hair when you're driving. Or the wind in your scarf.

Merritt and I zipped along Highway 101 with the windows down, my sunroof open, and my red scarf flapping in the breeze. My *Best of the Sixties* compilation belted out a reminder that we were indeed "California Girls." But what I was actually feeling at the moment was free.

And loving it.

"Free at last, free at last. Thank God Almighty, I'm free at last," I shouted into the wind. Merritt threw me a conspiratorial grin. Evidently she was feeling free too.

We were running away from everything and everybody.

Especially anything remotely connected to cancer.

Cancer. Cancer. Cancer. I was sick to death of hearing the word. And sick to death of being sick. And desperate to get away from it all for a few days, from everyone who knew me and everything that reminded me of hospitals and blood draws and chemo and emesis basins.

Seeing my frustration, Merritt had ridden to the rescue with this newest version of our traditional weekend getaway.

For years now, whenever one of us was feeling frustrated or discouraged or just plain in a bad mood, we had pointed my car west to the Pacific. Which was where we were headed now—at ten miles above the speed limit. Merritt had actually taken a personal leave day so we could go in the middle of the week and beat the Labor Day rush.

The Mamas and the Papas clicked on, and we sang along lustily to "California Dreamin'." Thanks to Merritt and her eclectic retro tastes, I've developed a thing for pop music from the sixties and seventies. So we're very compatible when it comes to road music.

We found a cheap motel a block from the beach in Pacific Grove, a little town that hosts Monarch butterflies when they migrate there every winter.

"This is just what the doctor ordered." I breathed in the fragrant ocean air as we walked along the beach, searching for sand dollars and collecting shells. "There's nothing else like it."

I spotted a guy throwing a Frisbee to his German shepherd. The shepherd would leap and catch the plastic disc in midair every time. "Hey, Mer, if we get bored, I can always whip out these two Frisbees in my chest and we can play catch."

"Not a good idea." Merritt shaded her eyes against the sun. "Rover over there might intercept them, and then where would you be?"

Ten minutes later I had to stop and rest. My stamina wasn't what it used to be. But I insisted Merritt keep going. "We've only gotten one sand dollar so far, and it's broken. I need a whole one for my collection." I eased down to the sand. "I'll just kick back and enjoy the view."

After I had repeatedly assured her that I'd be fine, Merritt pulled the hood of my sweatshirt up over my thin scarf and tied it firmly beneath my chin. Then she reached into her backpack and pulled out a fleece blanket, which she tucked around me.

"Now don't get chilled," she told me, sounding like my mother.

"Okay, okay. Stop fussing already." I waved her off. "Go find some sand dollars."

"Yes, ma'am." She scampered away.

I hugged my knees against my chest—gently—and gazed at the pounding surf. As I watched wave after wave crash onto the beach, I thought back to the day my life came crashing down around me and about everything that had happened since.

Three months earlier I had both breasts, all my hair, a boyfriend, a good job, a nice neighborhood church, great friends, a close-knit family.

Now I had no hair, no church, no boyfriend, and my breasts were under construction.

I glanced down at the twin mounds just beginning to take shape beneath my sweatshirt. Then I looked out to sea again. From the corner of my eye I could see Merritt digging in the sand.

But I also had wonderful friends and family who had been with me every step of the way and shown me unconditional, sacrificial love.

As for the "good job" part—*good* is a relative term. It was a good job in the sense that I was good at it, and I'd felt good about carrying on in the family business, working alongside my parents.

Plus, it had good pay, benefits, and stability. It was a safe, secure, nine-to-five occupation that brought in a steady paycheck and kept my evenings and weekends free, and I knew my mom and dad cut me a little more slack in terms of vacations and such than they would an ordinary employee.

But the thing was, every time I thought about going back there to work, I felt my heart begin to sink.

Guess that ought to tell me something, huh?

I thought of how Merritt and Jillian were always urging me to unleash my creative side. Then I thought about what Rashida had said and the offer she'd made.

To love what you do and feel that it matters.

Okay, I had to admit I loved decorating. Rearranging furniture and sewing slipcovers and making rooms cozy and welcoming was fun for me. But how did that really matter in the grand scheme of things? It wasn't like I was curing cancer or anything.

And typing and filing accounting reports was noble how, exactly?

I rested my chin on my knees and thought of Jane. And in my mind's eye I saw again the cluttered chaos surrounding her in her tiny home. Then I looked out at the sea and the wide expanse of unfettered sky and breathed deeply.

Merritt came running up. "Hey, I found one!" She loosened my right hand, opened it palm up, and placed in it a perfect sand dollar—still slightly wet.

• • •

We were making the 17-Mile Drive (yes, that's its name) from Pacific Grove into Monterey when my cell rang. I looked at the number and groaned. "It's my mom." I shot Merritt an accusing glance. "You were supposed to remind me to call her when we arrived."

Merritt looked at me over her sunglasses. "She's *your* mother."

"I know, but I have chemo brain, remember? I forget everything." I flipped open my phone and made my voice bright. "Hi, Mom. Sorry I didn't call. I was so caught up in the ocean and everything I forgot." I mouthed *Shh* to Merritt, who was making gagging sounds in the background. "Yes, we're fine. Tell Dad hi. I'll call you when we leave. Love you. Bye."

I'd barely flipped my phone shut when it rang again. "Yes?" I made a face at Merritt. "Uh-huh. Okay, I'll tell her. Oops, you're cutting out, Mom. Gotta go."

Then, in deference to Merritt and our getaway, I turned off my cell.

And didn't set it to vibrate.

Merritt refused to even own a cell phone. "Talk about slavery. My boss wanted to give me a company one so he could contact me at any time." She shuddered. "I don't *think* so. It's just a job. My nights and weekends are my own."

She grinned over at me. "Not to mention those all-important go-to-the-beach days."

• • •

In Monterey, we visited the town's world-renowned aquarium (where I went straight for the playful otters while Merritt adored the "ethereal" jellyfish) and my family's favorite seafood restaurant (where I quickly learned that chemo and fish smells do *not* mix). Then we picked up a few souvenirs before heading to

Carmel-by-the-Sea, which has to be one of the most beautiful places on earth. And one of the most expensive. Clint Eastwood was once mayor there, which should tell you something.

As Merritt and I wandered through the myriad high-end contemporary art galleries, a hand-painted silk vest caught my eye. I wanted to shout out to Merritt, but one doesn't shout in these upscale kinds of places. Instead, I tugged on her sleeve and led her over to the display of textile art.

"Yours are so much better," I whispered. "You really need to do more. The women in group all loved theirs."

Merritt fingered the silk thoughtfully. "Hmm. Maybe scarves too."

• • •

That night in our hotel room, we took up the game we'd been playing since our freshman year in high school.

I pulled out a pen and notepad and faced my best friend. "Okay, if you had a million dollars, what would you do with it?"

She gave me a dry look. "I think it's time to raise the amount due to inflation. We need to make it two million."

"Whatever. So what would you do with it?"

She shifted on her uncomfortable queen-sized bed. "Buy a pillow-top mattress and carry it with me wherever I go."

"For real."

Merritt took a handful of grapes from a bag on the nightstand and popped one into her mouth. "Well, first, I'd quit my job." She grimaced. "In a heartbeat. Then I'd travel all over Europe with my sketch pad for two or three months."

"Where would you go first?"

"Florence," she replied without hesitation. "To see the *David*. That's a lifelong dream. Then I'd return to Paris—without your parents this time—"

I made a face at her.

"—where I'd prowl the Louvre and the Musée d'Orsay all day long and then hang out with the sidewalk artists in Montmartre at night."

She flopped back on the bed and looked up at the ceiling. "And when I finally came home, I'd buy a little house on the coast—maybe somewhere around here—"

"Not for less than two million you won't." I grunted. "Not in California, baby—at least not on the coast."

"Well, then I'd come inland." She sighed. "All I need is a little house with enough room for an art studio where I could paint all day long."

"What about a car?"

"Oh, I forgot about that." She shrugged. "I guess that might be helpful. Then I could take off for the coast whenever I wanted. But I definitely wouldn't buy new." She sniffed. "I'm not about to spend twenty or thirty thousand bucks just on transportation."

She held out her hand for the notepad. "Okay, what about you?"

"Well, since I'm not a car person either, I'd probably just pay this one off, along with all my other bills—"

"Which still leaves you with what—about one million nine hundred and ninety-three thousand?"

"More or less." It was my turn to look up at the ceiling. "Let's see. Since my parents have already paid off their house, I think I'd send them on a second honeymoon. Maybe a Mediterranean cruise—without *me*. Gotta start getting them used to that empty nest thing sometime." I grinned. "I'd set aside money for Josh's college, of course. And I could donate some money to some of the cancer groups like Komen and the American Cancer Society and some of the children's charities like World Vision."

"Very nice, Ms. Bountiful. But what about *you*?" She jabbed the pen at me. "What would you do for *you*—if money were no object?"

"That's easy. Ride in a gondola in Venice, scuba-dive in the Caribbean, see a Broadway musical, and visit the Grand Canyon."

"Is that it?"

"Well . . ." I chewed a hangnail. "I've always wanted to see New England in the fall."

She wrote it down and did some calculations. "Okay, so unless you give most of your money to charity, that still leaves you with maybe a million and a half. Then what?"

I hesitated.

"C'mon, 'fess up," Merritt urged.

I took a deep breath. "Well, I've been thinking I'd like to own my own business someday."

"Now you're talkin'!" Merritt clapped her hands. "You should do it!"

"What?"

"Open up your own business."

I scrambled off the bed, opened the door, and stepped out on the concrete balcony, grabbing the iron rail and peering up at the sky.

"What are you doing?"

"Looking for the two million dollars that should be falling from the sky."

"Get back in here, you idiot."

"The only way I'll ever get two million dollars is if I can get Zoey in group to sneak me the state lottery numbers." I plucked a couple of grapes and sat back on my bed cross-legged. "Unfortunately, she's honest. So—returning to reality now—what are you going to do when Jillian moves out after her wedding?"

"Advertise for a new roommate. Without my two million, I can't manage the rent on my own."

"But you don't have to advertise. I know the perfect roommate for you."

"Who?" She gave me a wary look. "One of your church friends?"

"Sort of." I stuck out my arms in a "ta-da" gesture. "Me."

Merritt did a double take, then high-fived me. "Well, it's about time. I've only been asking you for eight years."

"Well, I figured I'd better do it now, 'cause I could be dead next year."

She threw her pillow at me.

chapter **twenty-one**

Tuesday

4:30 PM—*Today was a red-letter day. FINAL CHEMO TREATMENT! Yippee! Strike up the band, start the parade.*

Paul was so sweet. He brought me a helium balloon with "Congratulations" written on it.

Be still, my heart.

When he walked away to tend to another patient, Merritt leaned over and whispered, "I think maybe someone has a little crush." Well, yeah. But she actually meant he might have a crush on me.

I got all excited by the prospect—he had rubbed my arm, after all, and I've always felt there was a spark between us—until one of the other nurses walked past and admired my balloon.

"He's a doll, isn't he?" she said.

"That's an understatement." I tried not to pant too hard.

"Too bad he's engaged. To a doctor, no less."

I rolled my tongue back up into my mouth. Pop went the fantasy bubble.

"I give up," I told Merritt and Jillian later that evening when I

was bemoaning the loss of my dream man. "All the good ones are taken."

"Not all," Jillian said. "In fact . . ."

• • •

"So, Tony, are you a breast man?"

My date gave me a startled look, clearly wondering why I would ask such a question, then seemed to resolve it in his mind as he glanced down at the chicken on his plate. "Well, I prefer breasts," he said carefully, "but I also like the occasional barbecued drumstick." He took a bite of his chicken Marsala.

"No, no. I mean on a woman." I leaned forward over my pasta primavera. "'Cause I don't have any. Breasts, that is."

He choked on his chicken.

"Oh, I will again. Eventually." I stole a glance downward and whispered, "In fact, they're under construction right now." I looked him straight in the eye as he gulped his wine, his cheeks stained to a dull red.

Maybe I had been a little too blunt.

"What I mean is that I have breast cancer and underwent a double mastectomy. I wanted to get that off my chest right up front." Then I realized what I'd said and grinned. "Ha! That's pretty funny, huh?"

Tony gave me a weak smile and excused himself to go to the restroom.

And never came back.

But at least he paid for dinner. My last blind date left me holding the check. Maybe it was the whole wig-moving thing when I scratched my head . . .

• • •

"You really asked him if he was a breast man?" Jillian stared at me as I inhaled the rest of my pasta in their living room. "I can't believe you did that."

Merritt snorted. "I'd love to have seen his face."

I swallowed the last bite of sourdough roll and wiped my lips with my napkin, grateful I was finally able to keep food down again. "I don't want to waste my time on people who can't handle the truth."

"Ooh, you're getting all Jack Nicholson on us." Merritt crossed her eyes.

Jillian, who had set me up on the blind date with Tony from her church singles group, sighed. "Nat, I know you pride yourself on being up-front and open. But there's such a thing as being too up-front."

"I disagree." I glanced down at my shirt. "If there's one thing I'm learning through all this, it's that life's too short to mess around with people who can't accept me as I am, warts and all."

Merritt gave me an innocent look. "Don't you mean implants and all?"

I nodded, and my wig slipped forward. Snatching it off, I tossed it up in the air and caught it. "Yep. Chrome dome and all too."

We giggled. Even Jillian. Briefly.

"I'm surprised you didn't take off your wig in the restaurant," she grumbled.

"I considered it, but I thought that old 'Waiter, there's a hair in my soup' scenario had been done to death."

"But there's egg drop soup," Merritt said. "Why not wig drop soup?"

"Eew." Jillian and I shuddered in unison.

"Besides," I reminded her, "we were at an Italian restaurant, not Chinese."

Jillian, who has a little Italian on her father's side, grabbed my wig and clapped it atop her long, silky blonde hair. "Then it would have been *wigestrone*." She began dancing around the living room, singing "Funiculi, funicula."

Merritt and I joined in, trying our best to be passionately Italian, but not knowing any lyrics besides "funiculi, funicula," we soon switched over to "That's Amore." Since my dad has all the tapes from the old Dean Martin show and played them over and over again while I was growing up, I did a pretty good Dino impression.

At last we collapsed in helpless laughter on the couch. Jillian handed my wig back. "Boy, that thing gets hot."

"You're tellin' me."

"Nat?"

"Yes, Jilly?"

"Next time could you please at least let the guy finish his dinner before you drop the bombshell on him?"

Merritt patted her C-cups. "You mean boobshell, don't you?"

Jillian groaned. "Enough with the boob puns already. They're getting old."

"I second that." I looked at Jillian and held up three fingers in the Girl Scout pledge. "I promise to let the guy finish his dinner before I break the boob news to him. Scout's honor." I wrinkled my nose. "*If* I remember, that is. Chemo really does a number on your memory."

"Speaking of memory . . ." Merritt gave me a penetrating look. "Have you remembered to tell your folks that you're planning to move in here after Jillian gets married?"

"Uh, not yet." I shifted on the couch. "I keep forgetting."

"Ri-i-ight." Jillian exchanged a knowing look with Merritt.

"Okay, so maybe I haven't forgotten exactly. I'm just waiting for the perfect time."

Merritt sighed. "There will never be a perfect time. Just do it!"

•   •   •

I thought I was going to die on the drive home.

My head was hot and sweaty beneath the wig—I shouldn't have even put it back on, but I'd taken pity on all my fellow drivers. And my bra against my taut tissue expanders was growing increasingly uncomfortable. While my new breasts were still undergoing construction, I wore a prosthesis in each bra cup just to give me a little form when I went out in public. But those suckers can really get heavy. And hot.

The minute I got home, I yanked off the itchy wig and tossed it on the ottoman, then reached beneath my blouse to unhook the double-loaded bra and yanked that off, too, dropping it on the couch before heading to the kitchen.

"Knock, knock." Andy's voice wafted through the living-room screen door.

"C'mon in," I called out. "I'm just getting some milk and cookies. Want some?"

"What kind?"

"Oatmeal raisin."

"Do you even need to ask?"

Entering the living room with the tray of goodies, I found Andy sitting on the couch, my wig askew on his head, juggling my two breast forms. "You dropped something," he deadpanned.

With anyone else, I'd have died of embarrassment, but this was just Andy. I tilted my head. "Hey, you look good as a brunette—a little like Johnny Depp in *Pirates of the Caribbean*—minus the gold teeth, of course."

I startled myself a little when I said that. Did Andy really look like Johnny Depp? I looked again and decided—not really. His eyes were a little like Johnny's—warm, brown, and soulful. I'd always thought Andy had nice eyes. But he was taller and not as fine-boned, and his smile was different.

I sighed. There just wasn't anybody quite like my Johnny. Which was why he was a star in the first place.

I set the tray of cookies and milk down on the ottoman. "Okay, juggle-man, hand 'em over." I extended my hand, and he plopped the two breast forms into it, grinning.

"I'm glad you didn't sit on them. You might have popped 'em." I plucked my wig from his head and snatched up my bra from the couch. "Be right back."

In my bedroom, I returned both fake boobs to their hollowed-out compartments inside their pretty pink boxes, then quickly shed my uncomfortable date wear for a pair of green-plaid pajama bottoms and a baggy T-shirt—my standard uniform for whenever guests dropped in. I thought about covering my bald head with a scarf, but my head was still hot and itchy. Besides, it was only Andy.

He was dunking a cookie when I returned. "So how was the big date?"

I plopped down in my club chair and took a long drink of milk before answering. "I scared him off."

"You?" He grinned. "I can't believe it. How?"

"Well . . . I asked him if he was a breast man and then told him I didn't have any."

Andy sprayed milk all down his shirt.

"Hey, careful! Don't get milk on my couch."

He blotted his shirt with a napkin, wheezing with laughter the whole time. "Only you." He shook his head. "Gotta love ya."

"Tell that to my date. I don't think he was feelin' the love."

"His loss." Andy angled his head, which now sported nearly an inch of stubble. "Although . . . can you really blame him?" He adopted his familiar big-brother air. "You might want to consider waiting until at least the second or third date before you hit the guy with both barrels."

I quirked a penciled-on eyebrow at him and looked down at my tissue-expanded chest, which was finally starting to poke out a little. "Even if those barrels aren't fully loaded yet?"

chapter *twenty-two*

H ey, Natalie, you want crown molding in the master bed-room too?"

"If it's not too much trouble, Antonio."

"No problem. Piece a cake."

Rashida poked her head around the hall corner. "You want me to tell the guys to pull up *all* the carpeting?"

I nodded. "Every last bit. That carpet is really old and worn and full of dander, which isn't good for Jane's immune system. Besides, there are gorgeous hardwood floors underneath"—which I'd happily discovered the last time I was there.

We were doing a weekend extreme-makeover surprise on Jane and Mitch's house while they were out of town for some much-needed alone time. Our support group had given the couple a gift certificate to a beautiful bed-and-breakfast in the nearby Gold Country town of Sutter Creek, and Mitch, who was in on the surprise, had arranged for his parents to take the boys while they were gone. (Although grateful for the unexpected respite,

Jane had initially been hesitant about leaving baby Matthew, but her mother-in-law had assuaged her concerns by reminding her that she'd managed to raise four babies of her own without mishap.)

Mitch and Jane had already begun some improvement projects around the fifty-year-old house. They'd steamed off most of the seventies-vintage wallpaper, for instance, but hadn't gotten around to hanging the cheery yellow-and-white-checked wallpaper for the kitchen or the Thomas the Tank Engine border for Luke's bedroom. Jane's pregnancy and then the cancer had intruded. But we were prepared to take up a little of the slack and make the place a little more comfortable to live in.

In addition to our support group, I'd enlisted Jane and Mitch's family and their friends from church to help in the quickie cosmetic renovation. We didn't have the kind of budget they have on those home-and-garden TV shows or a team of designers and carpenters at our beck and call or a major department store providing free appliances, but we did have a lot of willing hearts and hands eager to pitch in.

I was delighted to discover that Antonio, Anita's husband, was a carpenter by trade, so I put him in charge of installing the crown molding and any other woodworking details—such as repairing the wobbly entertainment center and smoothing out the deep scratches in the front windowsill where Lady conducted her daily frenzied greeting to the mailman.

Johnna's brother Jason was a retired plumber, so he fixed the leaky dishwasher and replaced the old kitchen faucet. While Jason worked his plumbing magic, a couple of church ladies hung the sunny wallpaper. They also stocked the freezer with bland food for Jane and prepared dinners for Mitch and the kids.

Andy, who had painted houses every summer in college, was

in charge of the outside painting crew. He rented a couple of sprayers, and after water blasting off the old, peeling paint, the guys went to work turning the dirty tan ranch into a Wedgwood-blue charmer with white trim and shutters.

Several of the kids from the youth group Mitch pastored pitched in outside. One team of kids cut and edged the grass and cleared away debris, while another group weeded the flower beds and planted new flowers under my dad's green-thumb tutelage.

Inside, we yanked out old carpet, painted the walls with a special new non-lingering-odor paint, and installed crown molding. I'd had a blast picking the styles and colors from discount home improvement and department stores. (Paint and trim are two relatively inexpensive ways to make over a room and really make it pop.) I chose a vivid cobalt blue for Luke's room that was a perfect complement to the Thomas border and a light celery green for the master bedroom and bath. The trim was a steal—I'd almost danced when I found some returned trim and crown molding in a half-off bin.

I'd also located some great bargains for floor coverings and window treatments. So after the master bedroom walls were painted a soothing celery green and the doors, baseboards, and new molding a soft marshmallow cream, we Murphy-soaped the oak hardwood floor and laid down an oatmeal-colored Berber area rug so Jane would still have something soft to step on when she got out of bed in the morning.

I longed to fill the house with flowers. But chemo patients and those with compromised immune systems can't be around fresh flowers—the soil and water often carry germs. So I had to come up with an alternative.

Easy, you're probably thinking. *Just go with silk.*

Except—how can I put this delicately?—I *hated* silk flowers.

The whole artificialness of them turned me off. (And I was in good company here. Nate from *Oprah* agreed.) So many of them look plastic and fake—especially the stuff I grew up with. My mom had silk flower arrangements in every room and silk ivy trailing from the plant shelf in the kitchen.

Can you say dust magnets (especially in my mom's house)?

Anyway, dust was the last thing Jane needed. So silk and fresh flowers were both out of the question.

Knowing how much Jane loved flowers, however, I'd instructed Dad to have the high-school girls plant masses of them outside her bedroom window. And for the inside I had a brainstorm. I enlisted Merritt to stencil a large bouquet of daisies and daffodils on the bedroom wall.

Except she wouldn't do it. "*Stencil?*" Her lips could barely form the word. "I don't *think* so."

Instead, she painted a gorgeous freehand bouquet of not only daisies and daffs, but also tulips, day lilies, irises, and feathery stalks of lavender.

All of the women kept coming in to ooh and aah over the breathtaking wall bouquet.

"Could I hire you to do something like that in my house?" one asked.

"Me too," another added. "But I'd like all roses. What would you charge?"

Merritt looked bewildered.

"Ladies"—I clapped my hands—"we need to keep working if we're going to get everything done before Jane and Mitch return. Those of you interested in hiring Ms. Chase, please write down your name and phone number before you leave, and we'll get back to you."

As the women filed out, chattering about the wall flowers they would want, Constance gave me an approving smile. "Good thinking on your feet there, little Ms. Entrepreneur."

Merritt looked at me as if I'd lost my mind. "What were you *thinking*?"

"We'll talk about it later," I said briskly. "For now, we've got work to do. Come on. Chop-chop."

• • •

One decorating principle I'd absorbed even before all the home improvement shows flooded the TV channels was that whether you're sitting in a living room or lying in bed, the eye should always be able to gaze on something beautiful.

For Jane, I thought, what could be more beautiful than her children? So I removed the pictures of Luke and Matthew she kept on her nightstand and had them blown up to poster size. Constance and Merritt then framed them and mounted them on the wall opposite the bed.

That way the first thing Jane saw every morning when she woke up would be her boys.

My goal with the master bedroom was to provide a serene sanctuary where Jane could rest surrounded by beauty. And to accomplish that, I needed to reduce the clutter. I bought several sturdy yet inexpensive wicker baskets—small ones for the top of Mitch's dresser and nightstand where he could empty his pockets each night, and larger ones that could slide beneath each nightstand and hold a variety of books, magazines, and CDs.

For Jane, I splurged on a lovely hand-painted white wooden trinket box with a hinged lid and cascading roses tumbling down the sides for her nightstand. That way she could still keep essentials like pens, paper, reading glasses, nail clippers, and her daily devotional close by but out of sight in something beautiful.

The last time I'd visited, Jane had pointed out a curved piece of driftwood that Mitch had picked up for her on their Mendocino honeymoon. "It was the last day of our honeymoon," she'd said, caressing the wood with her eyes. "We'd spent the entire day on the beach—picnicking, chasing each other in and out of the surf, building sandcastles, necking on the sand . . ." She grinned. "Then it was almost dusk, and we had to go. But I didn't want to leave." Her bloodshot eyes (a few days earlier she'd burst the blood vessels in her eyes from vomiting so hard) had softened at the memory. "Mitch picked up that piece of driftwood, pulled out his pocketknife, and carved our initials and the date on the back. He gave it to me, saying that every time I looked at it, it would remind me of that day. And it does."

The romantic wood earned a place of honor in the center of Mitch and Jane's dresser.

Zoey's contribution to the bedroom sanctuary was a small rock-garden fountain. "The sound of the cascading water helps relax the mind, body, and soul," she explained. Faye, who'd surprised all of us by showing up, added unscented cream candles. "Romantic lighting is always nice." And Rashida said that Jane liked listening to praise music before she went to sleep, so we brought in a portable CD player and set it on her side of their bookshelf headboard.

In the bathroom, I'd noticed a Scripture on a sticky note in the center of the mirror, and I'd asked Mitch about it when Jane was out of earshot. "She likes to see that every morning when she brushes her teeth," he said.

This time it was Constance's turn to work some artist magic. After we'd finished painting the bathroom a shade lighter than the cool bedroom green, she lettered the verse above the bathroom mirror in beautiful calligraphy: "For our light affliction, which is but for a moment, worketh for us a far more exceeding and eternal weight of glory. 2 Corinthians 4:17."

We added thick, fluffy towels and plush area rugs to the room, and Mitch's family invested in a portable whirlpool machine that would turn the basic tub into a luxurious Jacuzzi bath where Jane could soothe her aching body. As a final touch, Nurse Johnna, our group leader, placed a certificate on the counter that entitled Jane to twice-weekly therapeutic massages from her own certified fingers.

Anita and I were on stepladders in the bedroom, hanging the simple tab curtains I'd found at Target, when Antonio rushed over. "Hey, babe," he said to Anita, "you don't need to be straining your arm like that." He helped her down and nodded at me. "You either. Let me do that for you."

I arched my starting-to-grow-in eyebrows at Anita as we walked down the hall.

Her cheeks pinkened. "Things are getting better," she whispered.

• • •

At the end of the day, I looked around at everything we'd accomplished, and it was good. It was just what I wanted for Jane—still her house, but now more peaceful and serene. And with the touches of beauty she needed.

Glancing out the front window, I noticed Andy pull up in his truck with Josh in the passenger seat. He'd told me awhile ago that he had to go run an errand, but I'd forgotten all about it. Now as I watched, he motioned one of the teenage boys to help him remove an unwieldy object covered with an old army blanket from the back of his truck. The two carried it in through the front door, an excited Josh close on their heels.

"What in the world?"

Josh jumped up and down with delight. "It's a surprise." He grabbed my hand and led me after his dad and the mysterious box that had just disappeared into Luke's room.

Merritt, Rashida, Anita, and the straggle of remaining workers followed behind us Pied Piper fashion.

"Let's set it in the corner," Andy instructed his helper. He looked around the cluster of curious faces for his son. "Okay, Josh, you ready?"

"Ready." Josh raced over to the other side of the box opposite Andy, his eyes sparkling, and started to lift the blanket.

"Not yet, buddy. On the count of three, okay?" Andy grabbed his back corner of the blanket. "One, two—"

"Three!" Josh shrieked as they removed the covering.

Beneath it was a large wooden box, painted red, with a hinged lid and Luke's name stenciled in blue at the top. The whole thing was plastered with crooked stickers of toys.

"Daddy made this for Luke and decorated it with stickers 'cause he's my friend, and we both like Legos and Thomas the Tank Engine," Josh said proudly. "And Bob the Builder too."

Behind me I heard a chorus of sniffling.

I knelt down and hugged Josh, blinking back my own tears as my eyes sought Andy's. "Thank you. It's absolutely perfect. I knew we were missing something, but I just didn't know what it was."

chapter *twenty-three*

Y ou done stopped going to church?" Rashida shot me a penetrating look.

I had accepted her decorating-job offer and was over at her house taking measurements for the window treatments. "Hang on a sec." I held the metal tape between my thumb and forefinger. "Write this down before I forget."

She did, but I wasn't getting off the hook that easily. "Why'd you stop?"

"Lots of reasons." I sighed. "I've been there my whole life. I needed a change. But mainly I just wanted to be somewhere where everyone wasn't staring at me."

Rashida's church wasn't exactly the place for that. As the only white face in the crowd, I felt like the lone vanilla wafer in a sea of Mallomars. But there was no help for it. Rashida had insisted I get my skinny white butt back to church, and to make sure I did, she was taking me to hers.

"My butt's not skinny," I had protested.

"Well, it sure ain't bootylicious." Rashida snorted. She patted her own slim-but-rounded behind. "You white women got no butts at all."

"Uh-*huh*. What about Jennifer Lopez?"

"Don't count. She's Latina."

"Marilyn Monroe?"

"And she's been dead for *how* long?"

She waved a finger at me and feigned a frown.

"You better give up now, girl. You know you don't have a case."

• • •

"Preach it, brothah! All right now. Go 'head. Yes, Jesus."

Rashida's church was the most talkative church I'd ever been to. And the singingest. And the dancingest. And Rashida was right there in the thick of it—singing, clapping, waving her arms, and dancing in the aisles.

I shook my head. Hard to believe she was a buttoned-down lawyer during the week.

Well, sort of buttoned-down.

"C'mon girl. Go 'head and move," she whispered to me.

"I *am* moving."

She took in my feeble step-slide from one foot to the other. "Ya call that movin'? Get *down*."

But I was a little too white-bread to get down, although I sure enjoyed watching everybody else. Talk about the Spirit moving.

After the service, Rashida was introducing me to some of her friends when I noticed a good-looking man smiling at us and trying to make his way in our direction. "Oh my," I whispered. "Be still, my heart. That guy looks like Denzel Washington."

"Who?" She looked up and grunted. "Oh, that's just Fred. He's no Denzel. Too short."

"Short, tall—I don't care. He's drop-dead gorgeous."

"You think?" Rashida tilted her head and critically surveyed the Denzel look-alike as two Faith-and-Angie types waylaid him to talk.

"Have you ever gone out with him?"

Rashida pulled herself up to her full five foot nine. "Do I look like a short woman?"

By the time Fred managed to extricate himself from the flirtatious duo, we were starting to walk out the door, but he fell into step with us as we started down the outside stairs. Rashida introduced us, and we made small talk for a while.

But Fred, although warm and polite to me, only had eyes for her.

* * *

Sunday afternoon

Sometimes I think the nuns and monks have the right idea—that whole quiet and contemplative bit.

Today after weeks of visiting myriad churches and worshiping in multiple styles, I'm sitting near the duck pond at McKinley Park enjoying the sun on my legs and a cool breeze coming off the water.

Just me and God.

I need this time alone. Seems like I'm surrounded by people all the time. And I know my friends and family mean well, but they're taking such good care of me that I never seem to have a moment to myself. Even in my own home.

And I desperately need that.

To think.

And be.
And pray.
And heal.
Thank you for this sanctuary, Lord.

• • •

"How's that cinnamon roll, Dad?"

"Delicious as always." He wiped icing from his mouth. "You sure know the way to your dear old dad's heart. Or should I say stomach?"

"That's an only daughter's job." I held out the teapot. "More tea?" I'd had to declare my house a coffee-free zone for the chemo duration, and I hadn't restocked it after the chemo ended.

He shook his head, drained his Earl Grey, then looked at me over the rim of his mug. "So what is it you have to tell me that you don't want your mother to know?"

"What do you mean?" I widened my eyes. I might not have had eyebrows or eyelashes anymore, but that didn't stop me from trying my standard wide-eyed look of innocence.

He chuckled. "I've been your father for twenty-seven years. I think I know you pretty well by now."

"Busted." I returned the teapot to the counter, then sat down across from him. "Well, you see . . ." I worried a hangnail between my teeth.

"Would this have anything to do with your wanting to quit your job, by any chance?"

I bit down on my finger. "How'd you know?"

"I watched you at Jane's, and you were in your element, sweetheart." Dad covered my hand with his. "You were so animated and clearly loving every minute of it." He chuckled. "I don't remember ever seeing you that excited around the office."

"It's not that I—"

"Hey, I'm not complaining, just making a simple statement of fact. It was wonderful to see you come so alive." He squeezed my hand tight. "*Wonderful*. Life is short. You've got to grab the gusto!"

"You sound like a beer commercial," I teased.

"Where do you think I get all my words of wisdom?" My tee-totaling dad winked. Then he grew serious. "Honey, I was never more proud of you than when I saw what you did for that family." His eyes misted.

"I just wanted to help. That was the only practical way I knew how."

"You did help—a beautiful job. You definitely have a gift." He wagged his finger at me. "We can keep you on the books awhile because of your insurance, and we can probably work out some kind of arrangement to hold you until you get another job. But I'd rather not see you back in the office again." He eyed the plate of cinnamon rolls. "I think that merits another cinnamon roll, don't you?"

I pushed the plate his way. "Sure do. Although there's something else—"

"There you are, Jim." Mom poked her head in the door. "I've been looking all over for you." Her eyes crinkled when she approached and saw the sticky rolls. "Should have known you'd be here satisfying your sweet tooth. Just make sure you don't spoil your appetite. We have dinner reservations at Scott's."

Mom turned her attention to me. "Everyone was asking after you at church today, honey. Mrs. Wheeler said to tell you that you're in her prayers, and so did Pastor Dave. He misses you.

Everyone does." She fiddled with her wedding ring. "Do you think you'll be coming back to church soon?"

"Maybe," I hedged. "Hard to say."

She beamed, certain of victory, then plucked up one of my home magazines and began riffling through it. "You know, I was thinking that maybe we could remodel your bathroom. Maybe put in a shower-and-tub combo so you could take baths too. And perhaps a pretty pedestal sink?" Her eyes danced. "What do you think, Ms. Decorator?"

"Well, uh, that sounds really nice. But"—I sent Dad an apologetic look—"actually, I'm going to be moving out."

She dropped the magazine. "What?"

"What?" Dad echoed.

Mom's mouth opened and closed.

"You can't move out," Dad protested. "You've just finished your chemo."

"It'll be two weeks on Tuesday." I laid my hand on his. "Don't worry," I said gently, "I'm not moving out tomorrow."

"When, then?" Mom asked. "And *why*?"

"End of the year, after Jillian's wedding. And as for why"—I squared my shoulders—"it's high time I was out on my own. Although, technically, I won't be on my own, since I'm going to move in with Merritt." I smiled with anticipation. "We'll be two single girls on our own."

Mom whirled on Dad. "Did you know about this?"

"First I've heard of it."

I decided I might as well go for broke. "I've actually started taking a night class at the community college. They let me miss the first class because of the chemo."

"A night class?" Mom furrowed her brow. "In what?"

"Interior design. The teacher actually has his own design firm and great contacts in the area. He said that if I do well, he might even be able to land me an internship."

"But why would—"

"And something else. After I finish my reconstruction, I'm going to find a tap-dancing class."

"Tap dancing?" Mom arched her eyebrows. "What—are you Ginger Rogers now?" She threw up her hands. "Next you'll be saying you're going to quit your job."

Dad and I exchanged a look.

· · ·

Later, after my folks left, I took a deep breath and started doing a clean sweep of my cottage. Although I wasn't a clutter bug like my mom, I did have a lot of stuff. Too much stuff. And I spent way too much time dusting it, cleaning it, and taking care of it.

Now that I was going to make a fresh start, it was time for some serious purging. Nothing too extreme—stark minimalism is *not* my style—just a little less-is-more action.

I was in the bedroom examining my "Boob Voyage" poster—definitely a keeper—when I heard a light rap at the screen door.

"Is it safe to come in?" Andy called.

"All clear." I carried the poster into the living room and propped it up against the armoire.

"Cool artwork. Merritt's, I assume?"

"Yep."

"The woman sure knows how to paint." Andy gave me a cautious look. "Hey, it sounded like World War III in here earlier. I didn't want to get hit by any exploding Ruth-bombs, so I took cover. So what was the big battle about?"

"I just told my folks I was moving out and quitting my job."

"*Just*, she says?" He grinned. "If I'd known, I would have taken even better cover."

"It's time for me to get out from under my parents' thumbs." I pinched the bridge of my nose. "I mean, I love them, but I'm nearly twenty-eight years old, and I'm still living in their backyard. What's wrong with this picture?"

"Nothing's wrong with it. Nothing at all. You and your parents are just really close." He smiled. "But you're right. I do think it's time for you to spread your wings a little. To find out who you really are, apart from your parents."

chapter *twenty-four*

"Look! There's Mickey!" Josh waved frantically. "Mickey, Mickey! Over here!"

Andy, Josh, Merritt, and I were at Disneyland celebrating the end of my chemo. It was Josh's very first time at the Magic Kingdom, and seeing the park through the eyes of a child was fun for all of us. Seeing it from the seat of a wheelchair was another thing entirely. But I was still pretty weak and didn't have a lot of stamina, so the wheelchair was a necessity.

Anyway, Josh thought the wheelchair was cool. Especially since it let us go to the front of all the lines.

Merritt gave me a wry look. "We should have tried the wheelchair trick years ago."

We made quite an interesting foursome. I was the only baldy remaining now, but I kept my chilly head covered with a silk scarf and a cute denim cloche hat. Everyone else's hair had grown back in, although Josh liked his short cut so much he'd told his dad he wanted another buzz cut "just like it" next summer. Andy's hair, which he'd always worn a bit longish, had now grown out into sort of an updated crewcut.

And Merritt had gone spiky platinum blonde.

Wherever we went, people stared—or started to, then flushed and quickly looked away.

"Gee!" I gave my platinum pal a wry grin. "You'd think they'd never seen a woman with no eyebrows or eyelashes in a wheelchair before."

"They're just trying to figure out what rock group we belong to."

I giggled. "Chemo Girl and the Buzzheads."

"No, we're the Skin—" Josh clapped his hand over his mouth. "Sorry, Dad. I forgot."

I bought Josh, Andy, and Merritt a set of Mickey Mouse ears from one of the stores on Main Street.

Josh gave me a puzzled look as he reached up to feel his new headgear. "Where's yours, Aunt Nat?"

"They wouldn't fit over this." I gestured to my hat.

"I think we can fix that." Andy whipped a plastic princess tiara out of a Disney bag and clipped it over my hat.

"Aw, thanks, Andy. You're such a prince. But it's coming loose." I reached up just as the little crown lost its hold on the denim.

"Hey, no problem." Merritt pulled a couple of safety pins from her shoulder bag and handed them to Andy, who carefully secured the tiara back in place.

"You keep safety pins in your purse?" I asked Merritt suspiciously.

"A Girl Scout is always prepared," she recited.

"You weren't a Girl Scout."

Merritt winked. "I know. That's 'cause I was prepared."

Josh laughed excitedly on the Pirates of the Caribbean ride, but with a hint of nervousness. "It's really dark in here."

I put an arm around him and whispered. "Don't worry. Aunt Natalie will protect you."

He turned in his seat. "Nuh-uh. You're a girl. I'm s'posed to protect you."

"Well then," I told him solemnly, "I really need you to cuddle up close." And I smiled to feel his little body mold itself to mine. *Maybe we need to protect each other*, I thought as the little boat bounced around the bend.

• • •

After lunch at the Blue Bayou, Josh was eager and impatient to ride on the flying Dumbos and kept urging all of us to hurry up.

"Hey, buddy, remember what I told you?" Andy said. "Aunt Natalie's still sick, so she can't go as fast. We need to take it a little slower, okay?"

"She's always sick!" Josh pouted and kicked the side of the wheelchair. "Why can't you hurry up and get better?"

"Josh!" Andy took a firm grip on his son's arm. "That's not nice. You know better than to act like that." He squatted down and looked him square in the eye, his tone stern. "Do you want a time-out?"

Josh shook his head.

"So what do you need to do?"

His lip trembled. "Say I'm sorry."

"Don't say it to me. Say it to Aunt Natalie."

Josh's big blue eyes brimmed with tears that caught in his lashes. "I'm sorry, Aunt Natalie." He hiccupped.

"That's okay. I feel the same way. I'd like to hurry up and get better too."

He clambered up into my lap and patted my arm with his sticky hand. "You're gonna be better real soon." He looked at the wheelchair, his eyes widening. "Hey, c'n I have a ride?"

"Sure." I turned to Andy. "Make this baby fly!"

Andy and Merritt each took a handle and broke into a run. Parents and children scattered as we flew down the avenue.

"Whee!" Josh squealed. I reached one hand up to grab my hat while I held tightly to Josh with the other. We made it to the flying Dumbo ride in record time.

• • •

While Merritt took Josh on the Dumbos, his dad and I relaxed. I tilted back my head to catch the rays, enjoying the feel of the sun on my skin.

"I'm really sorry for what Josh said back there." Andy ran his hand through his sandy stubble. "Too much sugar, too much excitement, I guess. Maybe he's too young. Maybe I should have waited another year to bring him."

"I don't think so." I removed my hat tiara and scratched my itchy head through the scarf. "But maybe it wasn't such a good idea for me to come." I gestured down at the chair. "Then the two of you could have had more fun and wouldn't have had to worry about taking care of me."

"We wanted you with us. That's what friends are for."

"Still, I—" My voice broke off.

"What?" Andy looked at me in puzzlement.

"Jack," I whispered, staring at the familiar figure fast approach-

ing on the walkway, laughing and holding hands with a perfect
girl-next-door type.

I froze, praying he wouldn't see me.

The long-haired, apple-cheeked brunette with him noticed
the wheelchair first and averted her eyes, moving in closer to
Jack.

What? In case I'm contagious or something?

Jack's eyes flicked toward the chair, and he, too, started to
look away. Then he spotted Andy. His eyes flew back to the chair
and locked on mine. He faltered.

The brunette gave him a quizzical look. He leaned down and
said something to her. She stood awkwardly on the pavement
while Jack made his way warily to us.

*Great. Just great. You couldn't wait 'til my boobs were finished
before you let me run into Jack, God? Or at least until I had eyebrows
again?*

"Natalie . . ." Jack averted his eyes from my scarf-clad head
and nodded at Andy, who laid a protective hand on my shoulder.

"Jack." I answered coolly, willing my voice not to quaver.
"Haven't seen you in ages." I sat up straighter. "You haven't
changed a bit."

"Uh, thanks." He cast about for something to say. Jack always
knew just what to say.

But not this time. The realization gave me confidence. I knew
I could do this.

Andy started to speak, but I silenced him with a glance.

Jack obviously didn't know where to look. Finally, he zeroed
in on the safe spot of my chin. "You, uh . . . how are you?"

"Me?" *Relieved I'm sitting down so my knees don't buckle
beneath me.* "I'm great. Just great." I gave him a bright smile. "A

little disappointed though." My fingers inched up toward the ends of my scarf, which dangled down past my shoulder.

"Um, I—"

Slowly I tugged on the scarf, letting it fall to my shoulders to reveal my bald head. "Disappointed because I was expecting a wolf whistle. I know that thing you have about women's hair, so I thought you'd really appreciate my latest style."

Jack blanched and started to back away.

"Not so fast," I told him evenly. "I have some things I want to say to you. That I *need* to say to you."

His eyes got that deer-in-the headlights look.

"Thank you," I said.

Jack's eyebrows flew up.

"You did me a huge favor," I told him. "By dropping off the face of the earth like that when you found out I had cancer, you showed me what a shallow, superficial, looks-obsessed jerk you are."

Andy made an indistinguishable sound, but I didn't look over at him. I was on a roll.

"You also showed me exactly what I want in a man," I continued. "Someone who's not going to cut and run at the first sign of trouble, someone who understands that a woman is not defined by her breasts or her hair." I inclined my bald head proudly. "Or any other outward physical manifestation."

I got to my feet, breathing hard, and laid my hand on my tissue-expanded chest, over my heart.

Jack backed up, his face a dull red.

"A woman is heart, brains, spirit, soul, and tenderness"—I lifted my chin—"and any man who can't see what lies beneath the boobs and the hair just isn't worth my time."

"Go, Nat!" Merritt's voice rang out behind me.

"And if you're not man enough to see that, you can—" I fumbled for just the right phrase, keeping in mind that we were at Disneyland. "You can just . . . kiss my . . . head."

By now the hunted look in Jack's eyes had turned to pure panic, and I noticed that apple-cheek girl had disappeared entirely. I took pity on him and sank back down in the wheelchair, my legs wobbly. "See you later, Jack."

He scuttled away, and Merritt and Andy applauded.

Josh too. "Why are we clapping?" he asked.

I just shook my head. "Kiss my head? I can't believe I said that."

• • •

I was dreaming again.

But no Hulks and red octopi this time. Instead, I was running in a field of wildflowers, wearing a gauzy white dress like in one of those douche commercials. Only on TV, the girl usually has long blonde hair flowing behind her. Mine was a rich brown and looked remarkably like Belle's from *Beauty in the Beast.*

So I was running in this field of wildflowers in this white gauzy dress, my thick Belle hair bouncing behind me, arms extended, running toward something fuzzy in the distance. As I drew nearer, I saw a man on a white horse, but his face was still fuzzy and indistinct. (Even from this far away, though, I could tell he had an amazing body—rippling abs beneath his white shirt and great pecs.) I ran faster and faster, trying to make out his face.

"Time to wake up, Sleeping Beauty."

Fuzzy-faced guy galloped away.

"No!"

I reached my hand up to run it through my bouncy Belle hair, but all my fingers grasped was air. Then they touched smooth skin stretched over a Humpty Dumpty head. I burrowed into the pillow, trying to put all the dream pieces back together again. It wasn't happening. Instead, I remembered I was in the hotel with Merritt. We'd taken the monorail so I could take a much-needed nap and also allow Josh and Andy some father-son bonding time.

I opened one eye. "What time is it?"

"A few minutes to five," Merritt said. "I woke you up a little early."

"Thanks. You ruined a perfectly great dream—and I was Belle, by the way, not Sleeping Beauty."

"Sorry." She bounced on the bed, not acting the least bit sorry. "But I wanted to share my good news. I found out just before we left but haven't had a chance to tell you. It's a dream as well." Her eyes danced.

"What?" I was wide awake now. "Spill."

The usually mellow Merritt's words tumbled over each other. "Constance asked me to bring a couple of my pieces to her gallery, and she really liked them, so she came over to the apartment and looked at some more, and . . ."

"And . . . ?"

"And she wants to do a show of my work!" Merritt shrieked.

"Your first show!" I squealed.

Then we squealed and shrieked again together.

• • •

We hooked up with Andy and Josh for dinner at the Rainforest Café in Downtown Disney. While we waited for our food, I proposed a toast. "To Merritt and her first show!"

We clinked water glasses.

Andy took a sip and raised his glass. "And to the end of chemo."

"Hear, hear." We clinked again and started to drink.

"Wait!" Josh said. "I wanna toast too."

"Okay, buddy, what do you want to toast?" I grinned at him. "Mickey Mouse or the Pirates of the Caribbean?"

He raised his child-sized glass. "To Aunt Natalie not being sick anymore."

My eyes blurred, but I managed to clink my glass with the rest.

"And to new beginnings," Merritt added.

"To new beginnings!" we all chorused.

* * *

All four of us oohed and aahed at the park's stirring grand finale. And once again, my wheelchair parted the Red Sea. We got great seats down in front.

Josh gasped when the fan of water sprayed up high in the air with all the images of Mickey Mouse projected on it. "Daddy, look!"

"I see, buddy. Pretty cool, huh?"

Josh's eyes shone.

Okay, so I couldn't really *see* them shining in the dark. But I know his every tone and inflection, and I just knew his eyes were shining.

"Totally cool," Josh said. "That's the best thing I ever saw."

I gave a smiling Andy an enthusiastic two thumbs-up.

Merritt and I loved the cinematic water spectacle, too, but what really set my heart aflutter was when the rafts floated by with all the different princesses dancing on them with their princes. I sighed and reached up to touch my tiara. When I was little, Snow White was my favorite, but Belle later replaced her. I mean, her *hair* moved. That one lock kept falling down over her forehead, and she kept pushing it back. What other animated princess's hair did that? Plus, she was a book lover just like me.

I sighed again. *God's in His heaven; all's right with the world.* I couldn't wait to write in my journal when we got back to the room. As Mary Poppins would say, it had been a "practically perfect" day.

Well, except for the Jack encounter.

But I was proud of how I'd handled that.

New beginnings.

Mickey had just slain the dragon and the show was almost over when my cell rudely went off.

I fumbled in my purse while people all around me turned to look. "Sorry," I whispered. At last my searching fingers found the off button and I pushed it.

Then Andy's cell rang. At least he didn't have to hunt around in a purse. He yanked it from his pocket and slapped his off button too.

After the fireworks, Andy and Merritt started gathering all our stuff, including a sleepy Josh. I checked my messages to see who'd called right in the middle of the finale.

Six missed calls? Mom, give me a break already.

Then I noticed that only two calls were from my mom. Two more were from Rashida, one was from Constance, and one was from Johnna.

And I knew.

re you gonna die like Luke's mommy, Aunt Natalie?" Fat tears rolled down Josh's cheeks. He stood in front of the wheelchair, his little body quivering.

I looked up at Andy helplessly.

He enfolded his son in his arms. "Aunt Natalie's not going to die," he said softly. "Not for a long, long time." He hugged his son tightly.

"But she had an owie just like Luke's mommy," Josh gulped out.

"Yes, but Luke's mommy's owie was not in just one place like Aunt Natalie's," Andy said gently. "Remember where I told you Aunt Natalie's owie was?"

Josh nodded and patted his narrow chest.

"That's right. But Luke's mommy had an owie there." He touched Josh's chest. "And there." His neck. "And there." His side. "And a lot of other places too. She had way too many owies for the doctors to be able to make her all better." He wiped Josh's nose. "But Aunt Natalie's already getting much better. That's why we're here—to celebrate her getting better."

I stroked Josh's growing-out buzz cut with a trembling hand, brushing my tears away with the other. "Your daddy's right, honey. I'm not going to die for a long, long time—probably after you're all grown up and old, maybe even a grandpa." I smiled and sent him an encouraging look. "But when I do die, you know where I'll go. Right?"

His lower lip trembled. "To heaven with Jesus." He clutched his thin little arms around my waist and wailed. "But I want you to stay here with me." Josh's body shook with sobs.

Andy's fingers tightened on the side of my wheelchair, his knuckles white.

I kissed the top of Josh's head and held him close, nuzzling him with my cheek. "I won't leave, sweetie. I promise." Then I tilted his head up to look at me. "You know what?" I said softly. "Now that Luke's mommy is in heaven, he's going to be very sad and missing her a lot, so we need to do what we can to help him feel better. Okay?"

He nodded through his sniffles. "Maybe I can bring him some of my Legos." Josh looked down, deep in thought. "And . . . maybe my Bob the Builder front loader—for just a little while," he added hastily. "Huh, Dad?" He lifted his tear-stained face. "Think that might make him feel better?"

"I'm sure it would," Andy said thickly. "That's a really good idea, buddy." He knelt down and gently extricated Josh from my lap.

Josh laid his head on his father's shoulder. "I'm thirsty, Daddy. And exhausted."

Andy and I both smiled at the big-boy word.

"Me too, bud. We all are." Andy gave my shoulder a comforting squeeze. "Let's go get some sleep."

• • •

I lost it in the hotel room.

I'd tried to hold it in as much as possible in front of Josh. But once the door clicked shut behind me, I dropped on the bed weeping.

"I'm so sorry, Nat." Merritt rubbed my back. "So sorry. I never met Jane, but from everything you and Constance said, and all the people who came over to help with her house, I could tell she was really special."

"She was." I grabbed a tissue from the nightstand. "Very sweet and kind. Humble too." I blew my nose. "But also very real." I smiled through my tears and told Merritt about Jane's bustier-and-thong suggestion for Pat.

"And she was so in love with her husband." *Her husband . . .*

My eyes flooded again at the thought of Mitch and his two motherless sons.

There was a soft knock at the door.

Merritt opened it to a worn-looking Andy. "Josh is asleep," he said. "Would you mind keeping an eye on him for me for a little while?"

Before the door even shut behind Merritt, I was in Andy's arms. Crying for Jane. And Mitch. And quiet little Luke. And baby Matthew.

For a long time, he just held me.

• • •

Later, after Andy had returned to his room and Merritt was sleeping, I pulled out my journal.

Saturday
    Jane died today.
    I knew it was coming, even thought it had happened once before.

Now I can't believe she's gone. I just saw her a few days ago at group. She was so happy about the house and couldn't stop talking about it.

How could it happen so fast?

I can't seem to stop crying. I don't even know why I'm so upset, but I am. Like I said, I knew it was coming. And I know Jane's home now— she's free from pain, and she has that whole new body she was looking forward to. But I just keep thinking about all the people who are going to miss her. I'm going to miss her.

I've been reading in the Bible tonight—I thought maybe that would help. Jane told me once that Psalm 91 was one of her favorites, so I looked that up in the hotel Gideon. It's all about God's promise to rescue and protect the people who love Him. And this is the way it ends: "I will be with him in trouble; I will deliver him, and honour him. With long life will I satisfy him, and show him my salvation."

But the thing is, Jane didn't get her long life! And who's to say I will, either? I know my cancer's not as advanced as hers was, and the doctors say I have a good prognosis. But it's still CANCER! I could die too.

I put down my pen and stared at what I'd just written.

Was that why I was so upset? Because I was worried about me—not about Jane and her family?

Ashamed of my selfishness, I cried myself to sleep.

● ● ●

Jane had asked that I read the Twenty-third Psalm at her memorial service.

"Me?" I gaped when Mitch told me of her request. "Why me?"

"I don't know." He gave me a sad little smile. "But Jane always had her reasons. And they were always prayerful ones." He looked at me with his wise youth-pastor eyes. "Maybe she thought you needed to actually hear the words."

When the time came, I read from the King James slowly. Haltingly. Glad there was a microphone.

"The Lord is my shepherd; I shall not want.

"He maketh me to lie down in green pastures: he leadeth me beside the still waters.

"He restoreth my soul: he leadeth me in the paths of righteousness for his name's sake.

"Yea, though I walk through the valley of the shadow of death, I will fear no evil: for thou art with me; thy rod and thy staff they comfort me . . .

"Surely goodness and mercy shall follow me all the days of my life: and I will dwell in the house of the Lord for ever."

After I finished reading, a peaceful stillness hovered in the air.

I slipped back into the pew next to Constance. We were clearly the cancer pew—all the women wore hats. Half didn't need to, but they did anyway to show their solidarity.

I will fear no evil, for thou art with me. I kept running the words over again in my head while Rashida stood to sing "Just as I Am"—another Jane request.

But what wouldn't have been a Jane request was the endless parade of people who went up after that, one by one, to share how she had touched their lives in some way.

Faye, gorgeous and immaculate as ever in her chic black Italian suit, designer hat, and Prada bag, leaned forward, listening intently to each one, the tears cascading down her perfectly made-up cheeks.

• • •

The sign on the grounds of the state capitol read "Making Strides against Breast Cancer." And that's what we were going to do.

Every October, which is Breast Cancer Awareness Month, the

American Cancer Society holds these walkathons in cities across the United States. The main purpose is to raise funds to fight breast cancer, but people also walk to celebrate their survival and to honor those who didn't make it.

Our whole support group—even Faye—had signed up to do the walk in memory of Jane.

It was a gorgeous fall day, with a snap in the air. The leaves on some of the trees had just started to turn amber and scarlet. But the main color I saw as we arrived on the capitol grounds was pink—a sea of pink T-shirts massed at the starting point. (I later read that more than twelve thousand people showed up.)

Many of those pink shirts bore the name or picture of a loved one emblazoned across the back. Our shirts showed Jane's name and photo.

Mitch came, too, holding tightly to Luke's hand, with little Matthew strapped to his pink-shirted chest in a canvas baby carrier. Their little white dog, Lady, trotted proudly alongside them in her own pink shirt, providing a welcome laugh in the midst of our tears.

As our little group wound its way through the streets of downtown, we linked our arms together, and Rashida led us in a chorus of "We Are Family." And when we got to the line about having all my sisters with me, I sang out loud and lustily, not caring for once that I couldn't carry a tune.

I even surprised Rashida by shaking my skinny white butt.

And who cared that I didn't make it to the finish? I just didn't have all my stamina back.

But I had the will.

Next year, I was going to go all the way. And not only that, but I also planned to proudly run in the Komen Race for the Cure in the spring.

chapter twenty-six

T a-da! Look at my new girls. Aren't they gorgeous?" Thinking of Pat, I proudly flashed the group my completed B-cups. The implants had finally gone in the week after our cancer walk.

Wolf whistles and loud clapping resounded through the room.

"You go, girl!" Rashida gave me a thumbs-up.

"Nice and perky." Faye nodded approvingly.

"Of course, I don't have my nipples yet, but Dr. Taggart will tattoo those next week."

"Congratulations, Natalie. Definitely a red-letter day." Johnna inclined her head to the end chair with a little smile. "However, we have someone new in group today."

"Oops. Sorry." I pulled my sweater down and nodded toward the attractive thirty-something brunette with the quirked eyebrows. "The same thing happened to me my first time, and I wondered if maybe I'd wandered onto the set of *Calendar Girls* or something."

"Pat loved that movie," Constance said, smiling. "Me too."

"Who didn't?" Anita said.

"Don't worry," I reassured the newcomer. "Flashing is not a group requirement."

"Good thing." Rashida snorted. "'Cause y'all ain't never gonna get a look at mine. They're only for a privileged few. Like my doctor and my husband—*if* I should ever decide to get married again."

"Got anyone special in mind?" I teased.

Johnna turned to Rashida. "Is there something we should know?"

"Nah, Natalie's just playin'." Rashida shot daggers in my direction.

"Well then, since we've gotten that out of the way, I'd like to introduce you all to Jennifer." Johnna indicated the woman beside her.

Jennifer was thirty-five, a freelance writer, and had just had a lumpectomy.

"You know, I'd been a little neurotic about cancer," she said wryly. "Every little symptom I had, I would imagine myself hearing those words, 'I'm afraid it's malignant.' But I'm finding that obsessing about cancer and actually living with the cancer reality are two very different things."

"That's why we have this support group." Johnna sent Jennifer a gentle smile. "Because we've all lived with, or are living"—she caught herself and looked at the chair where Jane used to sit, took a deep breath, and continued—"the cancer reality. And it's important to know you're not alone."

"Hear, hear." Constance clapped.

"Now does anyone else have anything they'd like to share"—Johnna glanced at me, her eyes twinkling— "other than a peep show?"

A more subdued Faye, now in the midst of her divorce, raised her hand tentatively. "My oncologist told me that his breast cancer patients who have a defeatist or negative attitude and just let the cancer have its way don't seem to do as well as those who exert some kind of control over it. So I'm trying to be less negative and more—"

"Easy for him to say," Jennifer interrupted with a sneer. "He's a man. He can't get breast cancer."

"But men *can* get breast cancer." I looked at Johnna, who gave me an encouraging nod. "It's a low percentage, but it does happen."

Johnna repeated to Jennifer the same statistics she'd given all of us awhile back. "And guys have prostate cancer to worry about too," she added. "At least we don't have that sword hanging over our heads."

Rashida jumped from her seat and did a little Zorro action in the air with a pretend sword. "Ha! Score one for the women."

*   *   *

D-day—or rather N-day—at last!

Today was the final step in my breast reconstruction. Last week, Dr. Taggart had removed my now-full tissue expanders and replaced them with my permanent saline implants.

Now it was nipple time.

She made a crosslike incision in the center of the pinkish-beige areola that she'd tattooed on each breast. Then she folded the edges of the cross into the center and stitched around the base to create my little nipple buttons.

"It's a good thing." Martha Stewart's catch phrase ran through my head when I first touched them. They looked amazingly real.

The only downside was I couldn't feel them.

Or rather they couldn't feel me.

My fingers felt the handcrafted nipple, all right. But the nipple itself didn't have any sensation. Neither did the breast around it.

There was a pressure from where my hand was touching, but that was all. Dr. Taggart said it would probably always be that way because of all the nerves that were cut during surgery. Not a mistake, she explained. It's just that the nerves are so infinitesimal—finer-than-thread strands invisible to the naked eye—that it is almost impossible to avoid cutting them.

She had told me all this before. And of course I hadn't been able to feel the tattoo or the nipple reconstruction, so I knew she was right. But I still couldn't help but be disappointed . . . and hope she was wrong.

I asked the doc to indulge me in a little experiment. I would close my eyes, and she would touch my breasts—first the one and then the other. I wanted to see if I could feel anything without the tactile confusion of my own fingertips getting in the way.

"Ready?" I shut my eyes.

"Ready."

"Okay, go."

"Dr. Taggart?"

"Yes, Natalie?"

"When are you going to start?"

"I already have."

Sigh. There go those wedding-night fireworks I'd been counting on.

After Dr. Taggart left the room, I cupped my new, beautiful, totally numb breasts. And wept.

•   •   •

Okay, so maybe my new breasts and nipples were just superficial, good-looking appendages without any feeling. They were still *mine*.

And gorgeous.

And without cancer.

I wanted to do something special to mark the occasion. And I made Merritt accompany me.

I'd considered getting the tattoo on my ankle, but I'd heard that it hurt less if you went for a fattier spot. And while I had mostly conquered my fear of needles, I saw no reason to go out looking for pain.

Since I have slim ankles, I opted for my stomach.

"Why not here?" Merritt asked, pointing to my derriere.

"'Cause then I couldn't see it." I flashed back to Rashida's comment about my skinny white butt. "Besides, I have a little more cushion on my tummy."

Doubtful that what I wanted would be found among all the dragons, snakes, military insignia, and motorcycle paraphernalia in the tattoo shop, I'd asked Merritt to sketch my choice for me. She handed the drawing to the tattoo artist, a bald guy named Chuck whose entire body—at least what we could see—was a canvas of black and purple ink.

"What is this?" he asked, staring at the quarter-sized leafy circle.

"A laurel wreath."

"A what?"

"Laurel wreath. Like Julius Caesar wore. In ancient times, it was worn as a sign of victory," I said.

"Cool." He began to tattoo me with the needle thingy.

Maybe my breasts had no sensation, but there was nothing wrong with my stomach's nerve endings. Ouch.

"I'm going to have to start calling you Cher," Merritt said as we drove away. "Three tattoos in one week." She grinned. "What next? A navel ring and a long platinum wig?"

"You never know." I plucked my jeans away from my throb-bing stomach. "Better watch out, or I might take over your wild-and-crazy artist territory, woman."

"In your dreams."

We stopped by Merritt's apartment—soon to be mine also—to show Jillian my triple tattoos. We found her sitting on the liv-ing room floor, awash in a sea of shoe boxes and tissue paper.

"Let me guess." Merritt looked at her roommate. "There was a closeout at Shoes-R-Us, so you bought out their whole inventory?"

Jillian burst into tears. "No. I'm trying to decide on my wed-ding shoes. But none of these look right."

"Well, if you want to see something that looks right, check out Nat's new nips."

"You got them? All finished?" Jillian's wet eyes lit up.

I stuck out my chest and kissed the tips of my fingers like a French chef. "C'est fini. C'est magnifique!"

"I wanna see, I wanna see," she clamored.

"Ooh, amazing," she said after I undid my blouse and bra. "They look so real!"

"That does it," Jillian said. "To mark this auspicious occasion, we're taking you out for a . . . drum roll . . . nipple celebration!" She pulled out her Nordstrom employee card from her purse. "And first stop on the nipple-stop tour: shopping." Her fashion-ista eyes gleamed. "I've been waiting for this day a long time."

"Wait a minute," I said. "I'm unemployed, remember."

"I happen to know you've got a hefty savings account from all those years of living practically rent-free. Plus, you'll need a wardrobe for your new career. And the first one is on me anyway."

"All right," I groused. "Just don't overdo it, Fairy Godmother, okay? And I'll tell you right now I'm not wearing any glass slippers." I looked at Jillian from beneath my grown-back eyebrows. "Especially ones with three-inch stiletto heels."

• • •

Jillian was a force of shopping nature.

Seriously, she was *good*. A real pro.

She whipped through racks of clothes like Superman flipping through *War and Peace*. "No, no. Not this. Too long. Too boring. Not a good color for you . . ." Periodically she'd pull something out, hold it up against me critically, then either return it to the rack or add it to the pile in Merritt's waiting arms.

"These are getting heavy," handmaiden Merritt finally whined.

So off to the dressing room we skipped.

Well, Jillian skipped. Merritt shuffled. And I dragged my heels.

• • •

"It's perfect." Jillian clapped her hands. "Every woman needs a basic little black dress."

I stared in the dressing-room mirror. "Uh, you don't think it's a little too *little*? And tight?" I plucked the clinging black jersey material away from my suddenly huge chest.

"Only if you're Amish." Jillian motioned for me to turn. "That fabric is supposed to mold to your curves."

"It's molding a little too much for me." My eyes sought Merritt's in the mirror. "Don't you think?"

"Sorry. Gotta go with shopgirl on this one." Merritt did her monotone Paris Hilton impression. "That's hot."

I plucked at the fabric again. "But my boobs stick out."

"They're supposed to, Sherlock."

"This much?" I stared at my profile.

"Welcome to the world of B-cups." Jillian came up behind me and gently put her hands on my shoulders. "I know it's going to take awhile for you to get used to your new breasts, Nat, but trust me—they only look huge to you. B-cup is a pretty standard size. In fact, it's more on the smallish end."

Merritt joined us at the mirror, smoothing down her poet's blouse. "I wear a 36-C. And I'm far from huge." She winked. "It's those double-D girls that need to worry. They can really do some serious damage with those puppies."

"But you're used to being voluptuous. It's a whole new world for me." I looked in the mirror again at the sleeveless, scoop-necked jersey matte dress and slowly did a 180-degree turn. Then I leaned forward and bent over slightly. "Hey, whaddya know? I've got cleavage!"

"That's what I'm talkin' about." Jillian high-fived me and handed me another black dress.

"Why do I need two?"

"One for night, and one for day. This one's a linen sheath."

I had to admit it looked good. Really good, in fact, with its clean, classic lines and boat neckline.

"Very Audrey Hepburn," Jillian said admiringly. "Now you just need Cary Grant."

"*Everyone* needs Cary Grant." I sighed. "Unfortunately, there was only one of him, and he's long gone. Although . . ." I lifted my index finger to my chin. "Isn't George Clooney still available? He's a close runner-up even though he's a bit on the old side."

I modeled a couple of more dresses, then tried on several tanks, sweaters, halters, and silky camisoles. But I drew the line at crop tops. "I'm not going to show my stomach. I'm so tired of seeing everyone's navels."

"But then you could show off your new laurel wreath." Merritt winked.

"Nuh-uh. Not for public consumption. Just for me."

"And the man of your dreams." Jillian smirked.

"Yeah, whoever *that* might be."

Merritt gave me a reflective look, which Jillian mirrored.

"*What*?" I put my hands on my hips.

"Oh, nothing." Jillian plucked a long, flowing deep-green skirt off the hanger. "Ooh, try this. You could wear it with a casual sweater for home or a jacket for business. Or dress it up with a glittery halter for, say, a wedding-rehearsal dinner during the holidays."

"And why in the world would I want to do that?" I asked innocently, well aware that her wedding was scheduled for just after Christmas, a little more than a month away.

She stuck out her tongue and handed it to me. "Just try it on."

Another one added to the pile.

I tried on a couple more skirts and pants, but when she returned with yet another dress, "a faux wrap with flutter sleeves," I held up my hand. "Enough. I'm exhausted. And hungry. I need sustenance."

They insisted that I wear one of my new outfits out of the store.

"Not the black dress." (Which Jillian had insisted on paying for.) I rubbed my arms. "I'm not quite ready for that public reveal." Instead, I chose a simple red knit wrap dress with a deep V-neck and a flirty skirt.

And walked out feeling slightly self-conscious.

But also pretty fabulous.

• • •

We headed across the street for Mexican and margaritas at El Torito—Merritt's choice to continue the nipple celebration. (To me, being able to eat the food was almost celebration enough!)

Merritt raised her salt-topped goblet. "Here's to my best friend, who is the bravest woman I know."

"Hear, hear." Jillian lifted her glass.

Merritt leaned in and whispered, "And who we're now going to start calling 'Lydia the Tattooed Lady.'"

We giggled and clinked our glasses.

Munching on chips and salsa, we discussed Merritt's art exhibition, which had been scheduled for February in Constance's gallery.

"Are you just going to do your canvases?" I crunched down on a chip.

"That's what I thought originally. But Constance says because I work in so many different mediums, she'd like to see a little bit of everything, so—"

"Hey, Nat," Jillian interrupted. "Sorry, Merritt." She leaned over and whispered, "That guy's checkin' you out."

"Where?"

"At the bar. And is he ever cute."

I started to turn my curly-capped head. My hair had grown out enough so that I now felt okay going out in public without my security-blanket hats and scarves. But it was still very short.

"No, don't look," Jillian hissed. "He'll see you."

"If I don't look, how can I tell what he looks like?" I started to raise my knife to use as a mirror, but Jillian stayed my hand.

"Too obvious." She sipped her drink, then stole another

look over the rim of her glass. "Matthew McConaughey with darker hair."

Be still, my heart.

"How do you know he's checking *me* out, Ms. Blonde and Gorgeous?" I scooped up some salsa. "You're the one who always turns guys' heads. Or maybe he's scoping out Merritt."

"Oh no, it's definitely you," Merritt said. "I noticed him when we came in. He couldn't take his eyes off you."

"Told you the new you was going to turn some heads." Jillian smirked.

"Ah, that must be it. My chemo head. Brings 'em running every time."

"Shh." Jillian hissed. "He's coming *over*."

A deep voice from behind me made me jump.

"I'm sorry. I didn't mean to startle you." Deep Voice moved into my line of vision. I gulped. Definitely a darker Matthew McConaughey.

Wonder if he has the abs?

"That's okay." I fiddled with my coaster.

"So what are you beautiful women celebrating?" But he never gave Merritt or Jillian a glance. He just looked straight at me.

"Uh—"

My new super-duper handcrafted nipples.

"A new addition," Merritt answered him with a devilish gleam. "Hi." She stuck out her hand. "I'm Merritt. This is Jillian—"

Jillian nodded.

"And the lady in red is Natalie."

"Hello, Natalie. I'm Brad." He touched my hand. "And may I just say that that is a fabulous dress? I noticed it the minute you walked in."

I blushed.

"Do you mind my asking where you got it? My wife has your same coloring, and I think it would look beautiful on her."

* * *

I pulled into the driveway and started unloading all my shopping loot, thankful for my savings account and my friends' generosity. Andy was playing hoops next door with a friend while Josh sat on the front porch, industriously building a Lego tower.

"Aunt Natalie!" Josh came running over, arms outstretched for a hug, but stopped short when he saw all the packages in the backseat of the car. "Is it Christmas already?"

"No, that's still a month away, sweetie." I grabbed a couple of bags and slung them over my arm. "I just went on a shopping spree."

"You look pretty," he said shyly. "Dad, Dad, come see."

Andy loped over to relieve me of some of the bags. Then it was his turn to stop short. And his eyes did something I'd never seen before—sort of a bugging-out-of-his-head effect. "Nice dress," he finally said.

"Hey, old buddy, you going to introduce me to this gorgeous creature?" His basketball friend slung his arm around Andy's shoulder.

"Oh, sure. Sorry." Andy ran his hand through his hair. "Ray, this is my friend Natalie. Natalie, this is Ray, a buddy of mine from college. He's in town on business."

"Pleased to meet you, lovely Natalie." Ray scooped up two or three shopping bags. "Here, let me help you with that."

Andy scowled, picked up the rest of the bags, and followed us into the house.

chapter *twenty-seven*

The next evening, right before I left for my support-group meeting, Andy knocked at my door to ask if I'd mind babysitting Josh on Saturday night.

"Of course. No problem." I swung open the screen door. "Come on in. I've got some oatmeal-raisin cookies."

"Uh, thanks, but I can't stay." He shifted from one foot to the other. "Got some work piled up I need to finish." He frowned. "You sure it's okay for Saturday? You're not busy or anything?"

"Nope. Free as a bird." I gave him a teasing look. "Unlike you. Got a hot date?"

Andy squirmed. "Well, um, Sara Sedberry wanted to thank me for fixing her sprinkler system, so she's taking me out to dinner."

"You *do* have a date."

"It's not a date. It's just a thank-you dinner."

"Men." I rolled my eyes. "You're so clueless. Trust me on this. It's a date." I smirked. "I've seen the way she looks at you."

. . .

When he brought Josh over on Saturday, Andy wore pressed khakis and a white button-down shirt, open at the collar, his hair still slightly wet from the shower.

"Well, don't *you* look nice?" I leaned toward him and sniffed. "Smell good too."

"Do *I* smell good?" Josh asked, stretching his neck out to me for a whiff. "Daddy put some of his smelly stuff from the black bottle on me too."

"Mmm, you smell delicious." I made chomping sounds by his neck. "I could just eat you up."

Josh giggled, then turned to his dad, his forehead puckered. "Don't let Miss Sara eat you up, Daddy."

"Oh, look at the time." Andy frowned at his watch, then kissed Josh on the head. "I have to go now, bud. Be good for Aunt Natalie. I'll be back soon." He flashed me an awkward smile and sprinted down the walk.

. . .

"Grilled cheese, peanut butter and jelly, or pizza?"

"Pizza!" Josh said. "Hawa—"

"I know." I grinned at him. "Hawaiian."

Josh slurped his root beer noisily as we put together a Mickey Mouse puzzle at the kitchen table. He pushed in a corner piece. "Look, I got Mickey's foot!"

"Good job. You are the puzzle king, bud."

Andy picked up a sleeping Josh at nine fifteen.

I raised my returned eyebrows. "Kind of early, isn't it?"

He didn't take the bait. Instead, he looked down at Josh. "I'd better get this little guy home to bed. Thanks again, Nat."

And just like that he was gone.

• • •

A week later, Andy's friend Ray was back in town on business again, and he called me up and asked me out to dinner.

Jillian thought I should wear the flirty little black dress, but I went with the classic linen sheath instead.

We had a nice time. Ray definitely knew how to charm a girl—he brought me flowers, took me to an expensive restaurant, opened my car door, and flattered me all night long.

I did pretty well too. I didn't once mention my boobs.

Over the pumpkin cheesecake, he covered my hand with his and looked intently into my eyes. "I can't believe some guy hasn't snatched you up yet. What's wrong with the men in this town? Are they all blind?"

I slid my hand from beneath his and took a drink of water. "Could be. Maybe that's why so many of them practice Braille."

Ray laughed and held up his hands, palms out. "Okay, I get it. I'm coming on too strong. I'll back off." He slipped his credit card into the leather folder the waiter had placed beside him. "You know"—he gave me a speculative look—"I don't think Andy liked my asking you out."

"Oh, he's just doing his protective big-brother thing."

"No." Ray shook his head. "I don't think so . . ."

"Trust me. You just don't know him the way I do."

• • •

After years as a double-A girl, I was having difficulty adjusting to my new B-cups. All of a sudden I felt like Dolly Parton. Every time I went out anywhere—the grocery store, gas station, around the block—I felt like every guy was staring at them.

I felt especially exposed at my Tuesday night tap, where we were required to wear leotards and jazz pants or kicky little Danskin skirts. The girls with the flawless bodies wore unitards or sports bras and bicycle shorts.

I kept putting a blouse over my snug leotard, which didn't sit well with Leonard, our French dance instructor. "What is zis?" he would say disdainfully, plucking the sleeve of my shirt between his two fingers. "A painting smock? Zis is not an art class. Zis is ze dahnce. And here we celebrate ze body."

I kept thinking maybe I was in the wrong class. "This *is* beginning tap dancing, right?" I whispered to the girl beside me the first night.

"Oh yeah, but Leonard's a frustrated Baryshnikov," she whispered back. "Ballet is his passion, but the tap teacher quit at the last minute, so he had to fill in."

Leonard frowned and clapped his hands. "Enough with ze talking. Let us begin."

He put on some Lawrence Welk–style music and started putting us through our beginning tap moves.

Which were not going well for me.

I had imagined myself as Ginger Rogers, Shirley Temple, and Liza Minnelli all rolled up into one incredible female dancing machine. I'd seen myself clad in spangle and glitters and tapping my way across a shiny dance floor, a spotlight highlighting my fancy footwork.

But for the life of me, I couldn't get the hang of the basic step-ball-change. There was some kind of disconnect between my brain and my feet.

"No, no, no!" Leonard would say, flailing his arms dramatically. "It is not ze step-step-change. It's step-*ball*-change." He would demonstrate. "You see? Is not difficult."

My face flaming, I would try again and again. And Leonard would tell the rest of the class to take a break while he worked with me on my technique.

I was much more successful in my other night class—interior decorating and design. "You have an innate flair," my instructor had told me after the fourth week. "You're a born decorator."

"That's what all my friends keep telling me."

I had blossomed under his tutelage and had a blast in class.

Maybe I *could* make a career out of this decorating thing after all. But the tap class—that was a problem. So after the third miserable week under Leonard's scathing impatience, I switched over to another tap class across town led by a transplanted Texas grandma with big hair, long fingernails, and lots of jewelry.

Charlene let us wear T-shirts and comfy capris to class. Her T-shirts had lots of embroidery, sequins, and glitter.

"That's it, honey," she'd call out in her husky drawl. "You're doin' great! Why, before you know it, you're gonna be the next Cyd Charisse." She'd tap and twirl across the room, leaving a trail of glitter in her happy wake. "Just wait 'til we have our first recital. Y'all are gonna be a sight to see." Then she'd crank up the Sinatra.

"Now c'mon and *dance*!"

chapter *twenty-eight*

I love the house! It's beautiful." My eyes drank in the original
crown molding, oak hardwood floors, and antique light fix-
tures of the old Victorian downtown.

Merritt peered around at the dusty drapes, peeling flocked
wallpaper, and doors hanging half off their hinges. "Well, it does
have sort of a vintage vibe," she said doubtfully.

Jillian made a face. "I know it doesn't look that great right
now, but—"

"But when it's all cleaned up, it will be absolutely gorgeous."
I ran my hands lovingly over the hand-carved built-in corner
cupboard in the dining room.

"I hoped you'd feel that way," the blushing soon-to-be-
homeowner said. "Bill and I want to hire you for the remodeling
and redecorating."

I backed up a step. "Whoa, there, Engaged One. I'm not a
contractor. I don't know anything about structure or electrical or
anything like that."

"But you know how to make a house pretty, right?"

"Well, yeah. But—"

"But nothing." Jillian waved off my concerns. "Bill's already had a building pal come in and inspect the house, and the structure's perfectly fine. There're a few spots of dry rot here and there. And of course we'll need to make some repairs"—she nodded at the rickety door we'd just passed through—"and update some plumbing and electrical and such, but that's what subcontractors are for."

She linked her arm in mine as we continued the tour of her new marital home, a sneezing Merritt trailing behind us. "Bill's given me carte blanche to do whatever I want in the house. And I want you to help me plan it." Jillian wrinkled her nose. "All he cares about is having a room where he can display his football trophies, watch ESPN, and smoke his smelly cigars in peace."

"Well, football was certainly an appropriate Victorian pastime," I murmured.

She smiled. "Obviously, we won't be a Victorian family." Jillian grew serious. "But I do want to maintain the integrity of the house as much as possible. And I know you feel the same way, which is why I especially want your help." She grinned. "And, of course, there's the fact that you're my friend, and I wanted to encourage you in your new career."

"Kind of an expensive encouragement, wouldn't you say?"

We finally arrived at what was going to become the master bath, just across the hall from Bill and Jillian's room. In Victorian days they didn't have master-bedroom-and-bath suites, but a former owner had already enlarged the hall bath to suit more contemporary sensibilities.

"This bathroom's in really good condition," I said. "We shouldn't have to do much at all." I ran my hand reverently over the original claw-foot tub. "Wow. What a beauty."

"Uh, there's only one other thing Bill was adamant about."

"What's that?"

Jillian blushed. "He wants a Jacuzzi tub big enough for two."

"And you want all this by when?"

"Oh, I know it's going to take awhile, and I want you free for some wedding stuff."

"Not to mention finishing my course. And Christmas is coming up. And—"

"Hey, relax." She linked an arm in mine. "It's going to be great. And you know what?" She gave me a meaningful look. "You've got all the time in the world."

* * *

"Ah, this is the life." I leaned my head back in the Jacuzzi and sighed.

"You're telling me." Merritt sipped her mimosa and stretched out her legs, her shiny new pedicure shimmering in the water. "A girl could get used to this."

"Even a nonmaterialistic Northern California hippie-chick artist?" Jillian arched her freshly waxed brows.

"Well, maybe not on a regular basis." Merritt looked at Jillian through blissful, half-closed eyes. "They might revoke my hippie-chick artist badge if they found out." She expelled a long sigh. "And I'd really hate to lose my discount privileges at the Co-op, the herbalist's, and all the Dead concerts. Not to mention my primo bicycle slot at the medicinal pot farm."

Jillian rolled her eyes and adjusted her bathing-suit straps.

"Have you ever thought of taking that routine on the stand-up comedy circuit?"

"Don't have to," she said. "All I have to do to be funny is parade around in one of those green herbal masks. Although," she added, touching her face like a model in a skin-care commercial, "it did make my skin touchably soft."

It was Merritt's first time at a spa. Mine too. And we were reveling in the luxury—though at first I'd resisted the idea of spending our "last hurrah" at such a place.

"It's not really my kind of thing," I'd protested.

"What? Being pampered?" Jillian stared. "Are you not a red-blooded American woman?"

"Well, I'm an American and I'm a *wo-man*." I gave a little Shania Twain lilt to the last word. "But after all the chemo, IVs, and blood draws, I'm not too sure how much red blood I've got left in me."

Even Merritt had joined in on the pressure campaign. "C'mon, Nattie, it'll be fun. Besides, it's a special occasion. How often does a girl get married?"

"Depends on the girl," I said. "If your name is Liz Taylor or Erica Kane, the numbers are legion."

Finally, I had succumbed to the spa pressure. And now I was glad that I had.

The full-body massage, especially, had been a revelation. Embarrassed at first about being almost naked under a sheet in front of a stranger, I'd tensed when the massage therapist first touched my leg. But once she started kneading my chemo-stressed muscles with sweet-smelling oil, I was Silly Putty in her hands. My body became a rolling mass of liquid Jell-O, and I fell asleep to the relaxing ocean sounds CD and her healing fingers.

When I woke up, I was drooling like a baby. And suddenly gung-ho for the entire spa experience.

"Hey, look, Ma. No hands!" I floated on my back to the center of the immense Jacuzzi, arms stretched wide at my sides, boobs straight up. "I'd probably never even need a life vest with these puppies." I giggled.

"Too bad boob jobs weren't around with the *Titanic*," Merritt said. "Could have saved a lot of lives." She smacked her head. "Plus, I could have made mucho bucks for my "Boob Voyage" signs from all those rich passengers."

Jillian slapped water at Merritt. "You're sick."

"Hey, hey. Watch the hair now," Merritt protested in a mock-prissy voice.

"Girls," I said sternly, "be nice, or I'll have to put you in time-out."

Merritt pouted. "She started it. 'Sides, you're not the boss of me."

"Yeah," Jillian echoed.

I glanced down at my new white one-piece that Jillian had ordered off-season for me through her retail contacts. "I'm sure glad we didn't do this until after my reconstruction was finished."

"How come?" Jillian shaded her eyes against the sun.

"I just remembered Constance telling me in group that whenever she went swimming, her prosthesis kept falling out of her suit. Sometimes she found it, but not always." I giggled. "People were always having to return it to her. Can you imagine?"

"I wonder if they returned it in a plain brown wrapper," Merritt mused.

"How'd they know it was hers?" Jillian asked.

We both looked at her.

"No. Really."

"Um, there probably weren't too many people in the swimming pool with falsies back then," I said.

"Don't be so sure of that." Jillian wagged her finger. "We do live in California, remember."

I breast-stroked over to them. "Hey, I know! Let's have a contest. We'll all float on our backs and see whose boobs don't flatten out to the sides. The winner gets a weekend here at the spa."

"I don't think so," Jillian said.

"Yeah." Merritt looked at me and then down at her full bikini top. "The odds are pretty stacked in your favor."

● ● ●

At last it was time for that walk down the aisle. I was a little nervous, but what girl wouldn't be on her big day?

The wedding music began, and Merritt gave me a quick thumbs-up from behind her bouquet before heading down the aisle in her strapless black-and-white maid-of-honor gown.

Now it was my turn.

I told the butterflies in my stomach to cocoon it and began the long white-carpet trek, grateful that my bouquet of red roses hid my trembling hands and praying that my new boobs would keep my strapless gown up and not crumple under the pressure.

I heard a few audible gasps from the guests, but I held my head high and kept walking. Slowly. Steadily. One step in front of the other.

At last I arrived at the altar, safe and sound. I let out my breath and turned as one with the rest of the church as the strains of the wedding march began and Jillian, escorted by her father, walked down the aisle to her Bill.

• • •

"You did it!" Merritt high-fived me in the ladies' room, where we'd dashed right after the ceremony. "You displayed your new cleavage in front of hundreds of people without fainting or having a wardrobe malfunction." She patted my shoulder. "See, it wasn't that bad."

"In what universe?" I shuddered. "I am *so* glad that's over."

But the reception was just beginning.

And, of course, it was fabulous. Jillian wouldn't have had it any other way. And she'd beautifully fulfilled her vow that "even though my wedding is right after Christmas, it's not going to be a Christmas wedding." From the top of the red-rose centerpieces on each hotel table to the bottom of the silver chairs, everything was elegance personified, including her dramatic colors—black and white, with splashes of red.

Our twin maid-of-honor dresses—Jillian couldn't decide between the two of us—were black, floor-length, sweeping, and strapless, with white satin piping around the fitted bodices. Jillian had gotten the idea from the vintage black-and-white gown Julia Roberts wore to the Academy Awards the year she won her Oscar. But Jillian, never one to copy *anyone*, had tweaked the look with a little help from one of her designer friends.

Hence the strapless conundrum that had had me hyperventilating about my new breasts, which were now so publicly, yet tastefully, on display.

At least to everyone else. It seemed no matter what I did, I couldn't get away from the bird's-eye view I had of Monica and Rachel.

Yes, I named my boobs.

Originally, I was going to go with Lucy and Ethel. But according to one of the myriad breast cancer books I'd read when I was first diagnosed, some woman had already done that. Or did I hear it on *Oprah*? Could it have even *been* Oprah? I couldn't remember. Chemo brain.

Anyway, the last thing I wanted to be was a copycat. So Monica and Rachel they became. They were roommates, after all. And no matter what I did, they were in my face—especially when I was sitting down. I'd reach for a glass of water, and there they were. Or I'd lean forward to talk to someone across the table, and bingo, there they'd be.

I didn't know how to act in my first strapless dress. Especially with my new girls. I was tempted to shove my bouquet down the front of my dress just to provide cover.

At the same time, I couldn't stop staring at my breasts.

It was like the first time you get a great new haircut. You don't mean to, but you catch yourself looking at it in the mirror every time you walk by. Or in store windows where you tilt your head from side to side to see your new 'do from every angle. Or catch a glimpse of it in your rearview mirror and angle the mirror to get a better look when you come to a stop sign.

Is that really me? Wow. I look so different. Lookin' good!

But there were no rearview mirrors here, and it really wasn't appropriate for me to spend so much time with Monica and Rachel at Jillian's wedding. So with fresh resolve, I headed to the buffet line with the rest of the bridal party. On the way, I overheard my mother say to Jillian's, "I can't wait for the day when I see *my* daughter walk down the aisle."

Jillian's stepmom dabbed at her eyes. "There's nothing like it, Ruth."

Oh, great. Now Mom's going to get all weepy and emotional.

Instead, she smirked. "Well, she'd better get a move on. We're not getting any younger."

I piled my plate high with shrimp, smoked salmon, stuffed mushrooms, shish kebab, and a few grapes and ducked out of her line of vision.

"Hungry, much?" Merritt stared at my loaded plate when I returned to our table.

I jerked my head over my shoulder. "Mother."

"Ah."

Then she took a closer look, and a wicked smile stole over her face. "Hey, isn't that a shish ke*boob*?"

• • •

Merritt and I watched Jillian and Bill move to the dance floor in a cloud of love.

After everyone applauded their first romantic couple dance to "Unforgettable," Jillian gave a nod to the DJ, who blasted out the Fifth Dimension's "Wedding Bell Blues." Jillian sang along lustily. "Billll!" she belted, grinning and shaking her finger at her new husband whenever the anguished cry of why he wouldn't marry her came on.

Bill grabbed his bride by the waist and caught her up in his arms, twirling and swinging her around amid much laughter and a few whistles and catcalls.

I was laughing along with the rest of the room when I heard a familiar voice behind me.

"Nattie?"

I nearly choked on my shish kebab. Realizing I was probably

not the only one with the bird's-eye view of my girls anymore, I clutched my hand to my bodice and turned. "Andy. You're back. Where's Josh?"

"Still with my folks in Texas. I came back early for the wedding."

Andy and Josh had been gone for a couple of weeks. For the past few years, he and his folks had developed the tradition of spending holidays with his sister's family in San Antonio and staying until after New Year's. Josh had always looked forward to the big family occasion, and I'd always been a little jealous. Christmas with just my parents and me was usually kind of quiet, and this year it had been almost swallowed up in wedding preparations.

"I missed you guys," I said softly. "It was nice of you to come." And it was strange to be standing there making inane small talk with my best friend.

Must be the boobs. And the dress. And these shoes. I'm about ready to get things back to normal.

"You look absolutely amazing." Andy's voice was strange, and there was a look in his eyes I'd never seen before. He wasn't staring at Monica and Rachel, either.

"You look all amazing, too, in your navy suit and crisp white shirt." *Smelling all fresh and manly.* All at once I had a wild and crazy impulse to nuzzle his manly neck and rip that shirt right off his chest.

Whoa. There must be something in the water.

Andy tugged at his collar. "Would you like to dance?"

I nodded.

"Hey there, Andy." Merritt gave him an appreciative wink. "Lookin' good."

"Uh, hi, Merritt." But his eyes never once left mine.

Andy reached down and drew me to my feet and into his

arms. We didn't say a word, just moved as one to the music, glid-
ing across the floor like Fred and Ginger. John and Charlotte.
Abbott and Costello . . .

I stepped on his foot.

"Ouch!"

"Sorry." I scrunched my eyes. "I'm not used to these high heels."

"They're pretty deadly." Andy grimaced. "You might want to
consider registering them as lethal weapons."

"I might if I was ever going to wear them again." I winced.
"But these Cinderella stilettos are being retired to the back of my
closet after tonight."

There was an awkward silence. Which was weird, because
this was Andy.

I cast about for something to fill it.

"So I guess I told you about my new internship, didn't I? I
start after the first of the year. Can't wait."

He didn't answer.

I babbled on. "Oh, and my tap-dancing class is going great. I'm
so glad I gave old Leonard-step-ball-*change* the heave-ho." I stepped
back, executed a flawless step-ball-change, and gave a little bow.

When I lifted my head, Andy was giving me a speculative
look. "There's something different about you."

"Hel*low*. I've got boobs again."

"No, it's not just that. Or the dress"—his eyes skimmed over
me, lingering on my lips, and he drew me back into a dancing
clinch—"amazing as it is."

My mouth went dry, and I was having difficulty breathing.

"You're more confident, more sure of yourself." His eyes darkened, and he pulled me closer to him, saying softly, "Could it be
that you've—"

A smooth, car-salesman voice punctured the air. "This can't be the same woman I met at church with Bill and Jillian."

We stopped dancing.

I saw him first. Wavy, too-perfect hair, buffed nails, silk suit (dark charcoal this time).

Justin continued. "Not this picture of health, this vision of loveliness . . ."

Andy released me and turned around, a quizzical look on his face.

Justin swooped in for a hug, his expensive silk arms squeezing me tight. "Natalie, it's so good to see you again. You look wonderful. I hoped I'd run into you here. It looks like our prayers were answered."

Andy excused himself and left.

I glared at Justin, longing to say what I was thinking but knowing it would be rude. *Oh, shut up and go polish your hair-spray cans.*

chapter *twenty-nine*

T ell me again why you're doing this." My father picked up the last cinnamon roll from the paper plate atop a stack of moving boxes in my kitchen.

"Because it's time, Dad. I'm nearly thirty years old, and I'm still living at home."

"No, you're not. You won't even be twenty-eight yet for a few more months." He made a sweeping circle with his hand. "And you've got your own nice little place here."

"Sure I do. And it's right in my parents' backyard." I sighed.

"Hey, Nat?" The front door slammed, and Merritt's voice rang out. "Ready to blow this popsicle stand?"

My father crumpled up the paper plate and tossed it in the open trash bag on the floor. "Well, I'd better get going if Andy and I are going to pick up that U-Haul by eight." He kissed me on the forehead and nodded to Merritt on his way out.

Mom showed up a few minutes later, a basket of folded laundry on her hip. "You know you'll have to do your own laundry now that you're moving out," she teased.

"I know. Not to worry. I'm a big girl." I taped another box shut and winked at her. "I think I can handle doing my own laundry."

She headed to the bathroom to help Merritt pack up the rest of my last-minute toiletries. While they were occupied, I took down the last thing in the kitchen—my gallery of hunks.

Slowly, I removed each one from the inside of the cupboard door, careful not to rip off any paint in the process. Then I dropped the pictures into the trash one by one, tearing them in half as I did.

"Bye, Ty."

"*Au revoir*, Jean-Luc."

"Bye, Clay."

"Later, Viggo."

Now only my sweet Johnny remained.

I looked into his melting brown eyes, which now reminded me so much of Andy's.

Andy. He'd been polite but elusive since the wedding, too busy to stop and talk about anything other than mundane moving details. I kept wondering what it was he'd been about to say to me on the dance floor. *"Could it be that you've—"*

That I've what?

I ripped Johnny in half and in half again.

• • •

Josh lost it once the U-Haul was loaded and we were set to leave. "I don't want you to go." He kicked at the ground, his lower lip trembling.

"I'm not going very far. I'm just moving in with Merritt." I stroked his arm and smiled. "You like Merritt. She's one of the Four Buzzheads, remember?"

"Why can't she move here instead?" A tear trickled down his face.

"There's not enough room, honey." I squatted down and wiped away his tear. "But we have lots of room at my new apartment, and you can come and stay over, okay? Merritt has lots of cool paint and stuff we can play with."

He sniffled. "Red paint?"

"And blue. And yellow."

"And maroon?"

I laughed. "A whole rainbow of colors." I hugged him. "And we can go down to the duck pond and feed the ducks." I gave him a soft butterfly kiss on the cheek. "Besides, I'll come over and see you all the time."

"You said you wouldn't leave." Josh wailed. "You promised."

Helpless, I looked on as Andy made soothing noises to his son, then scooped him up and took him inside to my mother.

I waved to Josh at the window as we pulled away, my heart clutching at the sight of his forlorn, tear-stained face. Then I made a note in my day planner to take him to the duck pond in a couple of weeks.

• • •

So this is how the other half lives.

I looked around at the suede walls (yes, *suede*), the marble floors, and the massive crystal chandelier.

Definitely not in Kansas anymore.

"Natalie? Come, dear, and bring your notebook."

"Yes, Magda."

Magda Evans was a chichi, in-demand local interior decorator who'd taken me on as a paid intern after a recommendation from my design professor. Today we were visiting one of her crème de la crème clients, a dot-com millionaire who'd cashed out his sky-high stock options just before the bust. He'd taken that bundle of cash and moved from the Bay area to the pristine foothills above Sacramento, where multimillion-dollar homes were de rigueur.

As I followed my new boss and mentor up the stairs, I looked down at the unusual stair covering beneath my feet. The pattern reminded me of something from the Florida Everglades. I crinkled my nose. "Looks like alligator."

"It is."

"Real alligator?"

"Of course."

I caught my jaw before it dropped.

Gerald Bates, Magda's client, was now bored with three of the six bedrooms and four of the six and a half baths in his five-million-dollar home, so he wanted her to do a major revamp. Gerald was in the midst of describing a look he'd seen at a Tuscan villa that he wanted to duplicate when I felt the call of Mother Nature.

"Excuse me; may I use your bathroom, please?"

"I'd like Natalie to see what I did in your master bath," Magda said. "Do you mind if she uses that one?"

"Not at all." He gestured across the hall. "Right through there."

I zipped through a large, albeit seriously minimalist, black-and-gray master bedroom with floor-to-ceiling windows and a great view I didn't have time to appreciate. The battleship-gray bathroom was bigger than my new bedroom, with lots of glass and stainless steel. I made my way past a walk-in glass-block shower to a spacious, private commode in a room all its own.

At last.

Wait a sec. A heated toilet seat? Clearly I was way behind on the high-tech commode curve.

Even farther behind than I knew.

I picked up a nearby remote control, wondering if a hidden flat-screen TV would suddenly drop down from the ceiling like I'd seen in one of my home makeover shows. I punched a few buttons and jumped as warm air blasted up from the bowl.

I hurriedly completed my visit and went to find my mentor. Magda beamed at me when I returned. "How did you like my masterpiece?"

"I've never seen anything quite like it."

"Isn't she amazing?" Gerald cooed. "She's always on the cutting edge."

"I'll say."

As I followed Magda from room to ridiculously expensive—and sparse—room taking notes, I thought again of Jane and her sweet little house. And how my friends and I had made it a little cozier and more comfortable.

Not cutting-edge at all. Just a great place for real people to live.

• • •

Back at her lavish office showroom, Magda and a few of her minion designers-in-training flipped through fabric swatches and paint chips for another one of her high-end projects—a nursery for a female banker and her lawyer husband expecting their first child.

"Pink and blue are so passé." Magda wrinkled her sculpted Rodeo Drive nose.

"What about yellow?" one of the minions suggested.

"Too obvious. I'm thinking orange."

"We could do a cute border print," I offered, remembering how much Luke had loved the Thomas the Tank Engine border Jane had selected. "Maybe classic Winnie the Pooh?"

There was a collective gasp. All eyes swiveled to Magda expectantly.

"Did you say *border print*, Natalie?" Her slashing Cabernet-colored eyebrows disappeared beneath her jagged, asymmetrical bangs.

I nodded.

"Darling, borders are so *yesterday*." Magda looked at me over her cat's-eye specs (tortoiseshell with embedded diamonds—"*not* rhinestones!"). "Unless, of course, you live in Small Town, USA."

The whole room tittered.

Then why do I always see them at Target and Home Depot? But I knew better than to utter any of those "common folk" store names in Magda's presence. I'd done it early on, and you'd have thought I'd killed one of her beloved cats or something.

Magda, who lived alone, had three Persian cats—Caesar, Cleopatra, and Marcus Antonius. They wore diamond collars, slept in satin kitty beds, enjoyed suede scratching posts, ate out of crystal food bowls, and luxuriated in a room of their own—in leopard print, of course.

In other words, the fabulous Magda was a spinster with multiple cats.

Except Magda and her kitties wouldn't be caught dead watching *Golden Girls* reruns. They're *Sex and the City* girls all the way.

• • •

"No way," Merritt said when I told her about the high-tech toilet that night over Chinese.

"Uh-huh. It was too bizarre. What will they think of next?"

She started to issue one of her standard witty comebacks but then raised her shoulders and said simply, "There's nothing I can think of to top that."

"The whole house was so stark and sterile. Nothing warm or cozy about it. Except for the suede walls downstairs." I shuddered. "And his bedroom—reminded me of a prison. It was massive, but the only furniture was this king-sized industrial-looking gray metal bed and this gray metal nightstand in the shape of a G."

"No dresser?"

"His closet is his dresser. He's got this huge island in the center of a gigantic walk-in closet that's nothing but drawers." I reached for an egg roll. "Not that I wouldn't like a larger closet myself someday, but the rest of the place was definitely not my style. Too cold and stark."

"As opposed to Jillian and Bill's place?"

"Exactly! Now that's going to be a warm, inviting home." I wielded my chopsticks to dredge up one last chunk of broccoli beef. "Speaking of which, how's the painting coming along?"

"Almost finished. Want to see?" Merritt asked shyly.

"Is the Pope Catholic? Are my boobs fake?"

Merritt's belated wedding present to Bill and Jillian was a painting of their newly purchased Victorian home, which we planned to have hanging over the mantel when they returned from their honeymoon.

"Ooh, it's gorgeous. I love it!"

"Really?" Merritt sent me an anxious look. She'd been struggling with the painting for weeks—first at Constance's studio since she didn't want to risk Jillian seeing it, then at home after Jillian moved out and I moved in. Usually Merritt worked in bold, vivid oils. But for some reason, they just weren't working for the gentle, old-world Victorian. After starting and stopping three different canvases, Merritt had finally given up and decided to try her hand at watercolor under Constance's helpful tutelage.

The finished result—or nearly finished; she still needed to touch up a few details—was soft and lovely, with a dreamy Impressionistic feel to it.

I sighed. "Makes me want to climb inside the painting and live in that house."

She squinted at it critically, in full-on neurotic artist mode. "You don't think maybe it's a little too *sweet*?"

"Maybe for you, O cynical one, but it's perfect for Bill and Jillian." I gave it another dreamy look. "Me too."

Merritt grunted. "Save it for the Hallmark channel." But I could tell she was pleased. "Just don't sign me up to paint these for the whole neighborhood now."

* * *

Two nights later, we hung the finished painting above the mantel in the newlyweds' bedroom.

"It's perfect, Mer. They're going to love it. Now when they lie in bed at night, they'll have something beautiful to look at."

"Oh, I think there will be plenty of other things they'll be busy looking at," she said.

I blushed. "We need to get busy on this room so it's finished before they get home tomorrow. Here, help me make the bed." I adjusted the Battenberg lace pillow shams and throw pillows. Not too many. One thing I'd learned from my male design instructor—most guys don't like an army of froufrou pillows on the bed.

"Why do we need all these pillows?" our instructor had told us he'd asked his wife. "We just have to take them off every night and put them all back on in the morning again."

Knowing Bill, I had decided less would be more.

While Merritt folded the antique quilt from Bill's grandmother to hang over the side of the white wicker rocker, I placed the solid beeswax pillar candles in staggered groupings at each end of the mantel, humming as I did.

When I turned around, Merritt was sitting in the rocker just staring at me.

"What? Do I have a rip in my pants or something?" I reached a hand to test the back of my jeans.

Merritt shook her head, and as she did, a tear fell onto her cheek.

"What is it? What's wrong?"

She gave me a tremulous smile. "Nothing's wrong. Everything's right. I was just thinking how great it is to see you all happy and healthy and in your element when just six months ago you were so sick." She blew air out through her teeth. "And I was so scared."

"You were scared?" It was my turn to stare. "You never said so or even acted like it. You were always my cheerleader, pushing me on, encouraging me to eat, and taking me to chemo. You and Andy both."

"Of course. That's what you needed. The last thing you needed was my tears and fears on top of your own." Merritt rubbed her eyes. "You had enough on your plate as it was."

"As I recall, I didn't have very much on my plate at all—other than a few Ensures and some ice chips."

She threw a magazine at me. "Hey! I'm tryin' to be all serious and emotional here."

"Well, snap out of it, would you? Otherwise I'm going to think aliens have taken over your body."

"E.T., phone home. E.T., phone home." She looked beneath another magazine on the table next to her, then set it back down and peered down at the floor.

"What are you looking for?"

"The trail of Reese's Pieces."

I lobbed the original magazine back at her.

"Seriously, Nattie." Merritt looked straight at me. "I . . . I . . ." She swallowed hard. "I was really afraid I was going to lose you. And I don't know what I'd have done if I had. You're my best friend." The tears rolled down her cheeks in earnest.

Mine too. And soon we were sobbing in unison.

I wiped my eyes and gave her a long hug. "It's okay. I'm fine now, and I'm not going anywhere. You can't get rid of me that easily." I brushed my hands on my jeans. "I don't know about you, but I'm starved."

Merritt looked at me. I looked at her. "We shouldn't," she said.

"No, we really shouldn't."

Then we hurried downstairs to the eighties-era kitchen, which I had yet to tackle.

Opening the dingy old refrigerator, we both stared at the lone item inside—the beautiful "Welcome Home!" picnic basket I'd painstakingly put together for Bill and Jillian. The wicker basket was loaded with gourmet cheese and crackers, smoked salmon, salami, Asian pears, Fuji apples, red and green grapes, chocolate truffles, and two mouth-watering slices of fruit-basket cake I'd picked up just today from the bakery. The same bakery that had made their fruit-basket wedding cake.

"We *really* shouldn't," I said.

"Right."

Then we looked at the basket again—the fat, juicy grapes, the extra-sharp Tillamook, the cake slices calling our names. "But we will."

I grabbed the basket, and we tore into it like hungry bears with a loaded ice chest.

I took a bite of smoked salmon on a water cracker and moaned. Vegetarian Merritt did the same with the cheddar.

After finishing off all the fruit, cheese, and salmon—neither of us are salami fans—we felt the need for something sweet. But which to choose—the truffles or the cake?

We inhaled them both.

"I can't move," I groaned afterward.

"Me either."

I undid the top button of my jeans and grimaced. "My laurel-wreath tattoo is fast becoming a laurel hedge."

Merritt stared at the decimated basket. "Now what are you going to do?"

I lifted my shoulders. "Get up first thing in the morning and replace it all."

We waddled into the living room, where we fell, sated, to the Oriental carpet.

"I feel sick," Merritt said.

"Well, don't puke on the vintage carpet. I scoured three flea markets and seven antique stores to find this baby."

Sinking into the plush Persian wool, I put my hands behind

my head and admired the original ceiling medallion molding around the vintage light fixture. There was still work to do in this room, too, though we'd cleaned it up and tried to make it inviting for Bill and Jillian to come home to.

"Hey, Mer?"

"Yeah?"

"Do you think maybe Andy was scared too?"

"Huh?"

"I was thinking of what you said upstairs and how you hid your fear from me. And wondering if maybe Andy might have been scared too."

"Nah." She rolled her eyes. "Ya think?"

"Is that why he's acting so strange now?" I shifted onto my side to face her. "*Strange* being the operative word. He's been such a stranger lately. I just don't understand what's going on with him."

I frowned. "He was so great throughout the whole cancer thing—amazing, actually. But now, poof, he's just disappeared. I hardly ever see him, and when I do see him, he hardly says anything."

"Basic Psych 101, Nat." Merritt scratched her arm. "Guys like Andy—strong, loyal, dependable, kind—are great in a crisis. They step up to the plate and do whatever needs to be done—take you to chemo, hold the puke basket, shave their heads in solidarity—nothing is too difficult for them. They rise to the occasion and do whatever needs to be done, no matter what."

I nodded. "Yep, that's Andy all the way."

"But"—she turned and gave me a searching look—"now that the crisis has passed, there's nothing more for him to do. You don't need him anymore. He's been your rock, your protector, your caregiver. But now you're able to do things for yourself again, and you're moving on with this whole new life—making changes, taking chances. And he doesn't know who he is anymore when it comes to you."

"He's my best friend, that's who he is. My best male friend," I added hastily. "And I miss him. I miss Josh."

Merritt rolled her eyes. "There are none so blind as those who will not see."

"What do you mean?"

"Figure it out, Sherlock."

I frowned. "Maybe he's met someone. He had at least one date with Sara back in November. I'd been trying to get them together for months. Maybe they finally clicked."

"Yeah, or maybe she's just a safe distraction." Merritt gave me a probing look. "Maybe during the cancer he got a little too close, and it scared him silly."

• • •

"Sara seems like a nice lady. Do you like her?"

Bent over his painting at my kitchen table in intense concentration, Josh shook his head. "Nuh-uh. She got too many teeth."

"Too many teeth?"

"Yes." He looked up and bared his teeth at me in a too-wide smile, scrunching his eyes up. "Like this. She always does that when she sees me and Daddy."

"Does she see your daddy a lot?" I asked casually.

"Nah." But he was bored with the dating inquisition. "Hey, Aunt Natalie. You got any more brownies? They were quite delicious."

As promised, I'd brought Josh over to my new place. Correction. Mine and Merritt's place. And my new roomie had graciously supplied us with some of her old acrylics that she rarely used so we could play artist while she ran errands.

"I think you may have had enough brownies, buddy." I smiled at him. "I don't want to spoil the dinner your dad has planned."

"You won't spoil it," he said earnestly. "I have a big appetite."

"That's for sure!" I grinned. "Tell you what. As soon as we finish our painting and wash up, you can have one more brownie. But just a small one, okay?"

"Okay." He started to push back from the table. "Let's go wash up."

"Not until we finish, Josh."

"But I am finished." He carefully turned his painting toward me. "See?"

I peered at the painting, which seemed to hold four figures—one small, two medium, and one very large. A wide swash of deep blue swept across the top, dotted with cheerful splashes of yellow.

"This is very interesting, Josh," I said carefully. "Can you tell me about it? Who is this? I pointed to the small figure."

"That's easy. Me."

"And this big guy?"

He looked exasperated. "It's Mickey. See the ears."

"Oh." I did see. Then I realized that one of the other figures had short, curly hair. My eyes blurred. "So this is . . ."

"That's us at Disneyland, but without the wheelchair," he said. "For the next time we go, now that you're all better."

Josh gave me an anxious look. "Don't you like it? How come you're crying?"

I jumped up and hugged him tightly. "I'm crying because I'm happy. I love my picture!"

His little voice muffled against my chest. "So c'n I have another brownie now?"

chapter *thirty*

It seemed like a crazy idea at first—going to the Grand Canyon in winter.

But once we got there, I decided that it was the absolutely perfect time to visit.

Yes, it was cold. I mean *really* cold. But most of the roads on the South Rim were open—uncrowded. The shuttles were running to the main overlooks. And the view . . .

"That's the most extraordinary thing I've ever seen." Dad sucked in his breath next to me.

I nodded, unable to speak. We stood shivering at the overlook just as the sun cleared the horizon. We stood staring at the magnificent chasm in absolute amazement. Even Mom was speechless at the sight.

And people think there is no God.

Dad gripped my arm and pointed. A bald eagle soared overhead, then dipped and swooped into the darkness of the snowy canyon, then rose into the light again, its magnificent wings spread wide.

On the other side of me, Merritt gasped.

The sheer size and depth of the canyon were beyond anything I could have imagined. Pictures simply didn't do it justice. We stood there transfixed as we watched the rising sun paint the exposed rocks near the rim a vivid red and set the snowy crags on fire.

I shivered in the crisp, frigid air and pulled my parka tightly around me as we crunched through the snow back to the car.

"You should have put on more layers, honey." Mom frowned at me. "Where's that thick cable-knit sweater we gave you last year for Christmas?"

"Uh, it kind of shrunk in the wash."

The laundry queen looked victorious. "I could come over and do your—" She stopped herself and sent me a wry grin. Then she put her arm around my shoulders and drew me to her. "Same thing happened to me the first time I washed your Dad's favorite fisherman's sweater. We wound up having to give it to Goodwill."

"Yeah," Dad grumbled. "Where I'm sure a couple of moms fought over it for their eight-year-old boys, since they're the only ones it would fit now."

Mom squeezed my shoulder and smiled. "The key is to block it back to size and dry it flat."

Now that I'd at last broken free of my parents and asserted my independence, it was nice to be able to choose to include them in the activities I wanted to. That's why I'd invited them and Merritt on this quick trip. I'd half-expected them to back out, since tax season was beginning to kick into high gear. (Our family had never done *anything* between January and April.) But maybe they were already beginning to think like retired people, which they would both be after the season was over. At any rate, they were eager to share this experience, one of the highest items on my to-do-before-I-die list.

Not that I was going to die anytime in the near future—the doctors had given me a clean bill of health at my last checkup—but I didn't want to waste any more time. Hence the midwinter getaway.

I'd invited Andy and Josh along on our Grand Canyon trip as well, but once again, Andy was too busy. When I offered to still take Josh, Andy had said he wasn't old enough for such a trip without his dad.

I sighed again, thinking of our conversation and reliving the same hurt and disappointment I'd felt at the time. *Andy, what is wrong between us? Can't we at least talk about it?* But his eyes had shuttered, and that was that.

The last time I'd seen Andy so closed off was when Sheila left him.

• • •

Over fajitas at dinner that night, I regaled my parents with some Magda stories from my short-lived internship. "Did you say *border print*, Natalie?" I raised my eyebrows in my best Magda impression. "And shabby chic? I *never* do shabby chic! Too scruffy. Too bourgeois. Too nineties."

"Guess we're really behind the times." Dad picked up another flour tortilla.

"Then so are all the women in my book club," Mom said.

"I wonder if Magda knows Leonard 'Zis is not an art class; zis is ze dahnce?'" Merritt mused. "If not, maybe you could set them up. Sounds like a match made in heaven to me."

After three weeks interning for Magda, I had switched over to another design firm. "Sorry, we're just not a good match," I'd told her when I resigned. "This just isn't me. You're champagne; I'm Coke."

She'd agreed, and we'd parted amicably.

The experience with Magda hadn't been all bad, though. Under her tutelage, I learned how to experiment with color. Now I was trying combinations I'd never have thought of before.

My new internship was with Joe and Elena, a down-to-earth husband-and-wife design team whose clients came from all walks of life and varying levels of income. Sure, there were a couple of millionaires. But mainly their clients were middle-to-upper-class regular folks who just needed guidance in realizing their visions for their homes—a much better fit for me.

"Someday"—I sipped my hot chocolate and sighed—"I'd like to have my own firm where I could help people who don't have the big bucks to spend. I'd go in and show them how to decorate within their budget by rearranging things they already have or spending just a little on just the right items. People need to know they can transform their homes on just a little money."

"Like you did at Jane's," Dad said gently, and I nodded.

"Uh, Nat?" asked Merritt. "I don't mean to pop your bubble, but how could you earn a living if you only work with people who don't have much money?"

"Probably just take on a few high-end clients to make up the difference." I grinned. "I have no problem taking rich people's money."

"You could be the Robin Hood of the decorating world," Merritt said.

Mom winked. "Just as long as they don't want silk flowers, right?"

• • •

That night after Merritt went to sleep in our shared motel room, I pulled out my cancer journal and reread the last entry I'd written, after another new woman had come to group railing against God and asking, "Why me?"

Thursday

Why shouldn't I get cancer? People always say, 'Why me?' But really, when you think about it, why not me? What makes me exempt? Cancer doesn't discriminate. It knows no boundaries of age, sex, good, evil. If that were the case and life was fair, Jane would still be here.

I think about Jane all the time now. About how I wish she was still here with us. But also about how she emanated peace and joy to all those around her, even when her entire body was riddled with cancer and she was filled with pain. She had this unshakable assurance that death would never touch her cancer-free soul.

I've come to believe that too—though I'm still a work-in-progress on that whole emanating-peace-and-joy thing.

After reading those last words, I sat in the quiet room for a long time, huddled in my warm robe under the single forty-watt lamp.

Thinking about Jane. And Pat. And God. And about all that had happened the past year of my life. Then I pulled out a pen and began to write.

Saturday night at the Grand Canyon

This will be my final entry in this cancer journal. My treatments are done, my hair has grown back (though not as long, of course), and I'm now cancer-free. Hallelujah!

From here on out, I don't think I'll be going to group every week, either. That was just for a season, my season of cancer, and that season has now passed. I'm entering a new one now—complete with new home and new career. It's time to move on.

I'll probably still go to group once a month or so, though—to see everyone and offer encouragement to scared newbies the way that others did to me. That's the least I can do to give back.

But the thing is, I just don't want to continue thinking and talking about cancer all the time. Cancer is not who I am. It doesn't define me.

I had cancer. I don't anymore. Now I'm ready to live this new exciting life God has ahead of me.

Strangely enough, I can honestly say I'm grateful for the cancer. If I hadn't gotten it, I wouldn't have been compelled to make changes and go after this new life. And I've learned some important lessons during my cancer journey:

That breasts do not make a woman.

That out of the ashes a whole new life can arise.

That the Man of my dreams was right there all along.

And He'll never leave me or forsake me.

. . .

"Now that is one gorgeous head." Rashida circled the bronze sculpture. "Girl," she said to Merritt, "you *definitely* got game."

"Thanks." Merritt gave her a pleased smile. "That's high praise coming from you."

The sculpture under discussion was a bust of my bald head with a lone tear sliding down the face. Merritt had done it from memory of the night when I first saw my shaved head in the mirror.

"Haunting," one woman said as she filed by.

"Heartbreaking," another said, searching for the price tag.

"I'm sorry. I'm afraid that piece isn't for sale," Merritt said. "It's a gift to a friend."

The night of Merritt's art exhibit had arrived at last, and the gallery was packed. But this exhibition wasn't just for her works. Merritt had asked Constance if the two of them could do a combined show and donate a large portion of the proceeds to the Capital Cancer Center.

Constance had thought that was a wonderful idea.

So had I.

Merritt and Constance had sent out invitations to all the cancer support groups in the area as well as to local artists and civic leaders. Also to doctors, nurses, and other hospital staff who worked at the cancer center. And, of course, to assorted friends and family, many of whom were milling around in the gallery right now.

All the women from group had come wearing their Merritt tunics and vests.

All except me.

Merritt had made me a special hand-painted silk stole instead, because I'd finally found the right occasion for the curve-hugging little black dress. I'd finally gotten comfortable with my new breasts and no longer felt the need to hunch my shoulders or hide them behind layers, so I simply let the wrap fall off my shoulders and hang loosely in the crook of my arms.

Merritt had given me a thumbs-up when I walked into the gallery. She hadn't seen me before then because she and Constance had spent the afternoon at the gallery, making sure all the details were in place for this show, which had taken up most of my friend's free time since finishing Bill and Jillian's painting.

True to her word, Merritt had refused to do another house watercolor, even though all Bill and Jillian's neighbors had clamored for one after seeing theirs. Merritt referred them to Constance, who specialized in soft, dreamy watercolor landscapes and portraits. Merritt's work tended to be more vibrant, passionate, even angry at times.

It was definitely provoking discussion.

"I don't see why it's necessary to show so many breasts," I heard one older woman in a buttoned-up beige pantsuit cluck to her friend. "I mean, I understand she's making a statement about breast cancer, but do we really need to *see* breasts?"

The breasts in question were mine. My new, rebuilt ones.

Never in a million years would I have even considered posing topless. I'd always felt my body was private and only to be seen by myself, my doctor, and my husband—*if* I ever got one. It was a matter of modesty. But that was B.C.—before cancer. When I recounted to Merritt how both Pat and I had excitedly flashed the support group when our reconstructions were complete, she'd gotten a thoughtful look in her eye.

The finished work (which wasn't obviously me) showed a joyous young woman, head thrown back, fists raised in victory, with perfectly round, symmetrical breasts, each bearing the clear red line of a scar across the center. I'd seen it while Merritt was working and absolutely loved it. But what I hadn't seen was the verse she'd lettered at the bottom, the words of a Psalm: "I praise you because I am fearfully and wonderfully made."

Tears sprang up in my eyes as I stood there looking at the finished painting and its inscription. My cancer journey had opened Merritt's heart toward God—an answer to many years of prayer on both my part and Jillian's.

Constance came and stood beside me, nodding to the painting in front of me and then another one to the left. "How do you like that one?"

This canvas showed a much older woman, her features blurred but wrinkled, with no hair, no breasts, and two faded scars, standing proud and defiant against a crimson background.

I stole a sideways glance at Constance. "Is that—"

"Yep," she said proudly. "In the flesh." She lowered her voice. "But don't tell anyone. I don't want to have to be beating the men off with a stick once they see my *Playboy* shot."

"Hey, your secret's safe with me," I said as we moved on to yet another painting.

In addition to the series of victorious "breastscapes," Merritt had also included a few fun and whimsical pieces. There was one of me with a huge grin creasing my face, my bald head tilted forward to show off the yellow smiley face painted on top while I smelled an oversized daffodil. Another one, which she'd dubbed "The Buzz-heads," showed a stubbly band of four—Andy on guitar, Josh on drums, Merritt on keyboards, and me wildly shaking a tambourine.

I wandered around the gallery sipping champagne and trying not to eavesdrop too obviously on what people were saying about my best friend's work.

"Wonderful."

"Honest."

"Compelling."

"*There* you are," Jillian said. "And you're finally wearing the dress! You look beautiful." She kissed me on the cheek. "Bill, doesn't Natalie look gorgeous?"

Her husband gave her a wry look. "How am I supposed to answer that question and not get in trouble?"

Jillian giggled and gave him a quick kiss. "You are so cute. But not to worry. You have my permission to tell Natalie she looks great."

"Natalie"—Bill turned to me—"you look great. Seriously. Fabulous dress."

"Thanks to Jillian," I said. "She's the one who picked it out. I never would have in a million years."

"My wife has good taste."

"I'll say." Rashida and her date, Fred, joined us again, with Rashida giving me an admiring once-over. "Girl, I never seen you look so fine." She turned to Jillian. "And you're the personal shopper at Nordstrom, right?" Rashida took another long look at my dress. "I need to set up an appointment with you, and soon."

A few minutes later, Merritt sidled up to me as I was munching on a piece of shrimp. "Did you see Nurse Paul's wife? I always expected she'd be this drop-dead-gorgeous model type."

"I know. I met her when I first came in."

The male nurse who'd always sent my pulse racing at the cancer center had proudly introduced me to a plain-Jane doctor with stick-straight hair, no makeup, and at least a seven-year head start on him. Yet she had the kindest eyes and the warmest smile, and it was obvious he adored her.

"Guess beauty is in the eye of the beholder," I added with a significant nod toward Merritt's new boyfriend, who was crossing the room toward us.

Merritt had recently started dating a guy who reminded me of Edward Scissorhands—without the hardware. And though I adore Johnny Depp, that ghostly white face was a bit too much even for me. Her boyfriend had jet-black hair, which he wore pulled back in a thin ponytail; a pale white face that never saw the sun; and a scrawny body constructed of sharp planes and angles.

Merritt thought he was adorable.

"His name is Vincent—after van Gogh," she'd told me after they met. "But don't worry. He's promised me he'll never cut off his ear."

"Just as long as he doesn't have a brother named Theo."

Vincent was an artist also, a sculptor who welded together wire and metal into fantastic shapes. And the two of them had met at church. Merritt had discovered a laid-back church downtown with lots of artists and hippie types—not the same one I visited—and pronounced it a perfect fit. Vincent seemed to be a good fit too. They'd been together ever since.

"Can I get you another glass of champagne, Natalie?" Vincent asked shyly.

"No, thanks. I'm afraid one's my limit." I laughed. "I usually just nurse the same drink all night long." I waved my glass to encompass the room. "So what do you think of all this?"

"I think it's great." Vincent laid a skinny arm around Merritt's shoulders. "Isn't she incredible? Such a gift she has."

"You're not kidding." Mom and Dad joined us. "I think the sculpted head is my favorite," Dad said softly.

"I don't know," Mom said. "I really love the painting with Nattie's hands raised in victory." They continued to debate their favorites, but I was no longer paying attention. Behind Mom's back, I saw that Andy had just arrived.

With Sara Sedberry.

Josh was right. She did have too many teeth.

I followed their progress around the room with my eyes. When Andy saw "The Buzzheads," his face flickered into a familiar smile, which was quickly gone.

Andy stopped and stared at the bronze of my head for a long time. Then he looked up, and our eyes locked. Then Sara tugged on his sleeve and he moved away.

I realized anew just how much I missed Andy and our friendship. And I was going to do whatever was necessary to get it back again.

The way it used to be.

I told this to Merritt in the restroom, where I'd pulled her for a quick best-friend chat.

"It can't ever be the way it used to be, Nat."

"Why not?"

"Because it's gone way beyond friendship. That's why Andy's acting so weird and distant." Merritt sighed. "Nat, the guy is crazy-wild in love with you, and you're in love with him, and everyone knows it except the two of you."

She shook her head. "Don't you get it? You guys are Harry and Sally."

chapter *thirty-one*

A re we *Harry and Sally?* I wondered as I drove home late that night after helping Merritt and Constance clean up.

I'd always thought of Andy as my big brother—the rock I leaned on and depended on. And loved. But you don't *fall* in love with your big brother. That would be incest, wouldn't it?

Only if you're actually related.

This isn't a soap opera where you're suddenly going to discover that Andy's your long-lost brother who was separated from you at birth. There's no blood tie that connects you—just heart ties and friendship ties woven over a lifetime.

Ties that were as natural to me as breathing.

Ties I didn't want to lose.

I thought of how my heart had quickened when I saw Andy at the gallery.

And how empty I'd been feeling without him in my life on a daily basis.

And how I'd wanted to chick-slap Sara and show her the door when I saw her hanging all over him.

I suddenly realized that *I* wanted to be the one hanging all over him. And not just that. I wanted to be the one kissing him. The thought of his sweet, familiar lips sent my stomach into backflips.

Guess that wouldn't be the case if he were my brother.

We *were* Harry and Sally!

Then how come Andy didn't do a Billy Crystal and rush up to me and declare his love for me in front of everyone? That's what the guy's supposed to do, isn't he? So why didn't he?

The answer slapped me up side the face.

Because of Sheila.

And because you might die and leave him too.

The plain and simple truth was Andy was terrified. That's why he had pulled back so far. That's why he had started dating Sara. And that was also why he would never make a move.

You have to do it.

Huh? But that wasn't how it was supposed to work. It was up to the guy to do that. A girl never tells a guy how she feels first. Talk about desperate.

Well, aren't you?

Am I what?

Desperately missing Andy—and Josh—and desperately in love with Andy?

Well, yeah, but . . .

But what?

Another one of Rashida's quotes popped into my head. I'd heard it in college, too; it was by Thoreau. "The mass of men lead lives of quiet desperation."

Did I want to lead that kind of life? And did I want my sweet Andy to?

My sweet Andy?

I pulled a U-ey, and ten minutes later I was pounding on his door.

He opened it partway, looking deliciously rumpled in a white T-shirt and plaid pajama bottoms. "This isn't really a good time."

"No time like the present." I pushed past him. "Sorry. Don't mean to be a cliché."

Andy followed me into the living room, a wary look on his face. "What's up?"

"If there's one thing I've learned over the past year"—I took a deep breath—"it's that life is short and you can't let opportunities pass you by. Because you may never get the chance again."

"Nat, I—"

I held up my hand. "Please. Don't say anything 'til I'm done, okay? I just need to get this all out."

He swallowed and sat down on the couch.

I paced the room. "First, I want you to know that you don't have to say anything. And you don't have to do anything with this information I'm about to give you. It's just something I need to say. Okay?"

Andy looked bewildered but nodded again.

"You may be willing to lose a twenty-seven-year friendship, bucko, but I'm not going to let it be thrown away." Another deep breath. "Here's the thing." My eyes bored into his. "I love you, Andy Jacobs. Always have. I've loved you since we first played in the sandbox together. And I loved you in the third grade, when you wouldn't let your friends be mean to me. And in high school, when you took me to prom after Billy Wilson dumped me. I've always loved you. I just didn't always know it."

I held my eyes on his. "And I love you for holding the waste-basket when I got sick and catching my puke. And for shaving your head when I had to shave mine." My eyes filled. "And for never once turning away in disgust or fear when I was going through the whole cancer thing—even when I was bald and breastless."

I swiped at my eyes. "I love you for the amazing father you are to Josh and for the wonderful friend you've always been to me. But you've gotta listen, 'cause this is important"—I paused—"I don't love you like a brother anymore. You've become so much more to me than that now."

I couldn't tell how he was taking all this. He just sat on the couch and looked at me, which made me nervous. I babbled on, "Yes, part of it is because of how you took care of me when I was sick. You showed me pure, unconditional love. You always have. But you did it in such a tangible way then.

"And I know you're scared to love again," I said softly. "You're scared I might die and leave you."

Andy made an inarticulate noise.

I lifted my shoulders. "I can't promise I won't die. But I can promise I'll never leave you by choice. I'll never pull a Sheila on you." I said softly, "I love Josh like he was my own, and I think we could have a wonderful life together. So. Well. I just had to say that. So. That's that."

Suddenly embarrassed, I turned to go. But Andy leapt off the couch, spun me around, and crushed me in his arms.

Then his lips were on mine.

And I tasted saltwater.

I pulled back to look at him. Tears were streaming down his face, his sweet, familiar, gorgeous face that now wore a wonderful mushy look.

"I love you too, Nat. Guess I always have. But it wasn't until recently that I realized I'd *fallen* in love with you." He kissed me again. "And I didn't know what to do with that. Especially now that you were beginning this whole new life, and, well—"

"What did you mean at Bill and Jillian's wedding?"

He gave me a puzzled look.

"When we were dancing, and there was this thing starting up between us, and you looked at me and said, 'Could it be that you've—'"

I gazed into eyes filled with love. "Could it be that I've what?"

"Grown up." Andy smiled down at me.

I smacked his chest. "Hey!"

He smiled and captured my hand. "You have to admit, you'd been tied pretty tightly to the mom-and-dad strings for a long time." He stroked my cheek. "But the cancer changed you. It made you reexamine your life and make some changes and start to live your own life. And that's what I saw at the wedding." He groaned. "That and that fabulous dress. I couldn't keep my eyes off you."

His eyes darkened. "Nor could every other man there. Including that Justin jerk."

"Well, you didn't have to leave." I stuck out my lower lip. "I thought he was a jerk too."

Andy playfully tugged at my lower lip. "I didn't know that," he said. "And I didn't want to get in the way of this whole new life you were building." He sighed. "I wanted to give you time and space."

"You gave me a little too much space."

He nuzzled my neck. "I won't do that again."

He moved back a little and looked deep into my eyes.

And then he said the words: "Natalie Louise Moore, will you marry me?"

And of course I wanted to sing out, "Yes, yes, yes."

Instead, I asked a question: "How do you feel about my breasts?"

"What?" He cocked his head.

"I don't have any feeling in them, you know. Probably never will." I blushed. "I know that's a big thing to guys, and I don't want you to be disappointed."

He cupped my face in his hands. "I don't care one bit about your breasts. Breasts or no breasts, hair or no hair, it doesn't matter. I love *you*. Now will you answer the question please? I'm dyin' here."

"Yes. Of course yes." I hugged him tightly. Then I pulled back a little and ran my finger across his bottom lip. "If I'd known what kissing you was like, I'd never have waited all these years."

"Well then, maybe we'd better make up for lost time, don't you think?"

"Yes, please," I said as he lowered his head to mine.

And it didn't even occur to me until later to think that my mom would be really pleased.

* * *

Some women climb mountains or run marathons.

Others bungee jump.

Some go kayaking or go whitewater rafting or skydiving to celebrate their victory over cancer.

Me?

I conquered the step-ball-change. And just in time for Valentine's Day.

It had been three months since I began taking—and loving—tap-dance lessons under the tutelage of the big-haired, big-hearted, twinkle-toed Charlene. Dancing made me feel so alive, so free, so uninhibited. And so strong.

Pretty too.

And tonight was my chance to show it all off—my official dance-recital debut.

In the cramped dressing room, I donned my glittery costume, making sure to adjust Monica and Rachel inside my black span-dex bra and wishing that just this once the lack of feeling in my breasts would extend down to the roller coaster roaring through my stomach.

"Places, ladies," Miss Charlene instructed. "You all look gorgeous."

She winked at me. "Now go out there and have fun. I mean . . . break a leg!"

I took a deep breath and sent a quick prayer that I wouldn't trip and fall. Then joyfully tapped my way across the spotlighted stage clad in a top hat, tails, bright red lipstick, and lots and lots of sparkly sequins.

I couldn't see the audience for the lights, but I heard the applause, even over the music. Music to my ears.

And just as I reached up to tip my hat to a jaunty angle, I heard a small voice pipe up proudly from the audience.

Josh's voice.

"That's my Aunt Natalie," he told everyone. "She's gonna be my mom!"

epilogue

I scanned the room and adjusted the printed napkins on the antique oak sideboard once again.

"Would you stop fussing already?" Merritt said. "Everything looks great."

"It looks more than great." Andy's arms stole around me from behind, coming to rest on my slightly protruding stomach. "It looks perfect, honey."

He kissed my neck.

"Yeah, Mom. Really cool." Josh eyed the plates of hors d'oeuvres on the sideboard, zeroing in on the miniature egg rolls. "So when do we get to eat?"

"That's what I want to know." My dad tousled his grandson's hair. "We men have to keep up our strength. Right, Josh?"

"You two. Always thinking of your stomach." Mom filched two egg rolls off a nearby platter and surreptitiously passed them to Dad and Josh.

"Mom!"

"What?" she said innocently. "I didn't mess up the display."

"Hey, babe," Vincent said to Merritt. "Looks like you've got quite a crowd forming out front." He looked from his wife to me. "You two ready to open the doors?"

I looked at my best friend and business partner. She looked at me. "Ready!"

The crowd streamed in. "Would you look at this sculpture? Wouldn't it look great in our foyer?"

"I'm checking out these fabulous window coverings. I've been looking for ages for just the right drapes for my bedroom."

"Hey, Josh!"

Luke started to sprint over, then slowed to a walk as his father gently admonished him. Mitch and Faye followed in his wake with five-year-old Matthew.

Faye had stopped coloring her hair, and it was now a soft brown streaked with silver. After Jane's death and the cancer walk, where she had talked a long time with Mitch, she had started attending their church. A couple of years later, she and Mitch, who was now the associate pastor, had begun to date. And last spring, with our entire support group in happy, tearful attendance, the two had married.

"There you are." Jillian's voice broke through my memories as she swooped in for a double hug. Bill stood behind her, smiling.

"Where's Emily?" I asked.

"Trust me, you don't want a two-year-old at a shop opening. Too many breakables. Besides, I needed a child-free night." Jillian rested her hands on her very pregnant abdomen and winked. "You'll understand what I mean soon enough."

"Can't wait." I patted sweet baby Jane inside my tummy. Andy and I had just learned we were having a girl, but we weren't telling anyone yet. We wanted to savor the knowing, just the two of us, for a while.

"Girl, you really startin' to show." Rashida, her silver hoops winking beneath her dreadlocks, gave me a speculative look. "So y'all know yet what this child going to—"

"Oh, there's Zoey. I need to say hi." I sped away before I confessed all to my lawyer friend.

Merritt intercepted me. "So, partner, what do you think?"

Before I could reply, a voice rose above the din. "Excuse me, everyone, could I have your attention, please?" Andy gave me a loving smile and raised his plastic goblet high. "I'd like to make a toast. Does everyone have a glass?"

I snagged a sparkling cider from a passing waiter. Merritt did too.

"This day has been a long time coming and is the culmination of a dream—for my beautiful, talented wife and for her equally talented best friend." He grinned at Merritt. "Hope you don't mind my leaving off the beautiful."

Merritt winked. "Not a problem. I know how jealous Nat can be."

The crowd laughed.

Andy continued. "If you'll please raise your glasses with me." His proud eyes sought mine. "To 'Less Is Moore'!"

"To Less Is Moore!" everyone cheered.

When the noise subsided, Merritt stepped up on a nearby stool. "My turn." She turned to me, her eyes misty. "We're not only celebrating the opening of our combination interior decorating firm and art gallery. We're also celebrating the fact that my partner, who happens to be my best friend, is now five years cancer-free." She raised her glass. "To Natalie."

"To Natalie!"

* * *

On the way home from the opening, my cell phone rang.

Our realtor.

She'd been showing us houses for weeks, but none had been quite right for the needs of our expanding family. But an older home in our price range had just come on the market, and she thought we might be interested. "It's definitely a fixer-upper," she warned me over the phone. "It's going to need a lot of TLC. But you can meet me there if you want."

Fifteen minutes later, we pulled up to an original Craftsman that was just a few blocks from our new church.

And I knew.

"Andy," I breathed. "It's our house."

"You may be right," he said. "But let's check out the inside before we decide." We held hands as we walked through the sixty-five-year-old house with dusty but original wood trim and moldings and amazing wide-planked oak floors.

"Would you look at this?" our realtor said. "There's been a flood here or something—the floors are warped, and I think those built-in bookcases lean to the left a little."

I squeezed Andy's hand. "Just like we like 'em; beaten and broken, but still standing."

Andy nodded and smiled at me. "We'll take it."

I am come that they might have life,
and that they might have it more abundantly.

—JOHN 10:10

Dear Reader,

As you can tell by reading *Reconstructing Natalie*, I'm a big believer in the power of laughter. And girlfriends. And relationships. They're what sustains and transforms Natalie, and they're what sustained me when I was diagnosed with breast cancer several years ago. That's why I'm a big believer in Women of Faith.

If you believe in these things too, you'll fit right in at a Women of Faith Conference. It's all about connecting: with ourselves, with others, and with God. It is two days where you can leave your day-to-day life behind and relax; get revitalized by inspiring speakers, energizing music, and most of all, connect with women of all shapes, sizes, ages, and denominations. One moment you'll find yourself laughing, the next, wiping away tears.

I encourage you to experience firsthand the joy of a Women of Faith Conference—where the women are real, the laughter is plentiful, and the message is eternal. Be inspired to replenish your spirituality and renew your faith. Come by yourself or with your friends, you'll be glad you did.

God bless,
Laura Jensen Walker

Visit womenoffaith.com

acknowledgments

Reconstructing Natalie would not have been possible without the gifted and amazing Ami McConnell and Anne Christian Buchanan. No one could ask for better editors to guide them through the world of fiction. Thank you for believing in Natalie and in me. You rock!

Deepest gratitude to Drs. Karin Klove and Dixie Mills for their medical expertise and willingness to answer so many cancer-related questions. Any errors are mine. (Karin, I will forever be grateful for your compassion when giving me the hard news those many years ago. I wish all patients could have a doctor as kind as you.)

Noel Wilson and Therese Pope from the American Cancer Society in Sacramento provided helpful information about cancer support groups. And thanks to the following for answers to many other questions—often at the last minute: Jennie Damron, Shane Galloway, Karen Grant, Nela Hammel, Marian Hitchings, Kari Jameson, Sheri Jameson, Nancy Maguire, Kim Orendor, Chris Pond, Debbie Thomas, and Laura Spencer—whose *Friends* obsession helped shape part of Natalie. Special thanks to Anne Peterson for the tap-dancing expertise. And to my old college pal Toni Terrell, for helping with Rashida's dialogue.

Heartfelt thanks to my friends and family who don't see me for long stretches of time as I hibernate in my writing cave, but who still love and support me. With special thanks to our Monday night Acts2U group. Couldn't have done it without your prayers.

Annette Smith, my dear Southern-fried writing friend, thanks for reading chapters under the gun. Again. You are a continual source of cheerleading and love in my life. Ditto to Cathy Elliott and Cindy Martinusen.

Getaway sighs of relief and thanks to Amy B. and Laura S. for my San Diego writing getaway and to Pat and Ken for my Sacramento one.

And as ever and always, my deepest thanks to Michael, my rock, my cushion, my heart, my home. Without you, none of this would be possible. Thank you for being my Andy and for kissing my mastectomy scar when you first saw it and saying, "I love this scar because it means I'm going to have you with me for a long time." *Je t'adore*.

Finally, all my gratitude goes to the myriad cancer-related groups and organizations out there that offer hope, education, and support to women fighting breast cancer. The following is by no means an exhaustive listing—there are way too many to list them all here—but I wanted to include a brief sampling:

American Cancer Society

Carol M. Baldwin Breast Cancer Research Fund

CureBreastCancer, Inc.

Susan G. Komen Breast Cancer Foundation

National Alliance of Breast Cancer Organizations

Young Survival Coalition

The Breast Cancer Site (www.thebreastcancersite.com), where a click a day funds free mammograms for women in need.

Reading Group Guide to *Reconstructing Natalie*

1. *Reconstructing Natalie* begins with "I'm obsessed with breasts." Natalie Moore isn't a vain woman, she's a casual girl-next-door type, but her diagnosis of breast cancer has her focusing on some body parts she never paid that much attention to before. Are you obsessed with some part of your body? And if so, which part and why?

2. Natalie is only 27-years-old when she's diagnosed with breast cancer. Do you think her age and the fact that she isn't married make that frightening diagnosis even more difficult? Do you think it would be easier to hear this if you were a married woman in your 50s or 60s?

3. Merritt and Jillian, Natalie's two best friends, throw her a "Boob Voyage" party the night before her mastectomy. Have any of your friends ever done something fun and silly like that to help you take your mind off a difficult or frightening situation? Would you do something similar for a friend?

4. After her surgery, Natalie is dependent on her friends and family to do things for her—many things she's accustomed to doing herself. Merritt demonstrates unconditional love and friendship to Natalie by doing things such as helping to bath her and shampooing her hair. Would you do something that intimate for a friend?

5. Some people pull away from or abandon Natalie once she tells them she has breast cancer. Have you ever had a friend leave or abandon you during a difficult time?

6. Natalie makes the choice to have a prophylactic mastectomy so that she won't have to live in fear of her cancer recurring in the non-cancerous breast. Did that seem like a drastic step to you? Would you consider taking such a step if you had a similar diagnosis?

7. Some people at Natalie's church say thoughtless things to her when she's first diagnosed. Do you think they were being mean or just clueless? Have you ever had someone at church or work say something insensitive to you when you were going through a trying time? How did you handle it?

8. In the breast cancer support group, Natalie meets and befriends a group of women, all very different from one another, who have this disease in common. Have you ever found yourself connecting with someone so different than you as a result of one shared experience? What lesson might there be in this?

9. Natalie's cancer and treatment compels her to rethink her life and, as a result, make major changes. Has your life ever done a similar about-face due to a life-changing event?

10. Andy, Natalie's neighbor and best male friend, is a rock for her throughout her treatment and yet, by the end of the book, their relationship has changed and grown into something deeper. Do you think it's possible for a man and a woman to be close friends without becoming romantically involved?

11. Jane is a kind and loving example of someone whose faith sustains her even through the darkest hours. Do you have that same kind of faith, and would it provide you comfort and hope if you found yourself in a situation similar to Jane's?

THE BOOK CLUB FOR TODAYS CHRISTIAN FAMILY

A Letter to Our Readers

Dear Reader:

In order that we might better contribute to your reading enjoyment, we would appreciate your taking a few minutes to respond to the following questions. When completed, please return to the following:

Andrea Doering, Editor-in-Chief
Crossings Book Club
401 Franklin Avenue, Garden City, NY 11530

You can post your review online! Go to www.crossings.com and rate this book.

Title _____ Author _____

1 Did you enjoy reading this book?

❑ Very much. I would like to see more books by this author!

❑ I really liked_____

❑ Moderately. I would have enjoyed it more if_____

2 What influenced your decision to purchase this book? Check all that apply.

❑ Cover
❑ Title
❑ Publicity
❑ Catalog description
❑ Friends
❑ Enjoyed other books by this author
❑ Other _____

3 Please check your age range:

❑ Under 18   ❑ 18-24
❑ 25-34   ❑ 35-45
❑ 46-55   ❑ Over 55

4 How many hours per week do you read? _____

5 How would you rate this book, on a scale from 1 (poor) to 5 (superior)?
_____

Name_____

Occupation_____

Address_____

City_____ State_____ Zip_____

Women of Faith Fiction

from WestBow Press

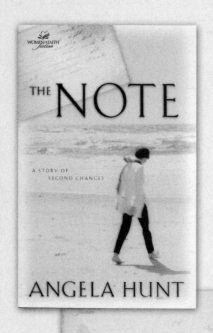

Women of Faith has shared the message of hope and grace with millions of women across the country through conferences and resources. When you see the words "Women of Faith Fiction" on a novel, you're guaranteed a reading experience that will capture your imagination and inspire your faith.

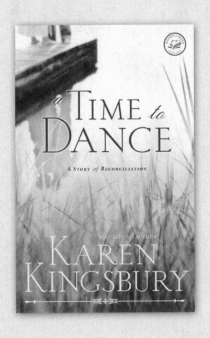

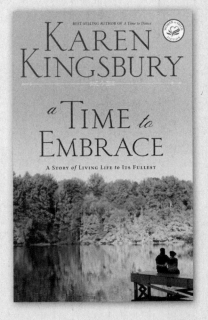

WOMEN of FAITH fiction

A novel

GARDENIAS
FOR
BREAKFAST

ROBIN JONES GUNN

from the best-selling author of Sisterchicks on the Loose

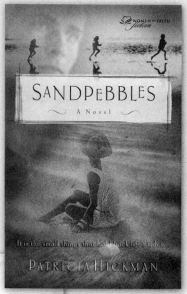

WOMEN of FAITH fiction

SANDPEBBLES

~ A Novel ~

It is the small things that hold back life's tides...

PATRICIA HICKMAN

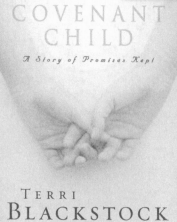

COVENANT
CHILD

A Story of Promises Kept

TERRI
BLACKSTOCK

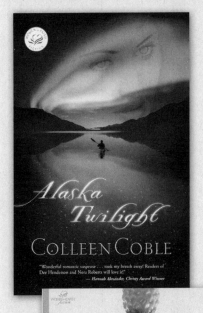

Alaska Twilight

COLLEEN COBLE

"Wonderful romantic suspense . . . took my breath away! Readers of Dee Henderson and Nora Roberts will love it!"
— Hannah Alexander, Christy Award Winner

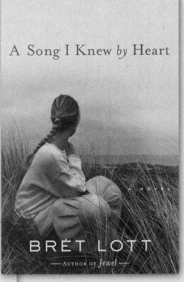

A Song I Knew *by* Heart

A NOVEL

BRET LOTT

AUTHOR OF *Jewel*

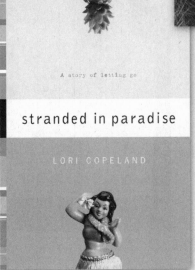

A story of letting go

stranded in paradise

LORI COPELAND

WOMEN OF FAITH
fiction

WESTBOW
PRESS
A Division of Thomas Nelson Publishers
Since 1798

Women of Faith
Novel of the Year

Enjoy these other books by
Laura Jensen Walker

Dreaming in Black & White

tradepaper
Publisher: WestBow Press
ISBN: 0849945232

Dreaming in Technicolor

tradepaper
Publisher:
WestBow Press
ISBN: 0849945240

Thanks for the Mammogram

Hardcover
Publisher: Revell
ISBN: 0800717783